FROM SCOTLAND
WITH LOVE

CLAIRE GILLIES

For my mum, Alice

Highland Heart

Nostalgic memories fill my mind
Of childhood days gone by
Neath summer skies we'd bathe and play
When winter came we'd skate and sleigh
And so the years did fly.

But still a highland heart can yearn
For the smell of peat and purple heather
For the boat on the loch, and the sheep on the hill
In my inward eye I see them still
And the whispering pines by the river.

- Mary Craik

1

Lori Robertson sat in a toilet cubicle staring at nothing in a daze. Cocooned inside its thin walls, she had the illusion of safety from the looming world outside. Breathing in and out slowly, Lori tried to calm herself using the techniques she had watched on one of her many favourited YouTube channels. She had now been in the ladies' for some time, and was sure people were beginning to wonder where she was. How could she let this happen? Right in the middle of a phone conversation with a supplier, she had the familiar overwhelming feeling start to take hold, and had had to place the receiver down unceremoniously. She would need to explain, or make up an excuse as she usually did when these episodes occurred. Maybe she could say something urgent had captured her attention: a fire? A robbery? No, Lori thought resignedly, she couldn't lie her way out of this one. She dismissed the rising pressure in her head and took a breath, trying to slow down her racing heart, which pounded in her ears, like a galloping horse with no intention of stopping. She breathed out, willing herself to calm down and to stop listening to the doubting voices in her head; evil whispers that she couldn't stop: *You're not good enough. Everyone will sooner or later find out you're a fraud.* She placed her head in-between her legs, and exhaled. This action helped a little, so here she remained, waiting for the tension to pass. She told herself as much as it felt like a heart attack, it really wasn't; she was not going to die – or explode, or even throw up! She closed her eyes in the quiet cubicle and allowed her rational thinking to creep to the forefront. The YouTube video had imparted some sound advice at least, and the thumping sound of her heart gradually stopped echoing in her eardrums. She was surprised that her assistant hadn't come into the bathroom already, banging the door down to continue the endless torrent of questions to which she was expected to know all the answers. Lori had recently been promoted to Buyer for the luxury fashion brand Costner's. It was an impressive company, and an impressive job; she just needed more time to get comfortable with the work, that was all. The ladies bathroom door opened and she heard two women laughing as they both went either side of Lori's cubicle and spoke over her unabashedly, chatting about the day's meetings and what they had chosen for lunch. Lori stood up, flushed the toilet and slowly walked out to the mirror opposite, taking in her appearance. She was stylishly dressed; wearing a tailored white shirt and smart pinstripe trousers. She tried her best to dress in a way that emanated the company brand – simple, sophisticated, understated and expensive. She reached for the paper towels and doused them in water, then lightly patted the damp squares onto her neck and forehead. She wiped the mascara from under her eyes, and smoothed a hand over her hair, which was pulled back into a high ponytail, showing expensive diamond stud earrings that her boyfriend Michael had bought for her birthday.

The two younger women emerged from the cubicles behind her.

"Hey Lori!" the two thin blondes said in unison, one was called Claudia, and the other Samantha, but Lori didn't know who was who; they looked so alike. She had already asked for a reminder a few times, and now it was too late; she should know how to differentiate them by now. Instead, Lori avoided pronouncing either name, and luckily hadn't been caught out yet. In any case, the pair certainly wouldn't look out of place on the front cover of a fashion magazine. Lori smiled weakly. She had always found it strange how so many attractive people worked in the office. Working in the fashion industry surrounded by bright, leggy blondes made her feel frumpy, and she hated it. But she was a product of her generation: happy in her own body to a certain extent, but sporting a confidence which had faded after years of being bombarded with the message that if you weren't immaculately toned and impossibly beautiful then you were no-one according to the fashion industry.

The slightly taller blonde looked at Lori in the mirror. "Will you be at the designers meeting?" She washed her hands and patted them dry with the elegance of a 1950s model presenting a pair of doeskin gloves - but in this case, it was paper towels.

"Yes – I mean, I believe so!" Lori edged her way to the door, smiling at the two models. She really didn't want to talk to anyone about meetings or schedules, especially after her recent episode: she needed deodorant, and to get out of the confined space. "Should be interesting to see what ideas they've come up with!" Lori nodded and grabbed the door handle. "I'll see you in there soon?"

"I'll save you a seat, just in case you're late again!" The taller girl laughed.

"Thanks!" Lori called as she left the bathroom. She was never completely sure about those two; they seemed nice enough, but there was always an aftertaste to their interactions that made Lori feel as if they were secretly laughing at her. She shook the thought from her mind and walked down the hallway which lead into the huge company office. Large windows looked out onto Manhattan streets, flooding the space with bright light, illuminating various groups of smart-looking, attractive people answering phones. Lori remembered the first day she had started working at Costner's; thinking she had walked onto a TV set. She had been excited, imagining she would live out the remainder of her working life through the lens of her favourite sitcom - but instead, it soon became clear that her days were to be filled by the daily grind of retail. It was noon, so she grabbed a sandwich from the bistro next door and went to eat at her desk. As soon as she sank into her seat, Julian's head popped up over the partition from the next group of desks. The young man's big eyes lit up as he saw Lori, and grabbing a pen and pad, he scurried over to her desk immediately. Lori inwardly groaned.

"Hi Lori! Can I double check some things with you?"

Mid-bite, Lori swallowed, nodding. In her new role she always felt she was eating whenever she spoke with Julian. She glanced over to her friend Alex, the buyer for kids-wear, who sat glued to her computer, endlessly reading and responding to emails. Lori thanked her lucky stars for having an assistant. Alex didn't merit a helping hand according to management, since the departmental targets for kids-wear was considerably smaller. Lori often felt sorry for her friend, and tried to help whenever possible. But those moments were few and far between. The only real time Lori could spend catching up on her own work was on her lunch break, as most of her days were spent in meetings, which in her experience never seemed to achieve very much. Lori tore her gaze away from her salad wrap to look back at Julian, who had already started listing some problems they were having with a certain production chain. Lori took a sip of water and pulled a nearby chair for him to sit on.

"OK, Julian." She could see the young man's face turning pink with panic, his forehead lightly sweating. "Sit down and breathe, we'll get through this. There are always going to be problems, we just need to work calmly, and together we'll get through them." Lori didn't know who she was trying to convince, herself or Julian.

Julian bit his lip "You're right Lori, thanks!"

Lori finished jotting down some notes on the back of an old catalogue, and glanced at her emails, so busy advising Julian that she hadn't noticed the popup window had been flashing a reminder on her computer. She chastised herself for not paying attention, she really couldn't be late for the designers meeting again... She sent Julian on his way, with solutions to work through, grabbed her phone and notepad and almost ran to the ninth floor board room.

She was ten minutes late when she walked in, and as quiet as she was, the whole room turned around and gawped at her. Frankie, her boss, was at the head of the table, legs crossed, pen poised and in discussion with the lead designer about a men's shirt pattern. She glanced at Lori briefly, then continued speaking, recrossing her legs, and tapping her pen impatiently on the tabletop. Lori couldn't see any seat available; the huge table was covered in paperwork and every place taken, the two blondes from earlier both conveniently did not look in her direction. Lori left her things on the table and popped outside the room to find a free chair. Very carefully but not very quietly she shuffled back in, chair in hand and sat down next to Alex, who smiled and made some space for her.

"But we need more. These styles are almost identical to last year's fall/winter collection." Frankie looked at sketches, dispirited, as she rested her elbows on the desk.

The lead designer moved uneasily in his seat and rifled through his drawings before picking up one and pushing it towards her. "We are going with the trends Frankie, this is what people will be looking for..."

She scrutinised the work before her and back at her notes, everyone in the room quietly waiting for her decision. Lori craned her head, trying to see the sketches, but she was seated too far away to make them out. Frankie coughed and the whole room held its breath: "No, it's not enough. We'll get lost in and amongst the other brands. I know our style is simple pointing definitively towards the classic, but I just don't think people are going to spend their hard-earned cash on a white shirt like this," she gestured with the flick of her hand to a design and sighed, "when they can just go to a cheaper brand! We need to go back to why people come to us; we need to set our own bar. Yes we need to look at trends, but not be so dictated by them!" She drummed her fingers on the outlines and sighed.

The designer looked over to his colleague, who nodded her approval. "Perhaps..." He spoke slowly, as if unsure what his next words were going to be, "we can revise these styles and get back to you? I'll get my team to work on some more."

Lori raised her hand at the far side of the table. "If I could make a suggestion?"

The whole room turned to face her as one.

"Yes?" Frankie asked, her eyes still on the designs.

"I thought... maybe we could look at our back-catalogue to see what our biggest sellers were a few decades ago? Maybe all the way back to when the brand started in the 1960s, if it's possible to access those design prints?" She lowered her hand slowly, immediately regretting her boldness as silence followed her words. Her heart gave a flutter, and she wished she was back in the safe toilet cubicle again.

Frankie looked at Lori intently as if solving a math calculation in her head, and Lori was sure she caught the designer rolling his eyes. Frankie clapped her hands with renewed energy. "We're coming up to our 60th anniversary next year, maybe this could be the start of the celebrations!" Frankie tapped the edge of her painted red nail gently against her red lips. "Lori could be onto something... I think we need to go back to our roots. Tie it in with the anniversary theme: more classic styles inspired by the 1960s - I'm thinking Steve McQueen, men love that look! And for the ladies-wear and kids-wear we should draw our inspiration from the men's style also... We *are* primarily known for our menswear, so that must be our overall focus."

The designer nodded, his eyes moving forlornly from Frankie to his scattered designs, already forgotten on the table.

"Shall we say this time next week for some new designs? Lori, you can assist; if you check previous styles that sold well around the 1960s and 70s and highlight which you think the men's range would benefit from."

"Of course, I'll get onto that!" Lori confirmed excitedly, the words fell out of her mouth before she could register her already substantial workload.

En route back to her desk, Lori stopped by the ever-smiling barista woman who had a small coffee stall in the hallway. Lori collected two takeaway cups, knowing she needed to sweeten Julian a little. She walked over to his neat desk and casually placed the paper cup of his favourite vanilla latte to the left of his mouse-mat. She grimaced looking down at his hopeful face, knowing he would be expecting her to lend a hand with his workload, when instead she was adding to it.

"So...we kind of have another job to do for next week...!" Lori smiled broadly, hoping he would welcome the work, but looking at his big eyes she found they turned from hope to alarm in a split second. *You and me both honey*, she thought ruefully.

2

Michael sat at the recently set, white-clothed table and glanced at his watch; Lori was running fifteen minutes late. The restaurant was fairly quiet however, so he wasn't too bothered. It was a rainy Wednesday evening; *what was it with people and rain? even the slightest trickle made them stay indoors?* Michael reflected as the waiter came to take his order. He looked at his watch again, and to keep the establishment and himself happy, he ordered a bottle of high end wine that one of the partners in his firm spoke about. He liked to keep abreast with his peers' tastes; if he cultivated the same interests then bit by bit he would gain trust, and investment, and work his way up the ranks. He had been with McClure and Wilkins for almost five years, and could now see himself there permanently. He smiled slightly to himself; in a few years' time he and Lori might be dining in this place more regularly. The waiter came back with the bottle, poured it with ceremony then waited until Michael had sipped the wine and nodded his approval. Inwardly he was disappointed; a verdict of fine, but not worth two hundred dollars was his conclusion. Really, it didn't matter what it tasted like: he could now say he sampled it if anyone asked at work – and the fact he hadn't been impressed might even stand in his favour. He glanced again at the door for any sign of Lori, just as the attendant opened it for an older couple wearing wool coats and carrying an umbrella. It was spring, yet people were wearing wool coats; New York weather amazed him sometimes, you needed to prepare for every season in one day. In the corner a man in a black suit played the piano; a gentle but very dreary version of Sinatra's *Stranger's in the Night*, reminding Michael of his father. This restaurant had been his favourite, to which he took Michael's mother on special occasions. His father, William Hadley had for many years owned a very successful estate agency, and for a time Michael believed he would step into his father's shoes and take over the business. After many family discussions, however, the role went to Michael's older brother Henry, and Michael was pointed in the direction of Law. He had been happy with the arrangement at the time, and now was positively relieved at the outcome. Law was much more his idea of a good stable job, and it also meant he didn't need to work with his father, which allowed them to have a far better relationship than would otherwise have been possible. As his parents had chosen this restaurant for celebrations, he thought it only fitting that he came here this evening; his own special occasion. He believed he had found the right woman for him: Lori Robertson. Hardworking, kind-hearted and graceful, she would make a very suitable partner, supporting him in his career, and being the mother of their future children. They made a good team, and he always felt relaxed whenever she accompanied him on work obligations, in a way he never had alone. She was admired by the wives of the partners, and secretly desired by the men, a fact he became aware of after overhearing Mr. McClure and a senior partner discussing Lori's attributes in the kitchen at a soiree. He was confident in Lori personally, and what she would bring to their marriage. He touched his breast pocket, feeling the small velvet box in which a marquise diamond on a gold band lay. It had been carefully selected after seeing one of his female colleagues show off her engagement ring in the office, and who had remarked on the rarity of the diamond and the specialist who had assisted her. She was right; the jeweller had helped Michael select a large but tasteful diamond, with smaller diamonds encrusted on the delicate band. The whole process was very easy, and he thought it would look very well on Lori's finger, and in turn, she would look very attractive on his arm. His intention had been to propose tonight, but as the minutes passed, it was looking less likely. If he did propose in the next hour or so, they would need to celebrate - which would affect his early meeting with an important client the following day. Michael looked at his watch again, now she was a full thirty minutes late. He checked his phone and a new message popped up on the screen: Lori was stuck in traffic. Michael put down his phone carefully as anger flared inside him. It was one of his pet hates; waiting on people. In his business, every minute mattered. *Time is money after all*, he took another sip of wine, then moved the glass aside to order a bourbon from the waiter. Lori really should make more of an effort; if he could get here at a certain time, there was no reason why she couldn't accomplish the same. So he decided there and then that he'd propose on another occasion, one where Lori arrived on time. It could wait, maybe until a long weekend at his parent's summer house in the Hamptons. In the meantime, he loosened his tie a little, swiped his phone open and began to answer some work emails. He sipped the strong smokey bourbon as he worked through what would have been waiting for him the next day. *Time is money, Michael*, he heard his father chuckle, *time is money!*

Lori walked through the door to the almost empty restaurant. A man played piano from the far side of the room making her feel like she was stepping into an old Hollywood movie. The whole scene felt like a late-night secret meeting place for two lovers escaping their hum-drum lives to begin an exciting affair. But it was barely 8pm, and upon closer inspection the restaurant wasn't terribly romantic; there was an air of stuffiness and outdated grandeur which permeated. Lori patted down her hair, which was still somewhat wet even though she had been sitting in a cab until the last forty feet of her journey. A waiter came to take her coat, and Lori gladly handed over the damp garment, hoping her appearance was acceptable. She wore a black dress that she kept in her drawer at work in case of emergencies, and after a day full of meetings, she scarcely had enough time to quickly brush her hair and apply lipstick in the ladies before she caught a cab. She had left Julian compiling Costner's best-selling looks, with still with a long way to go until he covered the styles from the early 1960s, but at least it was a start. Accomplishing whatever Frankie wanted was the main focus, and she mentally made a note to get Julian something special for his dedication to the cause.

Michael was typing on his phone, when the waiter escorted Lori to the table, and stood up to welcome her. Lori acknowledged Michael's traditional manners, holding doors open for women, and making sure he walked on the side of busy traffic when they strolled across the city together. These little things he did, showed her how much he cared - *and wasn't it the little things that mattered?* Lori leaned in and they kissed briefly, conscious of the few onlookers quietly eating their dinner.

"I'm sorry darling. It was so busy, traffic was hell!" Lori took a long drink of her wine that was waiting for her; the day's events had taken their toll, and all she wanted was to forget. "What a day!"

"Yeah?" Michael put his phone away and opened up the menu. "Why don't we order now then we can talk. I'm starving. I think I'll order the sea bass."

Lori pursed her lips, unsure if Michael was angry at her lateness. She looked down at the entirely French menu and was uninspired at what she saw; right now what she really wanted was a burger and a pint of beer. She glanced up, unaware that the waiter was standing close by, already waiting to take her order. Her burger would have to be put on hold for another night, so she ordered the first thing she could pronounce on the menu.

The pianist began playing an Ella Fitzgerald number, an upbeat piece of music making Lori want to dance in between the quiet tables. Michael reached across to take her hand in his, his blue eyes looking deep into her own. He was an attractive man, always smartly dressed and clean-shaven, and Lori rarely ever saw him scruffy, even on his days off work. She remembered the first time they met, she couldn't stop glancing at the handsome stranger leaning on the bar counter, talking to friends. That evening Lori had been with a colleague, listening to her mounting boyfriend troubles, but all the while unable to fully concentrate on her friend. The stranger was intriguing: magnificent, tall, and who exhumed a confidence that enticed her. After much of the

night looking in his direction, he had eventually recipro-
cated with a single smile and they locked into a new kind of
understanding. Lori knew not long after that night, that this
would be her man in life. That same smile she looked at
now had told her they were a good match right from the
start. Since being with Michael, she had been introduced to
a different world, a life of parties, glitz and glamour which
coincided with her career nicely. There was always some
event to go to, some fashion show, or one of the firm's
regular dinner parties. Lori's calendar was booked solid for
the next few months. She moved her fingers around his
smooth palm as he spoke about work. He was a fine man
indeed, someone to be proud of. Lori often noticed women
admiring him, even walking down the street she had on
occasion noticed heads turning. Even at the drawn-out
dinner parties, as dull as those affairs were, Lori enjoyed
seeing Michael in his element. He was the epitome of what
she had always wanted in a man. She sipped more wine and
felt her muscles relax, the music lulling her into a state of
contentment. Whether it was the wine, or her appreciation
of Michael's better qualities, she didn't know, but desire
pulsed through her body as if she were sinking into a hot
soapy bath. She kicked off her peep-toe shoe and touched
his leg with her foot. Running her toe up his ankle playfully;
she realised how much she wanted sex. Not just nice sex, but
hot, unrestrained up against a wall or in the restaurant loos
sex. She circled her finger around his palm wondering how
best to proposition him. But just as the words were about to
come out, Michael suddenly took his hand away and moved
his leg as the waiter approached them carrying big plates
sporting tiny portions of food. Lori felt a pang of disappointment and put her foot back into her shoe. She knew how
the evening would go now: they would finish the meal, get a

taxi together, and Michael would make sure the taxi dropped her off at her apartment first before continuing on to his. It was routine on a weeknight that they be in bed early, and in their own separate beds at that; a silent agreement between them for the last three years. She knew where she stood, there were no surprises, and everything was planned and in its place. It was what she wanted, it was the very reason she had moved to the big city, to plan and control her life of success. But just a tiny part of her wanted the thrill of the unknown, some adventure, something different. *Not tonight*, she inwardly sighed, as she picked at her boeuf bourguignon.

3

The early morning sun had just started to greet the New York streets, covering the city in a hazy pink glow. Lori woke up before her alarm, deciding that an early start would be best. She wiggled into a grey shirt-dress, and gently packed her black Versace jacket in her bag; hoping not to crease it amongst the other items. Michael had once commented that she was like *Mary Poppins*, lugging a bag around filled to the brim with assorted items. Lori had found the statement funny, and took it as a compliment. She liked to be prepared for any situation, which meant tape measures, a first-aid kit, makeup, scissors, and notepad – the list would go on. The bag itself was also replaced on a regular basis in favour of a bigger one. She looked at her face in the bathroom mirror, and carefully applied mascara on her lashes and pinned up her curls.

"Almost done?" Kim peered around the bathroom door, bleary-eyed.

"Yes, two ticks!" Lori pursed her deep pink lips on a tissue and patted her unruly hair once again.

Kim leaned against the hall wall, arms crossed "It's too early!" she groaned. "How can you be heading to work already?"

"It's not that early! I thought I'd get a head start on things!" Lori scrunched up her nose, looking at her reflection. Her curls could never be held in place, no matter how much mousse, hairspray, or oil she used. She had tried every styling product under the sun, all with the same result: her hair gave her the proverbial middle finger every day, and she had to live with it. She threw her hair clips on the floor in irritation. "Damn it!"

"Hey!" Kim croaked, "what's wrong?" She stood looking tiredly confused in an old Green Peace t-shirt, which Lori presumed was her boyfriend's rather than Kim's.

"I'm fine, I just have a lot on at work." Lori glanced at her watch, Kim was right, it was on the early side, but since not having Michael stay over last night, she had to put her energy somewhere else. "Have a good night?" Lori changed the subject and picked up the evidence of her little tantrum. Most mornings, the two housemates would meet in the hallway for a quick catch-up, that being the only time their schedules crossed. Kim's long hours as an event planner meant that Lori hardly saw her in the evenings, which may have been a big reason why the two enjoyed living together.

"Oh yeah: dramas and tears from the client, then halfway through they realise everything is going according to plan. It's always the same. Nobody listens to me, like I haven't planned a million of these events before!" Kim grumbled as she grabbed the door handle to steady herself.

"Darren here?" Lori was beginning to see Kim's new boyfriend at the apartment most nights. He was a nice guy, but not nearly as career focused as either of the girls, and was only too happy to meditate and eat cereal most of the day. And, to Lori's annoyance, would leave a dribble of milk in the fridge with no ostensible intention of buying more.

"Yes, he's not at the café today, so he might be here for a bit if that's OK?" Kim's eyes were now beginning to open properly, and focus in on Lori. Her dark hair was ruffled, and her eyes met Lori's with a cautious look; with the remains of last night's makeup still smudged around her eyelids.

Lori liked Darren, and he was a damn sight better than Kim's previous boyfriend, she had to confess. Ryan had been the biggest asshole she had ever met, and had cheated on Kim for months before she found out his true character. He had once even cornered Lori at the apartment and tried to kiss her, when Kim had left the room for mere moments. Lori was mortified about the whole incident, and had stressed over how to tell her friend. Each morning she would contemplate either leaving a note on the fridge, calling her at work, or scheduling an "apartment meeting" to impart the sad news that her boyfriend was a low-life. But luckily Kim had caught him out on the town with another girl, and dumped him on the spot. Darren was a lot better; a gentle soul, and Lori certainly wanted her friend to be happy.

"Of course," Lori agreed, but wondered if at this rate Darren should be contributing to the bills, or at least buying a carton of milk!

Lori had been living with Kim since she arrived in New York ten years ago. They had a relaxed friendship that didn't demand too much of Lori's time, which, with her work schedule, was an incredibly important factor in a house-mate. They had met at a fashion show, one of the first Lori had attended, in which everyone knew everyone else, and Lori found herself standing awkwardly by the free bar for most of the night. An outgoing Kim had approached her, eager to avoid her waitressing job and the pair instantly connected. Luckily for Lori, Kim had an apartment that her wealthy parents had bought her years before and had offered her the spare room. The two lived together ever since.

Lori left her small apartment and breathed in the city morning air. That familiar smell of New York she knew so well; freshly baked bagels mixed with salt and diesel that wafted through the streets from the Bay. Lori smiled to herself as she started to speed-walk her daily commute, bag packed and comfy shoes on, she let the world drift past her, and planned the day ahead. *Today would be a good day,* she told herself; no panic attacks, no anxiety, no stress. She left her suburb as shop-attendants rolled their shutters open, and the occasional early morning bakery lights glowed, spilling onto the sidewalk; the day had already started for so many others as Lori merged into the busy street. She loved living in New York. After her short spell in Australia, the years had passed in the blink of an eye. Brisbane had seemed so huge compared to anything Lori had known before, but after coming to New York, its sheer size had devoured Brisbane completely. When the opportunity to work as a coordinator for the New York branch had appeared, she had jumped at the chance to move countries and start her own adventure. Her goal of working up the ranks in the fashion industry was a reality now. After starting her career as a receptionist, to now be sitting as head buyer, she knew firmly that she would continue to progress until she reached the top. At first many people in the Manhattan office assumed she was Australian, which looking back, Lori had embraced as an easily-accepted identity. After several years had passed, and with staff always changing anyway, people just assumed Lori was another American from somewhere irrelevant outside New York. She was aware her accent had changed somewhat, but that wasn't really deliberate on her part. It just happened over time. She allowed people to assume what they wanted, and when colleagues asked where she was from, she would say she lived in Grameray Park, a great spot to live, do you know it? Ah, but where are you really from? they might ask. Then she would say Australia, which was true. But as she thought about it now, why had she never told the truth? Was she ashamed of it? No, it wasn't that. She just didn't want to be defined by it. She wanted to blend in. Be another New Yorker.

But blending in was not always something she had desired. An almost forgotten memory popped into her head as she waited at the pedestrian crossing, one involving her old school teacher Mrs MacMaster who had often told her to lower her voice when singing with the girl's choir. The small school was excited to be finalists in a competition and Lori couldn't wait to sing. But on the morning of the contest, her old school mistress had taken her aside.

"Now Lori I have an important job for you, you think you can do it?"

Lori had looked up at the tall matronly woman, in her waistcoat and long thick skirt that swished as she walked. For as long as she could remember, no matter the weather, Mrs MacMaster was always to be found in a woollen skirt.

"I want you to *pretend* that you're singing - we can only have so many voices with the kind of acoustics this church hall provides. So my girl: stand at the back, smile, and mime the words, and you will be doing your part for the choir just as well as anyone else."

Being so young and excited to be on stage, Lori had

nodded, and stood shoulder to shoulder with her classmates and pretended to sing. Now, looking back on that incident, perhaps it had made more of a lasting impact on her than she had ever realised. She could still see the small child standing in the echoing church hall, trying her best to ignore the scratchy ruffle collar of her blouse along with an even itchier tartan skirt.

A young, attractive girl wearing Doc Martens, a leather jacket and tartan pants walked past Lori, and she almost laughed at the coincidence. The tartan was a red Royal Stewart weave, which Lori noticed had become "on trend" of late. But the tartan she knew and loved well, was of course *Robertson*. It was her surname after all and a part of her identity. Even if the lingering memories of her wearing it were uncomfortable.

The truth was - Lori was Scottish, and from the very rural Highlands of Scotland at that. After moving to Australia when she was barely twenty, then onto New York for years on top of that, she had adopted a gentle American drawl. It worked for her. To be in a different country; being anyone she wanted to be. *Creating her own story.*

Lori crossed through Madison Square park, walking past the trees and small patches of green. She came this way to work almost every day, but somehow today she thought of home. Not Australia, but her real home: Scotland.

Another day presented more problems, with the usual small fires to be put out. Lori briefed Julian on the day's tasks, chased manufacturers to speed up a delivery and gradually worked through the emails that were now piling up in their hundreds. Alex had come to Lori's desk with a cup of coffee and a box of chocolates with a big red ribbon on top. "These are just a small thank you for helping me," her colleague smiled shyly.

"Oh, you didn't need to!" Lori took the cup gladly.

"I absolutely do, you've been so kind. I know you have a lot on your plate too!" Alex sat down at her desk, which was parallel with Lori's. "I just don't know how you do it, you seem so calm and collected. I'm freaking out at this workload every day." Alex grimaced at her computer screen.

"Do I?" Lori shook her head, and wondered if anyone had ever really come close to guessing how she actually felt inside. "I'm just trying to take each day as it comes." She sighed and drank more of her coffee, welcoming the caffeine. "I think the key is to remind yourself that we're not saving lives here – no one is going to die if we don't select the right style, or if we're late with a delivery or forget to prioritise a customer complaint. So what's the worst that can happen?"

Alex tore her eyes away from her computer screen. "Really? That's what you do?" She chuckled to herself in a daze. "You know, you're absolutely right!"

Lori had never asked Alex her age, it wasn't a thing that mattered to her usually. But as similar as they were in age, Alex had been a buyer for far longer and strangely, Lori felt that *she* was fast becoming the blonde girl's mentor.

"Sometimes we will just never have enough time to get through things. That's normal!" Lori leaned back in her chair and crossed her legs, resigning herself to make this her break time. She would work through lunch.

Alex sighed and suddenly put her hands over her face. Startled, Lori looked around to see if anyone was listening to their conversation, luckily no eyes watched them, all likely too engrossed in their own work to notice. She spun her chair closer to her upset colleague.

"Hey, it's OK! I can help you!"

"I can't take any more of your help!" Alex looked almost close to tears, she bit her lip and glanced around the office. "I'm not sure how long I can do this!" she whispered, as her eyes continued to dart about the other desks.

"It's just a tough spot, you'll get through it!" Lori put her hand on Alex's arm, trying to comfort her as best she could.

"That's just it - I don't think it is anymore!" Alex leaned her head on her hand and looked sideways at Lori, her eyes red. "I haven't slept properly in months!" she sighed shakily, and a tear fell from one eye. She wiped it away swiftly. "To be honest, I think it's more like years. I don't eat well either, everyday I make a sandwich or I plan to go out and get something, but things always crop up and I end up just eating shitty rice cakes all day." Lori had certainly noticed that even before she joined the menswear department, Alex had been rapidly losing weight. "And now... my boyfriend has split up with me!" another tear fell and she covered the side of her face with her hand, shielding herself from any onlookers.

Lori squeezed her arm. "OK breathe, don't think anymore on this for a second, just breathe." They both sat together in quiet companionship until Lori spoke first. "I think you may need a wee holiday? Maybe just some days away?" Lori suggested quietly.

"Wee?" Alex looked up blankly.

"Aye." Lori slipped up, the words came out of her mouth without her realising, and she quickly caught herself from letting her Scottish accent go any further. "I mean, how about going on a short vacation?"

"A vacation?" Alex shook her head in alarm. "No way,

who would do my job when I'm gone? I can't even take a day off when I'm ill!"

"OK well at least just take some time right now, go for a walk around the block. Clear your head; maybe switch off your phone and leave the office for a bit?" Lori patted her hand gently.

Alex dabbed her eyes slowly, her shoulders slumped. "You're right, I'll go out for a walk."

Lori spent the next couple of hours in front of her computer, consumed by the constant flow of emails. She noticed that Alex had been away for some time, and as a result had to answer her desk phone and take messages, writing each one down on a post-it note. The coloured bits of paper very quickly covered Alex's desk, with various departments chasing up outstanding issues. The day sped through to early evening, and Lori decided she needed an early night. As she started to pack up her things, her phone rang. It was Frankie.

"Hi Frankie!" Lori breezed. "Everything OK?"

"Hi Lori, well – yes, things are fine. I wondered if you could spare a minute? Could you come to my office?"

"Sure!" Lori ended the call and walked upstairs to the management offices. She liked and admired her boss; the older lady was ambitious, clever and valued her staff according to their talents rather than their contacts or personality. She almost always met Frankie each week for a coffee and catch-up. She had once overheard some of the other buyers talking about this fact: "She's so playing the game, all she wants is to be at the top and she's just using Frankie to get there!" Lori didn't blame them for being suspicious, but more than anything she simply liked Frankie, and enjoyed learning from her as a colleague - besides, it was the older woman who had asked *her* for a coffee in the first place. Since then the pair had developed a good working relationship, and Lori felt lucky to have Frankie on her side.

She walked up to the receptionist's desk, who immediately waved her through: "Just go ahead Lori, she's expecting you" the young girl with glasses smiled briefly, then cast her eyes back over sheets of paper before her. Lori found Frankie was standing with her back to the door, looking out the window at the city lights. The sun had already dropped behind the high buildings.

Lori hovered at the open door not wanting to disturb the moment, but coughed to get her boss's attention.

"Lori, come in! Sorry, I was somewhere else." She gestured to the leather sofa beside her that sat in front of the window, with the skyline of the city looming impressively at its back. She sat down on the sofa beside Lori, and took off her thick black glasses, pinching the bridge of her nose, her eyes closed. With short ash blonde hair, red lipstick and smart black dungarees, Frankie looked years younger than her age. But today she most definitely appeared exhausted.

"Everything OK?" Lori sat upright on the uncomfortable sofa, waiting for whatever news may be coming.

"Yes, it's all go here isn't it?" Frankie crossed her legs and leaned back. "How are you coping in your new role?"

"Oh I'm getting there, constantly learning something new every day. But I'm really thankful for the opportunity, and for Julian!" Lori had been an assistant for many years and if it wasn't for Frankie's promotion, she'd still be there. Lori felt indebted to her boss, her promotion was a huge compliment, considering all the many other girls who would claw each other out of the way for a similar opportunity. But Frankie had offered the job to Lori with no interview. Something unheard of, especially in the fashion industry. She also wanted to give a small shout-out to Julian, for his recent efforts with the back-catalogues.

"Good. Yes it'll take some time Lori, but I have every faith in you." She smiled briefly then took off her chunky black earrings and placed them on the table next to her discarded glasses. Massaging her earlobes, she sighed. "So I had a phone call from Alex earlier. She's resigned."

"What? But I was only talking to her a few hours ago!"

"Yes well, it turns out she's been struggling here... and she's had personal things going on too."

Lori couldn't believe the news. She had been sure Alex would be fine. They all had bad days; Lori had them too, that was the norm in the industry.

"Poor Alex!" Lori looked sheepishly at Frankie. "I better let you know, she had confided in me earlier that it was getting too much. But I thought she'd be fine after a quick walk!" Lori looked down.

"This job is not for everyone. I'm just sorry she never told me earlier, I could have done something." Frankie shifted on the sofa turning to face Lori. "I'm afraid this means we'll all need to do our bit until we find another person to fill in."

"Of course." The words came out of Lori's mouth instantly, and she wondered where she'd find the time to cover someone else's workload on top of her new task for the designers.

"I'm not saying just you, but I will need to split the work between the other buyers. I thought I'd let you know first before I call in everyone for a meeting tomorrow."

"Thank you," Lori said in a small voice.

"She'll be missed, and I know you both got on well."

Lori nodded unable to find the words. They did get "on well", as Frankie suggested, but if Lori really thought about it, she knew very little of Alex. Apart from what she had heard today, they would usually only talk about work. *But that was normal in high-powered office jobs, wasn't it?*

"I just want you to know, I saw what you were doing for Alex. You are a good team player Lori. And if you keep this up, particularly over the next couple of months...well I think there may be another promotion for you." Frankie nodded, and looked directly at Lori.

"Oh, but... I just started this role!" Lori backtracked, confused about what exactly was being suggested.

"Perhaps," Frankie nodded again, "but I need a hard worker, a member of staff who I can rely on. It may be the case that someone will need to take over from me at some stage..."

"Frankie, I don't know what to say!"

Frankie tapped Lori gently on the hand. "Nothing is finalised yet, but if you keep going the way I think you're going, you'll do very well here."

Lori walked back to her apartment that night reflecting on her day. Seeing her friend Alex leave without saying good-bye, and now with the idea of a promotion on the cards, she didn't know how to feel. She should feel happy that all her hard work was finally paying off; after years of toiling as an assistant she could be running the company soon. But all she could really think about was the workload to come. On the plus side, she hadn't locked herself in a cubicle today, although she barely had time to go to the bathroom. Lori took a deep breath in and out. Could she really keep this up? At some stage, eventually, she would burn out just like Alex. But then, wasn't this the career trajectory she had always wanted? Why wasn't she happier? Half-distracted, Lori felt her phone vibrate and answered it swiftly:

"Lori speaking."

The voice on the other side gasped and then shrieked: "Lori!"

"Tammy? Is that you? Is everything OK? Is it Gran?" Lori couldn't help the panic in her voice, she hadn't spoken to her family in so long, that her mind flew instantly to the negative.

She heard her little sister sniff loudly, then laugh down the phone. "The best news: I'm getting married!"

Relief spilled over Lori, and as the good news registered, a smile broke out on her face. "That's great! Is it to Alan?" Lori hadn't seen her sister in three years; *oh... wow, was it that long?* and knew that she had been seeing the very tall and cheery Alan Mackenzie, but since moving away from home all those years ago, she only vaguely remembered him from high school.

"Of course it's Alan!" Her sister sniped. "You think I'd get married to someone I'd just met?" Her tone had quickly changed, Tammy always had a hot temper.

"I'm sorry, I'm a bit all over the place at the moment. I'm so happy for you both, really, Alan seems like such a nice guy!"

"The best guy I know" Tammy reverted to her sunny self. "Can you believe it? I'm getting married! I can't wait!"

"Me too, what can I do for it? Have you thought about dates?" Lori was sure she'd be asked to organise most of the wedding. Tammy never shied away from asking every favour under the sun, and Lori was certain she would be happy to hand over the bulk of the worst tasks to her. She and their eldest sister Jean were the organisers in the family, while Tammy was the fun, carefree one.

"Would love help, I'll need my sisters with me. And you'll be so impressed - we've already set the date!"

"OK great! I'll pop it in my calendar"

"I'm so happy Lori! It's 1st of June!"

Lori mentally made a note to request holiday leave in plenty of time at the office. "OK, so: perhaps May next year I can come home and help organise whatever still needs doing the month before the wedding?"

The voice on the other end went quiet. "Oh – wait - you think I mean *next* year? No Lori, 1st of June *this* year!" She chuckled over the phone in astonishment. "Silly sausage, I'm not waiting a year!"

"But that's... like... three weeks away!" Lori blurted out, and stopped in the middle of the busy sidewalk. Passersby shuffled around her, some casting annoyed glances.

"Two and a half weeks, actually!"

"Absolutely not. I can't make that! We're losing people in my department; it's the worst timing. I'm sorry sis, you need to change the date – do it next year!" Lori gulped down her anxiety and continued walking. Tammy was out of her mind, there was no way Frankie would let her leave work for a couple of weeks, not now. It was out of the question.

"But we can't have it next year," came a small voice.

"Why can't you? I can be there and help with everything if I have time. Does Gran know about this?" Lori couldn't imagine her gran allowing such a quick wedding. It all sounded insane.

"We just can't, OK." Tammy sighed, the cheer lost from her voice.

"Well I can't come home at the drop of a hat! I work in New York, Tam!"

The other end of the line was quiet for some moments.

"Tammy?" Lori called out, worriedly. "Are you there?" There was another sigh, and a small grunt.

"OK... if you must know, Alan's parents are very religious, so... we need to get married soon. You see I didn't say -" She paused. "I'm... I'm pregnant and his parents would be just hideous if they knew it had happened before we got married!"

"Oh!" Lori was taken aback, her head was beginning to spin with all the announcements. "That's great too... I mean about the baby!" She stammered, unsure what to say. Was her sister actually happy she was going to be a mother?

"Thanks; it is good! The thing is, we've not lived together - his parents had stipulated we should get married before we live together, and as they live so nearby, Alan wanted to keep a good relationship going with them. They've done so much for us. It's just... well, they don't even think we've had sex! I think they reckon we'll wait until the wedding night...!"

"Oh, come on!" Lori laughed at the situation, despite herself. "In this day and age, there's no way they can possibly think that they can control their son's sex life! I'm sure you're mistaken Tam, they'll be thrilled you're pregnant!"

"No Lori, they aren't like that. They are lovely people, but I don't want to start our marriage on the wrong foot. They've been really kind to me; I can't do it to them. We're having the wedding next month, that's it – I'm sorry. Look, I'm sure work will give you time off, when was the last time you took a *real* holiday to see us?"

Lori didn't want to admit it, but she was sure it had been

a long time since she had had a proper break. Could it be two years? Was that even possible? Maybe she was already on the same track as Alex, without realising it. Almost at her apartment, she chewed the inside of her lip. "What about having it in August - or even July?" She clutched at straws, hoping her sister would reconsider.

"We can't. Alan is away on the rig for July and August, and any later than that I'll be showing big time."

Lori remained quiet.

"Please Lori, I need my big sis!"

"You have Jean too!" Lori wondered what their older sibling thought of this situation. But, as she was a single mother to two girls, and worked as the local school teacher, she was sure Jean didn't have a whole lot of spare time to even help out. Lori would need to go, but how could she leave her job at such a time? She walked up the steps to her front door then leaned against the handrail. The phone still glued to her ear, she closed her eyes; her sister on the other end waiting for her answer. "OK - I will see what I can do."

"Oh - yes, thank you thank you!"

"I can't promise anything mind you!"

"But you'll try, and I know that you'll do everything in your power to get here! Love you!" Her sister rang off leaving Lori numb, standing outside her apartment building.

Tomorrow was going to be awful; Frankie would announce Alex's resignation and that they all needed to pull together and take on more work, respectively, for the foreseeable future. And Lori was going to add to their problems, the worst timing to ask for a holiday! Oh how everyone was going to hate her!

4

"You're leaving?" Michael looked at Lori wide-eyed, as she took a sip from her martini. They were sitting at the counter of their favourite cocktail bar, which was fast becoming flooded with office workers, eager to find a spot for their well-earned after-work drinks.

"I'm not leaving, I'm just taking a break. A vacation." She let the effects of the alcohol wash over her.

Michael raised his eyebrows. "A vacation? It sounds like your sister is clicking her fingers and having her way again!"

"Oh come on, it's not like that!" Lori had had a long day. After discussing her situation with Frankie straight off the bat, she had spent the rest of her time working at full pelt. All the while feeling as though she was letting down her whole team. To her surprise, however, Frankie had suggested that perhaps a break would be good for her.

"I'm so sorry Frankie, my sister needs me..." Lori had warmed to her boss even more at her understanding.

"I know you wouldn't ask unless you had to," Frankie sighed, as Lori stood in front of her desk. "Though I won't say I'm particularly thrilled about it. But in this business there's no right time for anything. There's always something! It'll still be like this in a few weeks when you come back, I'm sure!" Frankie gave her a small smile. "What's more, my receptionist tells me you haven't logged a holiday for well over a year. I have to give you the time off!" She turned in her swivel chair and stood up.

"Thank you, Frankie. I can work off site. Just call me, I'll be available!" Lori bit her lip, trying to contain herself, slightly in shock that she was getting the go-ahead.

"I might just take you up on that - but in the meantime, I want you to give a handover to the other buyers, and to your assistant." Frankie walked towards her with a wry smile. "I can't imagine Julian will take this too well!"

"Frankie, we have a meeting with the board!" The spectacled receptionist had popped her head around the door, urging her boss to follow her upstairs with a gesture of her pen and pad.

"Of course!" Frankie straightened her jacket and nudged Lori playfully on the elbow as she passed.

"You have a good time. Come back refreshed!"

Lori had been relieved at the outcome, though it had not brought the same feeling to her department.

She turned to face Michael, his lips pinched tightly. "Your sister is getting her own way then?" He shook his head slightly, clearly not impressed with Lori's original news.

"If she doesn't get her own way for her wedding, when else should she?" Lori couldn't help but be exasperated at his tone. "You've never met her, or even spoken to her. Why do you say that?"

He squinted at her with surprise. "It's just how you speak about her." He moved his glass in gentle circles making his ice cubes knock together with a tinkle. "How long will you be away?" His eyes remained on the glass as he spoke, and

Lori had to stop herself from becoming even more frustrated.

"A couple of weeks."

"It'll take a full day just to get back to Australia!" He looked at her, earnestly this time, and Lori's heart stopped. She had been sure he knew where she came from! How on earth had they come so far together without ever getting round to her hometown?

"Michael... hun... I'm not sure you know everything about me...."

The next day allowed Lori to catch up on her chores for the week. Usually she worked her weekends, but now she needed to organise her trip back to Scotland; there was no time for conference calls. She had already booked her flight by 8am, and had started packing, rummaging around in her large wardrobe wondering what one wore in Scotland nowadays? The last time she had gone home was years ago, and usually she'd borrow clothes from her sisters, but things were different now. As she pulled out various examples of Versace, Armani, Dior and Westwood, all beautiful and luxurious, she smiled at how successful she felt just wearing them. On this occasion, however, they wouldn't be suitable: in the Highlands of Scotland it rained almost every day, and the thought of getting her Dior silk hacking jacket ruined couldn't be imagined! She put the majority of them back, and opted for the most practical clothing she could find. *Perhaps a few dresses would be nice too?* She folded everything in neat piles on her bed, as the sun streamed through the small window, casting its light over her calmly, warming her. Lori took packing suitcases very seriously; time and effort were important if you wanted the least amount of ironing, and the maximum out of the case's capacity. There was a system of packing she always followed whenever herself and Michael would leave the city for a quick getaway, and shoes were always to be packed first. She bent down on her knees and sifted through all the many pairs she had on the base of the wardrobe. She mostly came across high heels, which were all fabulous, but she knew that stilettos were not the best type of footwear to take. Lori grunted and padded her hands into the darker nooks, delving further into the back of her wardrobe. Her only find was a box hidden under a few scarves that must have fallen from their hooks. Her heart fluttered as she pulled it towards her; it was her old memory box. She lifted the lid, and gently brushed the photographs of her parents, her gran and her sisters. She smiled at a photo of her mum and dad cuddling her on the beach, her dad sporting a large moustache, which must have been the fashion at the time, her mum in a light, yellow flowery dress. It must have been taken at the beach near their village of Arlochy, years before the boat accident. A very small Lori sat beside them on a tartan rug, and from her expression, a little too distracted by the sandwich in her hand to smile at the camera. Her hair matched her father's almost identically. The colour of a rusty iron shed, exposed to the elements for a decade or so. A trait that passed to her sisters also. Lori smiled to herself; her parents had been truly in love, she had known that even at four years old, on the picnic blanket. Her mother and father did everything together; even on that fateful day out on the boat, they were together to the end. After all the many years that passed, Lori still felt a longing to know them more. But in the scheme of things, she had accepted the loss of her parents as one could, and now cherished the memories she had of them. They remained in the back of her mind, almost exactly as they were in the photograph; smiling on the beach. She flipped the photo over and visualised them for a moment, focusing on their features and characteristics as best she could. As much in love as they had been, she could still recall the fights they would often have. Her father had been laid off from his well-paid job at the forestry commission, which came as a blow to her mother, and for years afterwards he struggled to find work. He had taken up various subsequent notions of working for himself, from a stint as a very bad carpenter, to another as a sea-sick fisherman. He lacked the direction and drive that Lori's mother had. Whom if given the chance, would have got herself a good job no matter what, letting her father be a stay at home dad. But it was another time back then, the idea of a stay at home dad would have been unthinkable: a man's duty was to be the breadwinner, and the woman made the home. Lori hated the idea of society moulding her into someone she wasn't, just as she knew she could never allow herself to be unemployed, even the idea made her palms sweat. If she had not got her golden ticket with Costner's, she would have followed most careers, taking any work that she found. Thankfully, she need not rely on anyone else, only herself and she knew her sheer drive would steer her upwards. A part of Lori couldn't shake the thought that if her mother had supported them financially, things might have been different. Even though her father was the glorified breadwinner, the last few months before their death, the bread, so to speak, had disappeared almost completely. It was so long ago now, she had been very young when the news had come through. But her gran was there to take care of them all, and from then on they had lived with her in their parents' house. *Dearest Gran.* Lori hadn't spoken to her in a few weeks, but was undeniably excited to see her again and be enveloped in her loving arms.

Lori continued to pick through the contents of her memory box, and soon discovered several old envelopes addressed to Australia. They were from Callum. Lori shook her head slowly with a small grin; she hadn't thought of him in a long time. Callum, the gorgeous boy from her local school, who she had thought was "out of her league", but who had turned out by the end of school, to have the very same opinion of her. They had spent the most amazing summer together, before Lori had left for Australia. She opened the first envelope, and seeing his scrawl still made her heart flutter. She bit her lip, shaking her head again with a fond smile, and summoned the courage to read.

> *Dear Lori,*
> *I hope you landed safely, and are settling well into life "down under". I can't imagine how it must feel being in such an exciting place! Are you traveling around or staying in the same spot? It's bleak and miserable here, you really left at the best time - I believe it's summer with you now? Not much has changed since you left, I've been working at the fish farm — pretty dull work but the pay is good. I'm still playing shinty, last week we won a match against Newtonmore, so it was a crazy night celebrating — it's been years since we won a game against them!*
> *I'm thinking of saving some cash and maybe do a wee trip too, suggest anywhere? Your gran got a new puppy the other day I'm sure she's*

probably told you, the cutest little collie. She
took pity on old farmer MacAulay, he had a
litter of 8 puppies he needed to re-home. I was
tempted myself, but thought it best to stay
free at the moment, see where things take me.
Anyway, let me know how you are. I have been
thinking of you, and missing your laugh.
From Scotland with love,
Callum

Lori crawled towards the bed and sat resting her back against the frame. Was Callum her first love? She didn't know; all those explosive emotions were at a time when the only thing she wanted was to get away from her tiny home-town and explore the rest of the world. It was a rare thing to find a man writing letters, and reading the words now Lori felt a little guilty at how she had treated him. She hadn't wanted to stay and settle down in Arlochy right after high school. She knew deep down that she had to spread her wings. The idea of finding a mediocre local job, forever struggling to pay bills hadn't tempted her. And she was glad she had moved; not only was she living in the best city in the world, she had a dream job, a successful boyfriend and the luxury of being able to buy whatever she wanted. She had always yearned to live somewhere like New York ever since watching movies as a child. To live a glamorous life. And now she was.

Lori tucked away the few letters into her suitcase and finished packing; extinguishing any old memories before they came to the surface.

Michael walked under the rich green trees that lined the walkway, with the busy traffic passing on one side and the bright central park on the other, he stayed anchored to the street between quiet and chaos. He let his mind drift. He couldn't ignore his feelings another second more. Lori had never told him about her past, shouldn't the fact that she had lied to him all these years be a concern? He scratched his chin, which unusually sported a day's worth of stubble. She admitted that she was not in fact from Australia, but from Scotland - the other side of the world. She had stipulated it shouldn't matter where she was from, she was still the same person to him, but as Michael walked on the feeling of unease clung to him. *She had lied.* She was not the person he had thought she was. He remembered Lori's talk of going to the beach often as a child, which he always imagined as a place of white sands, and shark-filled waters. He had pictured Australia, because she had told him that was where she was from. How could he trust her now? What stories did she tell his colleagues when he wasn't there? He had wanted to be with someone who had an uncomplicated life, and thought Lori ticked that box. He needed a relaxed and peaceful home to return to each evening, with a wife who supported him without anything hidden in the closet. With the coming years ahead, he would need to focus more on his career, he needed someone who wouldn't cause any drama. *Was Lori that woman?* Or was she simply carrying around too much baggage for him to welcome into his life? Last night she had told him about Arlochy and about her mother and father dying in a tragic boat accident when she and her two sisters were young – *Christ, that explained why the youngest always got her way!* The story was sad, and he was sorry for her loss, but what still niggled away at him was the idea of trust. Could he trust her, or would she be forever hiding herself from him? Why hadn't she mentioned it all before? Michael walked on, passing chattering families, and couples strolling in the warm afternoon sun. He took off his blazer and folded it over his arm, turning onto a quiet path through the park. He wandered aimlessly around the reservoir and walked over The Gothic Bridge, pausing in the centre. Leaning on his jacket, he reached into the inside pocket, and opened the small box with its diamond ring nestled on a red velvet cushion. He had almost proposed to her before all this, and though a part of him felt he had escaped something unpleasant, another part of him felt an aching pang of disappointment. He stood still, watching ducks glide on the water in the far distance. If only he could have no cares in the world, just like one of those ducks, content to just drift on by, and bob down for the occasional grub. But he was a Hadley, and Hadley's didn't drift, they succeeded. His grandfather had made his money in the car industry, then sold the business in favour of buying property. From then on, the Hadley men didn't flounder; they were focused, and had nothing to want for besides ever-increasing ambition. Michael had initially imagined himself running away after his studies had finished, with ideas of backpacking. But when the day of his graduation drew nearer, he found he no longer had the desire to be sleeping in flea-invested beds, or mixing with people he would never meet again. His world was in New York. Everyone and everything that mattered was here. Eventually, opportunities had presented themselves often in the circles he moved in, and with time he had gained employment at a very exclusive firm in which he hoped he would continue to thrive. It was the way things should be, for people like him. Michael scratched his chin again, deciding to go home and shave before the day was over. Lori would be leaving soon, and as he put the box back into his pocket, he thought perhaps it was best that she did take some time off after all. At least so he could have space to think. He could set some new goals for his future, and decide what he wanted - and if that included Lori after all.

5

Before take-off, Lori scrolled through her messages on her phone. Since arriving at the airport she had received so many calls and messages from Julian, that she had lost count how often she swiped upward to hear his high-pitched 'Lori?' on the end of the line. Even after sending her own work to the other buyers, Julian still persisted in calling her instead of asking them for guidance. Although Lori didn't mind his troubled loyalty; she had thrown everyone in at the deep end and would do whatever she could to be reachable. But now, as the air hostess signalled for her to switch off her phone, she begrudgingly did so and focused her attentions on some paperwork instead. This trip would not be a complete waste of her professional time she vowed, she would still remain involved with the company. She would show Frankie her commitment, and would succeed, and as a result she would never want for anything - her job would be secure, and her salary generous.

∽

Lori ventured out of the tiny Inverness airport and immediately switched on her phone to find a message from Tammy:

> *"Sorry sis, too much going on here for anyone to*
> *come to the airport! But you could get the bus*
> *and we'll pick you up in Fort William?*
> *Soz! xxx"*

Lori suppressed the anger that immediately flared up inside her; this was just how her sister was. Even the way she had worded the message: trying to be so nice that it just ended up sounding passive aggressive. Against her better judgement, Lori stomped her foot like a child throwing a tantrum.

This was typical Tammy, her sister was so thoughtless at times. Even when they were little girls she was the same. One Christmas Lori got a long awaited and loved Barbie, only for her little sister to steal it, then hand it back to her come January - with one arm missing and ripped clothing! "*So soz!*" She could hear Tammy's voice ring in her ears. Well, there was no way she was getting the bus, even if Tammy did plan to pick her up from the bus station, so grudgingly. Lori huffed as she dragged her luggage to the car-hire desk.

"Hello lovey, can I help you?" A middle-aged man in a green and black uniform looked up over his computer.

"Yes - a car please, maybe automatic if you have one?" Lori realised her accent was still very much American, and she consciously made an effort to revert back to her old tones.

"OK then... do you have a booking?"

"No booking I'm afraid." She rummaged around in her bag for her driver's license.

He glanced at the computer screen in front of him and made a face. "Sorry lovey, we don't have anything available. It's very busy right now, tourist season and all!"

Lori bit her lip, she was exhausted but the last thing she wanted was to endure a twisty bus ride. "You have nothing at all? I need to get to Arlochy!"

"Oh lovely part of the world, that is." The man stopped looking at the computer and stood up beaming at Lori. "My sister takes her kids there every year. I always say though, 'Betty why don't you go somewhere else; there's a whole world out there!' But she loves it, think she plans to move there when she's old." The friendly man in his strong Invernessian accent carried on speaking as Lori daydreamed about leaving the conversation and hop in an Audi convertible. She mentally pinched herself to cheer up a bit, she should be happy to be home. But right now, all she wanted was to get to Arlochy, have a shower and check in with work before anything else happened or before Julian had an aneurysm.

"Do you have any suggestions on what I should do?" Lori interrupted the cheery man who was now talking about how many tourists the small airport was receiving over the last few days, and all the wonderful places they had come from.

"Oh! OK!" He stopped short, scratched his chin and looked at his computer once again. "Let me have a wee look, see what I can do!" He spent some time clicking the mouse and tapping the keyboard loudly, that Lori eventually began to wonder if he was actually doing anything, or just making appearances.

"Right love, best bet – get to Fort William, and we can have a car waiting for you there!"

Lori inwardly groaned, she hated getting the bus, the journey was a couple of hours and the roads tortuous. Her sister had said she would be there to meet her off the bus, but driving directly without having to rely on anyone else's schedule was vastly preferable. There was nothing else she could do, so she thanked the man, and set out for the bus into Inverness city.

It was early morning, and the shuttle bus took minutes to get to the city, everything seeming so shrunken to her after her years in New York. The bus went over the River Ness, to meet the charming old city standing proudly along the edge - though really the clusters of small stone buildings looked more like a town to Lori. Victorian red sandstone houses and churches lined the riverside in between trees. The whole scene looked like a beautiful painting; set against the backdrop of the castle with saltire flag perched on its highest point, blowing in the breeze as if waving at Lori to welcome her home. After Lori got on the connecting bus, she sat at the front to avoid any risk of nausea, which was something she was prone to. So much so, that her mum would always shout over her shoulder in their battered old Ford: "Look ahead if you're car-sick! Look ahead toots!", to a pre-teen Lori who would avidly watch buildings, trees and hills go past, without much consideration for the outcome until it was inevitably too late.

"Where you heading my dear?" the old bus driver asked her as he started up the engine, and Lori felt immediate and acute regret at sitting in the front. Perhaps two hours of mild nausea wouldn't have been so bad if she'd known it came with a generous dose of privacy at the back of the grimy old vehicle.

"Arlochy."

"Oh lovely, I went there with my wife once. Good place to be this time of year!" He looked at her brightly in his rear-view mirror.

"Yes, I'm looking forward to see it. It's been a couple of years." Lori smiled then looked out the window to see trees flashing past, but hastily reverted her eyes back to the front before the queasy feeling engulfed her.

"Are you from there? You sound American!" the man playfully winked.

"Yes I'm from there, spent a few years away. Well a lot of years away. I'm sure my accent will come back quick enough!"

"You just have a blether to me the rest of the journey deary and I'll get you talking as if you never left!" He laughed, and turned the first of many corners. Lori texted her sister not to bother picking her up, and lay back making herself as comfortable as possible. She chuckled quietly to herself; there was no way of getting through this land without people continually talking to her – *never in New York*, she mused.

"That's us in Fort William!" the bus driver bellowed as he stopped outside a supermarket.

The passengers piled to get off the bus: "Thanks driver!" they called one by one, passing by.

"Have a good time home!" the old man winked again as Lori was the last to alight and collect her luggage.

"Thanks, safe journey onto Skye!"

"Oh gawd, don't remind me!" He put his head in his hand in mock-despair as Lori laughed, the poor man would be driving some more hours still, though personally she couldn't imagine staying on the bus a minute longer. She walked along a row of parked taxis to a small car with a young woman leaning against the door and swiping on her phone. She was wearing the same green and black uniform as the man from the airport, and looked up as Lori approached her. Lori gave a sigh of relief: she could rely on herself to get home now.

After years not driving in New York, Lori found herself gripping the wheel and swearing loudly at any vehicles that came within a mile radius of her. Which so happened to be camper-vans and buses that kept her wedged between them without any real view of the road. Resigning herself that she was trapped between giants for the remainder of the trip, Lori reflected on the joys of living in certain areas in the Highlands. The roads being so busy in the summer that most locals avoided going anywhere, then when winter came there was nothing open until late spring! Luckily, the more she continued on the winding road, the quieter things grew as tourists turned off at various attractions. Eventually the twists and turns became open roads and Lori cruised the familiar last section of the way back home. The views were spectacular; she had forgotten how dramatic the landscape was, and after so many years living in between buildings upon buildings, she looked out to the wide-open space before her in awe. The sea spread out into a bank of glittering mist on one side, and jagged, heather-patched hills on the other. Past the opal water in the distance were a few islands that Lori hoped to visit on this trip home, probably for the first time in twenty years. She put on the radio and tuned into the local radio station, trying to remember the frequency, until she stumbled on an old familiar nineties dance song that she remembered only too well. Lori marvelled at how even now the radio station played old dated tracks, happy to remain in the past, with no intention to catch up with the rest of the world. She remembered days spent at the station volunteering after school - which mainly consisted of cleaning. But she had loved it, and often imagined being a dj herself - as well as a diver, an artist, an explorer, and a writer. All the endless career paths and possibilities she had desired as a girl came flooding back, making her laugh to herself quietly in the fading sun. She thought back to summer nights spent by the sea front; going to ceilidh dances; barbecues in their garden; cheering wildly at the Highland games, the smell of smoke and sea salt in the air... and everything else in between. A few miles from her home and she caught sight of the big estate house on the hill, looming over the surrounding countryside before the village came into view. Its grounds were often used for concerts by local musicians, and in the autumn months a music school would open up there, teaching traditional instruments and singing. Lori winced at her stint singing Gaelic songs in the MOD, or rather, miming them, as her teacher had demanded. It had been some time since she had spoken a word of her native language. She was sure her gran wouldn't be pleased, but what could the old lady expect when half of her life had been spent on a different continent. Gaelic was not the language of the future, though she had toyed with the idea of Mandarin, or Hindi, something that would help her career down the line, but always coming to the conclusion that there were only so many hours in the day. Lori reflected on Michael's talents, being fluent in Italian and French gave him a cultured air that Lori wished she had. What would Michael think of her home? Her heart ached at how things were left between them and she wished he was with her now, perhaps she could call him and ask him to fly over? Lori was momentarily distracted and almost missed the turnoff for Arlochy. Focusing her mind back to the task in hand, she turned into the small single-track road. Picturesque old crofters cottages stood on one side of the road behind a single line of trees, which were covered in a glowing candy-pink blossom. This was undoubtedly the best time of year to come to the village, as the bus driver had said; nature thrived abundantly, and there was a buzz in the air that Lori could almost smell as she turned the corner at the end of the road. The view opened out onto a stretch of shimmering sea, with yachts scattered along the shoreline. She couldn't believe how long she'd been away, but strangely enough, everything looked the same: even an old bright red fishing boat remained anchored in the same spot from summers past. The car crept past the village hall, the bookshop, the small super-market, the café and pub at just under thirty miles an hour. Tourists meandered in the sunshine, popping into the boutiques, and some strolling down the pier, pointing now and then at the scenery she knew so well. Her heart fluttered suddenly; with excitement or nervousness, she didn't know which. What she did know was that in just a few moments she would see her gran's house, their home, and she anticipated the accompanying bittersweet pang that would come tugging at her chest. Past the Post Office and another strip of houses she finally spotted the brightly-painted post-box at the side of the road, a replica of the original cottage, before all the many alterations her gran had orchestrated over the last two decades. Lori turned down the drive to the full-size, mismashed dwelling, snuggled in between trees at the end of the lane on a pebbled path. The car ground over the stones, rolling slowly to a halt as she parked by the front door. It was an unusual style of cottage compared to others in the area. With all the modernisation it had undergone, caused it to spill and bulge out in front, allowing little space for cars to park. The only means of exit was reversing out onto the main road, which wasn't exactly the safest option. Lori was amazed to see there were no other cars parked, especially since Tammy had already started on the wedding plans. She had been sure everyone else would have been installed around the table to greet her. A little disappointed that her family had not made much of an effort, having half-expected a party, or at least some kind of small welcoming back into the fold, she collected her bag, and tried to shake off the feeling. She was expecting far too much, especially when she hadn't made much time for them over the years. Lori glanced at her watch; it was nearly dinner time - *where was everyone?* Her feet crunched on the pebbled ground as she walked under the green leafy archway that lead up to Gran's impressively large front door. She knocked a couple of times, and let herself in; it was normal in the Highland villages to leave your door unlocked, luckily enough, though something she would of course never do in New York. The door led into a hallway with immaculately polished wooden floors; her gran had always been a serious cleaner, and that was evidently still true. She tread over Moroccan rugs towards the open-plan kitchen and living-room. Colours and textures surrounded her. Since the girls were old enough, her gran had loved traveling to exotic countries to explore new cultures. Artwork and memorabilia hung on the walls and adorned the furniture, hailing from countries like Greece, Mexico and Brazil. It was a huge space, inside that house. Lori had always thought so, as though her gran wanted to be perpetually prepared for a large group at the drop of a hat. The fridge and kitchen table were similarly expansive for a woman who lived alone, as well as the lounge area, with its wide sofas that would sit a football team comfortably. Lori walked over to the sliding doors that stood between the rooms, and made her way onto the wooden decking and garden. The grass had been cut recently, but the patch where Lori and her sister Jean had spent many a nights practicing hand stands and cart wheels, was as scrubby and brown as ever. At the back of the garden stood a small wooden shed beside the vegetable patch. Lori smiled to herself, proud of the home her gran had made for them all; a cocoon that was safe and secure, but with space for freedom. Lori breathed in, and took off her shoes. Letting her toes wiggle in the soft cool green grass, she wondered if she was able to do a cartwheel now after all these years?

"Is that my wee Lolo?" came a familiar voice. Lori thought twice about the cartwheel, her heart leaping involuntarily at her old pet-name. Her gran was lying outstretched on a sun lounger on the far end of the veranda.

"How didn't I see you there!" Lori ran up the steps to give her gran a hug.

"Well aren't you a vision?" She rose from her lounger sleepy "I may have dozed off for a moment..."

Lori laughed, and suddenly noticed the border collie-dog stretched out underneath the lounger, with no visible intention of getting up.

"Bracken!" Lori petted the dog, which rolled over for her to pat his belly almost automatically with a heavy flop.

Gran shook her head gently and chuckled. "Bracken, my boy, you make a terrible guard dog!" The dog looked up at her with tired droopy eyes and remained still, welcoming Lori's attentions.

Lori gave her gran her arm and helped her up. She was bare-footed, and wore a turquoise kaftan over loose, palazzo trousers. Her gran loved clothes, and at every opportunity would aim to look her best. Today, she had dressed spectacularly for the warm sunshine.

She touched Lori's cheek. "You grow more and more like your mother." She beamed at her granddaughter, her keen blue eyes taking in every detail.

"I thought I was more like dad?" Lori smiled, leading her gran to the kitchen.

"Well yes, you certainly have our family's redder features - from your father and myself." She touched her own white hair, once a vivid shade of red. "But all women end up like their mothers in the end!" She stretched her arms above her. "Oh, I'm as stiff as a board, I need to get back to my yoga!" She selected two yellow cups from the colourful collection on the shelf next to the window.

"You do yoga?" Lori sat at the breakfast bar.

"Aye, down at the hall on Tuesday nights" She boiled the kettle and popped two teabags into a blue-spotted teapot.

"Well, you look amazing Gran!" Bracken slowly walked up to Lori and draped his furry side against her high chair. "Oh Bracken, you are the biggest sook aren't you?" Lori jumped down and petted the old dog once again.

"He'll be spoilt rotten with you around my dear. Just make sure to walk him, he's getting lazy in his old age." Gran poured the tea and leaned against the worktop, cup in hand. "How long are you here for?"

Lori stood up, leaving a huffing and puffing Bracken on the floor, whining softly for more attention. "I'll be away two days after the wedding. I have a big promotion coming up around then, at least I think so, and I need to be in the office to make sure it all goes okay." Lori took a sip of her tea and sighed with delight; her gran made the best brew in the world.

"But you were promoted? You're already a high-flying buyer now!" She raised her cup in congratulations.

"Yes, I know. Thing is, my boss kinda said I could maybe work up to manager, and potentially I could take her job some time down the line." Lori couldn't really believe the words that came out of her mouth; she was still excited about the proposed promotion, but not nearly as much as she thought she'd be. "Oh bugger!" she pulled out her phone from her side pocket, hastily switching it on and waiting impatiently for the home screen to light up. She had come to the realisation early on in her career that most women's clothing didn't have as many pockets as the opposite sex, so had commissioned a dressmaker in Manhattan to alter all her dresses, tops and skirts to include pockets. That way she could always have her phone on her, even when her bag wasn't to hand.

"Hey hey, a lady doesn't need to swear!" Gran raised one eyebrow, which made Lori draw back like a timid teenager.

"Sorry Gran! I just remembered I've had my phone off for hours!" Lori glanced at the screen, but there were no missed calls from Julian or the office; *that was strange. Maybe it was the time difference?* Lori anxiously weighed up the possibilities in her head, the prickle of panic darted down her spine at the thought of the office. Maybe she had turned off her answering machine and Frankie had been trying to reach her all this time? But before Lori's anxiety could get the better of her, she found the problem at the top of her screen: she had no reception for calls. "Where can I get signal?"

Her gran pointed behind Lori. "At the end of the lane, and if you don't get any there, then it's down by the pier. Honestly Lori, it's the same as last time, nothing's changed" Gran sighed and poured out the last dregs of tea from her cup in the sink, watching her granddaughter leave the house, absorbed in her phone.

A few calls to the office to iron out some issues and a text to Michael to say she was home safely, then Lori could finally relax. Gran had shown her to her old room, now the guest-room – with an en-suite and fluffy double bed. An improvement from the time Lori was a teenager, where a single bed and wall to wall posters of boybands Take That and Backstreet Boys were the principle features. Her gran seemed to have a bit of a seaside theme throughout the five bedrooms, and Lori applauded all the work she had put into making the whole place so warm and stylish.

"Seriously Gran, you should let these rooms out in the summer months, you'd make a fortune!" Lori placed her luggage down and spread out on the comfy bed.

"Oh no, I couldn't do that – I wouldn't even know how! Besides, it's you girls' home, and I want to keep all the rooms available for when any of you visit." She waved her hand and lead Lori back through to the kitchen, where she began preparing the meat for their imminent barbecue.

"Where is everyone anyway?" Lori sat at the kitchen counter and chewed on a piece of cucumber from the salad bowl. She hadn't seen either of her two sisters in years, and still felt a little hurt that neither had made an effort to welcome her home. Or truth be told, even visit her in New York for that matter, one of the most exciting cities in the world - and both had ignored her invitations to stay with her.

"Jean is at work, she'll be over with the girls soon. You'll not recognise Maggie and Anne, they are turning into little ladies, wee bairns no longer!" Gran took out some hand-made burgers, and more dishes of salads from the fridge, placing them on the counter before Lori. "You know you could give your old gran a hand?" She looked down at her granddaughter with a wry smile, the contents of the salad bowl rapidly disappearing under her gaze.

"What? I'm hungry, and I'm jet-lagged!" Lori giggled at Gran's outraged face. "OK, OK, what can I do?"

Just as her gran handed her a fresh loaf of bread to slice, the hum of cars arrived outside and there were calls at the door. "Anyone in?" Tammy shouted, and seconds later almost leaped into the kitchen. "Lori!" She ran up to her elder sister, hugging her tightly.

"Argh, I need to breathe!" Lori laughed, instantly forgetting her misgivings from moments ago.

"You look amazing Lori, New York agrees with you!" She grabbed the hand of the tall man behind her, his blonde cropped hair and blue eyes shining brightly.

"So nice to see you Lori, been a long time!" Alan grinned.

Lori lent in for a hug, but Alan picked her up and twirled her around, making her cry out laughing.

"I was not expecting that kind of warm welcome!" She smoothed her hair, composing herself as Tammy wrapped her arms around her soon-to-be husband. Lori beamed at them, Alan towered above Tammy, resting his chin on her head. They looked so blissfully in love. Lori felt a small pang for Michael.

"We're so happy you're here, and we definitely need all

the help we can get!" Tammy admitted with hands raised up in front of her.

"I thought as much!" Lori rolled her eyes. "We'll get there, starting first thing tomorrow morning."

"We have plans for tomorrow: picking the bridesmaids dresses, my wedding dress, and Alan's kilt – and one for his best man too!" Tammy said quickly, and squeezed Alan's hand.

"Who's the best man?" Lori narrowed her eyes suspiciously. "And where exactly are the bridesmaids' dresses coming from?"

"We'll head to Inverness, I'm sure we'll find some there!"

"Tammy, I've just come from there!" Lori felt light-headed at the thought of having to undertake the winding trip all the way to Inverness again in less than twelve hours' time.

"Aye, well, we have appointments at a few boutiques!" Tammy folded her arms "Don't look at me like that Lori, I can't help it if we need to go tomorrow, and we do – so we are all going to make a trip of it."

"I just wish you had let me know, I could've stayed there this evening, or arranged my flight to arrive there tomorrow, or -"

"Well it's done now." Gran interrupted "OK girls, you've just seen each other for the first time in I-don't-know-how-long, so no squabbling like teenagers! Let's enjoy this evening!" Gran handed them both plates of food. "Now - start the BBQ please, at this rate it'll be dark by the time we're eating!"

∽

By the time the food was finally cooked, and the large table outside was set, Lori was almost dizzy with hunger and a little tipsy after two glasses of wine. Once everything was laid out on the table, she was able to devour whatever she could find and lay back into her chair deliciously full and sleepy. In the garden, fairy-lights and Chinese lanterns glowed over the veranda on a thin wire in the gentle breeze. Lori smiled to herself and watched Jean's two girls dance to music from Tammy's phone.

"You put on quite the party, Gran." Lori declared, watching the scene.

"It's to welcome you home, my Lolo." Gran patted her grand-daughter's hand affectionately.

Lori put her head on Gran's shoulder with a sigh just as Jean sat down next to them both with glass of wine in one hand, and the other balancing a plateful of food. The two children ran over trying to nuzzle into their mother as she was just about to eat.

"Mummy come play!" Maggie the youngest, pulled at Jean's hand with a pout.

"No girls – not now sweetheart, careful! I haven't eaten all day. Go play by yourselves for a wee while!" She shooed them both off her.

Lori took the opportunity to distract her nieces and began tickling the youngest. "You give your mummy a break!" Lori chased Maggie around the garden, her squeals of delight echoing in the night air, then she moved to her quieter niece Anne, who stood by the table, pretending to pick at her food.

"The tickle monster is coming to get you girls!" Lori chased the pair, and both children screeched, their laughter growing all the louder the faster they ran.

"Auntie Lori!" Maggie taunted from the edge of one side of the garden.

"No, no - over here Auntie Lori!" Anne shouted from the opposite end of the lawn, leaving Lori in the middle, with the chance to take a breather. She slumped down with a giggle onto the grass, exhausted. Her nieces ran over and piled on top of her.

"Oh you girls are so heavy! What's that mother of yours feeding you?" She wriggled underneath them but gave up with little fight. The jet-lag had started to press down upon her like a heavy stone. The two girls ignored their aunts pleas and buried themselves under her arms.

"Come on Auntie Lori, get up!" Anne put her face next to Lori's trying to revive her. Lori smiled to herself, she had missed this. Nothing had prepared her for the swelling in her heart, filling up the spaces she didn't realise she had. Eventually Maggie and Anne gave up on their aunt, but continued to lay there with limbs wrapped around one another. Very soon Lori's eyes closed, and sleep caught up with her, her mind lulled by the gentle soothing sounds of their breathing under the glow of swaying lanterns above.

6

"OK, time to get up!" Tammy yelled at Lori's door, entered without invitation, and promptly threw open the curtains.

Lori squinted "Do I have to go? I need to catch up on sleep... You just pick a dress for me, I'll fit into it..." Lori turned over on her side away from the glare, and snuggled into her soft pillow.

Tammy draped herself on the bed, her face right next to Lori's own. "I need you there, please Lori. You can sleep in the car, Alan's driving."

Lori lay still on the comfortable bed, feeling groggy from the previous night. Why had she thought it would be a good idea to drink wine? She groaned her agreement, knowing that resisting her sister wouldn't be an option and flung herself in the shower before she could think anymore on the subject.

~

After much grunting and moaning, she emerged from the bathroom and put on a black linen shirt dress. She tied a deep blue silk scarf around her neck and with her sunglasses and sandals picked out, she ventured out to the kitchen where her grandmother was rustling up a hearty breakfast. The smells were intoxicating, making Lori's stomach gurgle loudly in response.

"Morning, sleepy head!" Her gran picked up a sizzling skillet, and emptied out eggs, bacon, tomatoes and a large potato scone onto the plate on the counter. "Sleep well?" she smiled.

"Oh Gran, I could keep sleeping forever right now... That bed is amazing!" Lori walked up to the counter and sat down. "Is this for me?" Her stomach gurgled once again and her gran laughed.

"Of course, everyone's already eaten. Just you now!" She poured Lori a coffee from an orange percolator on the cooker and Lori lost herself in her gran's cooking.

"I need you in New York. Would you cook for me? I'll give you anything you want!" Lori promised faithfully, biting into the soft, floury potato scone.

Her gran shook her head chuckling. "Your place is tiny, remember last time you had to sleep in the same bed with me?"

Lori did admit her apartment was on the small side to accommodate guests comfortably, particularly when Kim had her boyfriend over. It had just so happened that the last time her Gran had visited, one of Darren's mates had also needed a place to crash.

"Yeah, I may need to find somewhere else soon." Lori drank the coffee deeply, and felt the caffeine hit her almost immediately.

"Things still going well with Michael? I'll need to meet him; he didn't want to come to the wedding?"

It only occurred to Lori that she hadn't actually asked Michael to come. Maybe it was because he had acted so strangely after discovering where she was from; that in itself had taken a while to explain tactfully. She had also wanted to focus solely on her sister, whom Michael had not actually met, after all. If he had accompanied her, well, she'd have had to show him around, and introduce him adequately to everyone, which she had no time for. The whole situation wouldn't really have been very fair on Tammy; *no, it was better this way.* "Things are good, yeah - he's doing really well in the company. He couldn't get away though, it was too last minute you see," Lori lied, feeling her gran's suspicious eyes on her.

"Oh, that's a shame!" Gran sipped her coffee, looking at her closely all the while. "Well maybe it's best, we can meet him when it's not so hectic up here!"

Jean walked in and sat down beside Lori. "Who are we talking about?" She smiled and nodded in thanks as Gran poured a coffee for her.

"Michael. Apparently, he's doing very well in the law firm." Gran brushed some crumbs from Lori's chin fondly.

"Oh that's good. Might be useful to have a lawyer in the family!" Jean gave a grim smile.

"The family?" Lori tried to cover the alarm in her voice. "We're just seeing each other. There's no mention of marriage just yet!"

"OK OK, don't get your knickers in a twist! It just might be good to know someone in that area of expertise!" Jean looked ahead, her expression taught, and her eyes tired.

"Are things not amicable with you and Douglas anymore?"

Her sister took a long sip from her cup, considering the question. "Things *were* good. He would always check in on the girls when he was back on shore. But since he's started seeing someone, he's said he'd like to take them on holiday for a month with this new girlfriend. But they've got school, he doesn't understand." She bit her lip. "I'm just worried things are going to get worse; you know how stubborn he is."

Lori put her hand around her sister's shoulder and rubbed it gently. "I'm sure Douglas doesn't realise about the school, and their grades; he's obviously all loved-up and being a bit selfish about it all. Try to keep lawyers out of this if you can. You guys have been doing really well all this time; I thought you both came to an official agreement?"

"We did, I got to keep the girls, and he could see them whenever he wanted. But now he has that new girlfriend, I'm just worried he's changing his mind." Jean looked close to tears.

"Hey, hey!" Lori smoothed her hand over her eldest sister's hair, feeling like her mother for a brief moment. "I can ask Michael if you really want me to, I'm sure it's different law over here compared to America, but he might know someone who could give you a bit of advice."

Jean blinked her red eyes. "Thanks Lo. You're right, I'll wait for now. Hopefully things will get better" She looked over to Gran who leaned against the cooker watching quietly. "And thanks for looking after the kids today Gran."

"Of course, it's my pleasure! I thought we'd go for a wee walk and get an ice cream by the pier. Then maybe I'll nip into the boutique in town."

The village of Arlochy was just ten minute's drive from the larger ferry town of Morvaig, which boasted more businesses and schools, along with a crazy number of holiday makers in the summer months. The Robertson girls had all attended Morvaig High School, where Jean worked as an English teacher.

"You really think you'll find something there Gran?" Lori wiped the last of her toast around her plate, gathering up any leftovers.

"Aye, I happen to know there's a gorgeous turquoise hat there, which would go just perfectly with my fancy dress in the wardrobe." She winked at Lori and collected the empty cups and plates.

"I wish we were all so lucky!" Jean joked. "I've told Tammy: no peach! I can't stand the colour; it makes me look so washed out and old!" Jean's hair was a slightly darker shade of auburn compared to her sisters, and she tended to stick to jeans and a jumper slightly more often than her sisters.

"Well you're no spring chicken, Jean!" Lori cackled.

"Hey! Cheeky cow!" She punched Lori's shoulder playfully.

"Gran, she hit me!" Lori looked up to her gran, her lip trembling deliberately.

"Och, away with you both! You think I don't already have my hands full with the two wee ones, and now you two behaving like children!"

Lori and Jean kissed Gran and the kids goodbye. They headed off in the early morning, as a mist hung over the sea, promising a day of sun in the hazy glow behind. The car journey mainly consisted of Tammy selecting various classic tracks for the three sisters to sing along to, as Alan cringed in the driver's seat.

"Jeezo girls, your taste in music is shocking!" He shook his head and rested his big arm on the rolled-down window.

"Come on! Who doesn't like Shania Twain?" Tammy batted her eyelids at him from the passenger seat.

"A lot of people! Me included!" He chuckled, grabbed her hand resting on her thigh, and clasped it lovingly.

"We have to like country music; it would be a cardinal sin if we didn't!" Jean piped up from the backseat.

"Why?" Alan yelled over the music.

"You know this, Alan!" Tammy rolled her eyes at her fiancé. "Remember Dad named us all after country and western singers!"

"Erm, I'm not sure... I don't think you've ever spoke about that?" He went slightly quiet, and Lori squeezed her head in between the front seats.

"Maybe we just presumed you knew. We got teased in high school for having weird names. Well I did anyway!" Lori scoffed.

"Me too!" Jean chimed in.

"Did you not think our names were a bit, well, strange for round here?" Tammy looked over to him in disbelief.

"I never really thought about it. But it's cool, I like it. It must have been very special to your dad, I mean for him to name you all after something he loved."

The girls smiled at one another, it *was* special, but it just went to show how eccentric their father had been too.

"I think we need some Dolly!" Tammy announced and the first chords of *Jolene* played out over the speakers.

"Class! I love this one," Alan said with enthusiasm. "But not one of ye are called Dolly? I thought she is the queen of country?!"

"God, can you imagine if dad called one of us Dolly?" Lori laughed.

"I'd die of embarrassment!" Tammy put her hand over her eyes.

"Me too!" Jean shook her head slowly, and then all three girl's launched back into a fresh sing-along without a moments hesitation.

Once they had arrived in the city, the entire morning was spent sitting in bridal shops and watching Tammy try on dress after dress. Lori made the most of her time and started scribbling down notes on all the tasks still to be done. Shouting to her entourage over the changing room partition, Tammy divulged that they had booked the church and the village hall for the reception, but that was about as much organising as she had achieved, it seemed. But that was alright, thought Lori, she knew this was her part to play. She sat perched on a sofa in the corner, planning in the new diary she had just bought, intermittently giving opinions on various dresses and accessories. Jean sat next to her and worked through a huge bundle of students homework she had taken with her on the journey. Tammy had ordered the shop assistant to fill their glasses with Prosecco, much to her elder sister's objections, but both eventually accepted the gesture after gentle threats were made.

"It's my wedding! We need to have fun!" demanded Tammy from the changing room, as she tried on her twentieth dress.

Lori and Jean packed away their papers, clinked glasses and gave in to the bubbles. Lori took her first proper look around. The shop was lined with various white dresses; tulles, silks, satins, and sequins all draped on rails waiting for their own special day. On the back wall behind the counter, was the bridesmaids dresses in a range of colours all clustered together and shining like jewels. Lori and Jean kept looking over, pointing to the styles they liked. But as Tammy was the bride-to-be, they waited with anticipation for her to select the wedding dress before a colour was allocated for their own. Tammy emerged in a beautiful lace off-the-shoulder ivory gown, with tulle poking out underneath the delicate splits in the skirt.

"It's gorgeous Tam, it's the best one yet!" Jean slowly walked around her and touched the trim on the back of her bodice.

Tammy admired herself in the mirror, smoothing her hands down the fabric and over her flat stomach, locking eyes with Lori at that moment. She looked away quickly, and paced around the room, gliding elegantly like a contestant in a Miss World competition.

"You're right, I think it's the one!" She turned to them both, and the shop assistant wasted no time in snapping into action.

"Delightful style," she remarked, and lightly touched the tiny buttons at the back with her extremely long fingernails. The woman's blond hair was piled high on her head in a bun with cat's eyes drawn on her eyelids and thick foundation heavily applied elsewhere. "It suits your skin tone too, just stunning." She stood back and looked Tammy up and down with approval. "And did I hear you wanted to take it?"

Tammy gazed at herself in the mirror once again and agreed. Lori was amazed at how quickly Tammy had made the decision, she was pleased how things were coming along. If her sister was going to keep this focused, then hopefully planning the rest of the proceedings should go far more smoothly than she had anticipated after all. *Here's hoping this wedding isn't a disaster*.

The shop assistant trotted behind Tammy back to the changing rooms to help her out of the dress, and the two sisters filled up their glasses again with the fast-disappearing Prosecco.

"I'll be marking the rest of this homework tomorrow, I think!" Jean clinked Lori's glass and they drank some more, until the blonde assistant came out with wedding dress draped over both arms, and packed it carefully at the front counter. Soon after, she came back into the room holding various coloured gowns, and Tammy emerged from the cubicle, evidently pleased with herself, and pointed out the first dresses she wanted them to try on.

The two sisters tried on hot pink off the shoulder dresses, which prompted Lori to pull her hair up in a high ponytail: "I need a scrunchie!", then dramatically pulled the curtain open belting out a Madonna number and making vogue-type hand gestures around her face.

"I hate pink!" Jean pulled her curtain, standing awkwardly with hunched shoulders and a crumpled face.

"Oh! I like it!" Tammy's eyes widened.

Jean looked down at herself with disgust. "I feel like a tart. A strawberry tart!" She cautiously looked over to Lori who joyously danced and gyrated on the spot, lost in her own 1980s music video.

"OK Jean, I don't want a surly bridesmaid! Try on the next one!" Tammy waved her hand and sank back on the sofa, clutching her phone. "Oh, girl's - Alan's just mentioned he's got a match on later, so we can't be too long!"

"Does he still play shinty?" Lori asked over the curtain, as her thoughts filtered back to a simpler time when she used to go and watch the local shinty matches. The principal draw for Lori however, involved lusting after all the strong boys in high school, and in particular, the broad-shouldered Callum Macrae. Athletic, but sturdy and strong, and with calf muscles to die for, Lori had been attracted to him almost from day one, and to her amazement, he had liked her too. She had experienced a lot that last summer of high school, including losing her virginity to him. Lori reflected on their hot nights together on the beach, wrapped in a blanket as he kissed every part of her body, taking her in like she was ice-cream on a spoon.

"Aye, I love my shinty men!" Tammy sighed.

Lori shook off the sexual distractions of her youth and squeezed herself into the next dress, only able to zip it up halfway before the fabric couldn't stretch anymore. She gasped in horror at her reflection: the bright lime-yellow made her look frighteningly like a luminous stuffed sausage.

Jean shouted over the curtain: "Didn't you like your shinty men too Lo? If I remember right, you used to stand at the pitch thirsting after Callum Macrae!"

"I don't know *what* you're talking about, I did nothing of the sort!" Lori tried her best to sound nonchalant, all the while trying to zip up the ghastly dress. She had never really been overweight, just an ordinary standard size, but today she bulged in all sorts of areas she hadn't realised she had; rolls of fat seemed to be exposed everywhere in this particular selection of garment. She struggled again with the zip and bumped into the dressing room wall, the Prosecco now certainly taking effect, and making her lean against it in one last attempt to squeeze into the dress, but to no avail. She saw herself in the mirror and almost gasped: her hair was still scraped back in a 1980s high side greasy ponytail and her cheeks were flushed. After her rush getting ready this morning, she should have reconsidered washing her hair: especially in this harsh light, she looked old, sweaty and unhealthy.

Her sister made hooting noises from the sofa. "That's not what I mind, Miss Robertson! You used to go and watch him when you thought no one saw you!" Tammy added: "Like, behind the bike sheds when you'd cop a look like some weird stalker!"

"Have you changed into the dress yet Jean, I don't wanna show until you do!" Lori wiped her eyes, noticing mascara had smudged over the tops of her eyelids, and somehow ended up making it look worse, smudging it under her eyes too.

"Almost, just give me a minute!" Jean groaned.

Lori continued thinking of Callum and immediately tried to clear him from her mind. She was a successful woman, not a silly teenage girl lusting after some schoolboy. "Callum might have been fit... Yeah, OK, he was hot! But he served a purpose, and I don't think he had much going on in that head of his anyway - God this dress! - I mean, he was great to look at, but not the sharpest tool in the box!"

"I'm ready!" called Jean.

The two girls threw open the curtains to a giggling Tammy, a shocked Alan, and a very angry-looking Callum Macrae. Lori froze on the spot like a deer caught in head-lights. She wanted to be swallowed up by the world, dress, ponytail and all. If the walls could have opened up and taken her at that very moment she would have been more grateful than words could express. Her cheeks burned, and she let her eyes fall to the ground, unable to make eye-contact with Callum.

"Cal - you remember my sisters, Lori and Jean?" Tammy said politely, very obviously trying to suppress her laughter.

"Callum.... hi...?" Lori was still praying for a distraction, for some kind of lightning to strike her down; *anything* to take her out of her current situation.

Callum nodded, his lips tight. "Yeah, hi."

The silence that ensued was unbearable, and Lori

wondered when the much-needed, sorely wished-for lightning was going to strike. Luckily Alan took pity on her, and broke the tension. "You asked who my best man was Lori, well - it's Callum!"

Callum gave a small smile. Lori groaned internally at how she must look, *and oh god what she had just said*. She hadn't even meant it. She just wanted her sisters to stop teasing her so mercilessly. Oh, how she was going to murder Tammy when she finally got a hold of her. Lori yanked up her tight sack-style dress, conscious of how low cut and strained the fabric was over her cleavage. "I – I don't like this bogey colour!" she announced to the room, feeling dizzy and hot.

The shop assistant shimmied over. "It's called chartreuse!"

Lori looked over to Jean, who somehow seemed to look acceptable in her dress, unlike herself. Her eyes then met Tammy's, with a threatening look. "It maybe chartreuse, but it's *not* happening!"

"You maybe just need a bigger size, that's all!" Tammy's finger tapped her mouth, scrutinising the dress.

"Nope! This is the worst dress in the world!" Lori dashed back into her changing room and pulled the curtains closed with a gasp. How was she to face him again? Would Callum now be stuck watching her try on each dress? Lori buried her head in her hands, mortified, but glad to be behind the curtain, hiding from her past. To her relief she heard Callum say his goodbyes to Tammy and leave the shop, and immediately after the tinkle of the shop bell, she wanted to cry with utter humiliation.

The journey home was silent. The dresses they had selected were in a royal blue silk, which Lori and Jean had insisted on paying for, and which Tammy had grudgingly accepted. Lori looked out of the car window, seeing the trees dart past. She avoided talking to her sisters in her current grumpy state, unable to see the funny side of the situation. Every bit of her felt humiliated; why had she said that awful thing about him? She didn't mean it of course, he wasn't dumb, that was the drink talking. What must he think of her? Callum had looked so furious, but even worse: he looked exactly the same as he had in high school; life in the Highlands obviously suited him. She leant back in her seat, welcoming the gentle rocking of the car, as the image of Callum and the memories of their nights together came flooding back.

7

L ori pulled open her bedroom curtains to greet the bright morning sunshine. She closed her eyes and bathed in its warm light, trying to forget the events from the previous day. She creaked open the window and a gentle sea breeze floated in with the scent of fresh beech trees. She had a very long luxurious shower, making sure she washed her hair this time, and went out in search for breakfast. Her gran had left a note on the counter top stating that she was away at a coffee morning over in the next town, so Lori walked out barefoot onto the veranda and sat on the wooden step, mug of tea in one hand and notepad in the other. In little time, she had drafted up the wedding table plans, making lists of potential guests and then moved onto dinner menu ideas, the photographer, table decorations and transport options. *Where was Tammy anyway?* Lori picked up the kitchen phone and called her sister's mobile phone, but there was no answer. *Oh, of course there would be no answer; no one has signal here,* Lori thought, her patience already waining. The perks of having a mobile phone, or cell phone as she was used to saying in New York, were all but lost in the Highlands of Scotland.

Lori ventured out along the harbour front in search of phone signal, and took in the familiar surroundings. Passing by the old bookshop, she had to resist the urge to peruse the basket of old classics outside its door, and focused instead on the task at hand: to find her sister. She continued strolling past both familiar and new faces, thinking how different she must now look to the young girl who had left Arlochy all those years ago. A quiet, shy, almost insecure girl. Now she was in an impressive job, working for a multi-million-dollar company, and able to do whatever she wanted with her life – aside from the occasional panic attack, admittedly. She loved the freedom that having money afforded her, perhaps she might buy an apartment, or maybe a house, and settle somewhere in the suburbs in the next couple of years. She had achieved everything herself, with no debt worries hanging over her like so many her age, and to top it all off - a possible future position as Managing Director of Costners, which sure had a nice ring to it.

Lori's phone bleeped, making her jump. She squinted at the device: it was a message from Michael:

> *"Thanks for letting me know you arrived safely.*
> *Remember what we spoke about. Just focus*
> *on your sister, and we'll talk when you get*
> *back. M"*

Lori reread the text message again; the words seemed strange to her. Suddenly, her phone erupted into a series of constant bleeping and vibrations showing all the missed calls, voice mails and texts she had received. Realising she must be near the hotspot for signal, she stopped in front of the bakery and scanned her phone for any real emergencies. Mainly the communications were from Julian, asking her for help and advice. *Poor Julian*, her heart went out to him. It was the middle of the night in New York just now, so she'd call later. She made a mental note to herself that when she got back she would give him something special, some treat to say thank you. Then it occurred to Lori, she didn't really know Julian; what his likes and dislikes were. Much like her colleague Alex, they hadn't spoken about personal things, because there was no time for that when the job brought such a demanding schedule each day. Should she know her own assistant more?

"Lori!" called a cheery voice behind her. It was Tammy, waving from behind a bakery counter, serving a long line of customers. "Do you want a tea bun too?" she asked a customer, gesturing with a paper bag and tongs. "Hey every-one, this is my big sister Lori!" she announced to the queue as Lori walked in shyly. "Sis, can you help a girl out?"

Lori could feel all eyes on her, and felt a little on display in her black wedge sandals and short cotton dress. She was certainly not in the get up to be dishing out bread and cakes. *And - oh no! look at all the flour on the counter!* Lori grimaced, but went to wash her hands; rolling up her loose sleeves reluctantly as Tammy tied an apron around her waist. Millionaire shortbread, glazed donuts, empire biscuits and rainbow cupcakes were on display under a glass counter, shining invitingly. Everything looked scrumptious, and Lori's stomach started to rumble in response; the jet-lag was making her hungry all the time! She dismissed the noises emanating from her and started packing up treats upon each customer's request. Pink and yellow French Fancies were proving very popular, and as Lori scooped another one into a bag she saw that at this rate they would be sold out soon. Her mouth watered, but she suppressed the temptation to pick one up and bite into the thin, glassy layer of icing. Just the promise of fluffy white sponge and sweet cream was enough to make her dizzy. She remembered her mum had always loved them; it would be her absolute treat, especially when money was tight, and on the odd occasion when special visitors would call to the house, she would offer them out on a beautiful blue flower plate: "French Fancy for madame? Oh yes, don't mind if I do!" Lori chuckled to herself. She had all but forgotten that memory of her mother, enjoying the little things in life, like the unadorned sweetness of those small pastel cakes.

"You're doing well, keep it up!" Tammy encouraged her sister as she typed up orders on the till. The bakery was tiny, consisting of a counter, a display and a small preparation area behind them, which lead onto an even smaller kitchen in the back. But as small as it was, it didn't seem to deter the mass of customers, as soon as one towns-person left, one more joined the queue outside.

"Do you have more stock?" Lori whispered.

Tammy looked down to see they were running bare. "Oh jeez! Yes!" She immediately left Lori to man the till.

OK... it can't be too hard...? Lori scanned the tiny buttons with numbers and words of various cakes, some of which she didn't even know. She saw 'scone', 'iced' and 'shortbread', but was unsure about the other price codes, so she edged away, apologising to the customers and waiting awkwardly for her little sister to return.

Tammy came back carrying a large box, and rolled her eyes at her sister. "It's not hard! OK you unload these, and I'll finish serving."

After an hour, the queue finally calmed down and only the odd customer popped in at a much less hectic pace. Tammy placed a bottle of water in Lori's hands. "Thanks for all your help!"

Lori leaned against the counter top, somewhat drained. "I didn't know you worked here?" She gratefully accepted the bottle and gulped the cool water, but drank too much too quickly, choking a little and wiping her mouth with embarrassment.

"Yeah, been here a few months, trying out the season. The bar work is good, but I'm trying to ease off the shifts there. Especially if there's a wee one coming!" She looked around to see if anyone was looking, and gently rubbed her stomach.

"How many people know about the baby?" Lori whispered.

"No-one yet, just me and Alan. I had to make sure you were going to come to the wedding, so I had to tell you." Her eyes snapped up from her belly to meet Lori's, with a wild penetrating look. "But don't pass that around to anyone else yet, OK?"

"Of course, it's not my secret. You tell people once you're ready."

Tammy sighed and massaged the back of her neck.

"I think you need to do another job though Tam, working behind the bar and in this environment isn't good, especially if you're pregnant"

"Shhh!" Tammy looked furtively around the small shop "You know how bad this place is for gossip!" She whispered. "I enjoy the work. Seeing people, being part of the community. You wouldn't know how that feels I guess."

Lori dismissed the slight dig from her sister. "But you can't keep it up in the long-term, you'll have to stop soon!" Lori leaned closer to her sister beside the till.

"I know but right now, we need the money for the wedding. Alan will be away back on the rig next month, and then the baby will be coming. So, we're on the hunt for any extra pennies we can get." She rubbed her stomach again, looking down at the space where there would soon be a bump.

"I can help you; I have money, I have savings."

"No!" Tammy raised her hand, bristling. "We don't need help; we've got the wedding covered." She sighed and shook her head, her face softening a little. "Thanks Lori, but we'll be fine."

Lori squeezed her sister's shoulder. "By the way, you were great out there today. With all the chaos, with all those customers!"

"I do put on quite the show!" Tammy flourished her hands in a theatrical gesture.

"You do though - I could use someone calm and collected in the office like you. Have you ever thought about maybe doing a bit more with your life? I mean, you could be so much more. Do so much more!"

Tammy stood still for some moments then folded her arms. "What? Do something *more* with my life? Jesus Lori, how dare you!"

Immediately Lori backtracked. "No I don't mean that, I just meant..."

"You think because we've all stayed at home, it means we don't have a good life? Just because I haven't traveled like you, and I don't have a nose for the finer things in life doesn't mean I don't enjoy my life! Should I be working all the hours under the sun for someone else, staring at a computer screen all day, and thinking about my next manicure? Frankly I don't think you seem to be enjoying *yours*!" Tammy picked up a tray of cold sausage rolls and took them out the back.

"Tammy, you're so sensitive!" Lori followed her sister. "I didn't mean that, I just want the best for you!" She couldn't help the anger rising in her voice. "And I didn't come here to get my head bitten off, I came to discuss preparations for *your* wedding. Then I get thrown into dishing out pastries to the locals, who some, in my opinion, should think about easing off the sugar and butter instead of clearing your trays!" Lori regretted her snipe at their customers the second the words had left her mouth, especially after her breakfast the day before, and her own appetite for sweet treats. But she wanted to irritate Tammy for her comment about computers and manicures, particularly as it had been rather accurate. Just before Tammy could retort, Gran entered the shop, diffusing the situation with a dazzling smile and a sweep of her skirts.

"How are my wee women?" She radiated summer and elegance in a yellow dress and white sunhat.

Lori took off her apron and laid it on the counter. "We're good Gran, just about to catch up on wedding business." Lori looked over her shoulder to Tammy, who was fiddling around with a box to put the sausage rolls in. "Tam, why don't you come over to the house after work, maybe we'll pour a glass of wine – or, er.. a cup of tea - and go through things. I don't want you to stress!" Lori moved around to the other side of the till, making her exit before any more customers appeared. She reached over and squeezed Tammy's arm, giving her an apologetic smile.

"Alright," Tammy mumbled, not looking up.

"Oh, and before I go – four french fancies please!"

Tammy finally met Lori's eyes, and relented. She packed four dainty squares, held up the box and gave a coy smile. "For madame!"

8

After various issues were put to bed in New York, Lori tried calling Michael, but after several missed attempts, she sent him a text, hoping that he was OK. His last message had seemed cryptic, especially after their chaste kiss at the airport had left her feeling somewhat empty. She was fairly sure she was being punished for not telling him the truth about her past. She knew it was wrong to be dishonest with him, but they had rarely talked about their childhoods; *Michael was just as much at fault.* Whenever she had asked him what his life was like as a boy, he had never divulged too much, making Lori feel bad for even asking. Besides, her early life in Scotland was intrinsically linked to the bittersweet sadness of her parents, that she avoided discussing it with anyone. She shrugged off her uneasy feelings and popped her phone back into her pocket. The late afternoon sun was dropping, but still shining brightly enough to illuminate the distant hills, enticing Lori to chase the light. She headed in the direction of their local church for a walk. The old stone building lay further out of the village, in a glen surrounded

by hills and trees. It was even more picturesque than she
remembered. There was something ancient and romantic
about the setting that took Lori's breath away. She believed
that if she were to travel forward or back into another time -
the church, and its lichen-strewn stonework would still look
exactly the same. She stepped up to the moss-covered iron
gates and pushed them apart with a creak. Inside the
grounds stood the old graveyard. Lori's shoulders tensed
and she paused. She had been here many times before,
nothing had changed. But something twisted inside her, like
a knotted rope. Lori slowly walked up to her parents' headstone: one single stone for them both; *even in death they were
together.* Above the grave stood a large Evergreen, its protec-
tive branches sheltering her parents from the wild west
coast weather. It was such a tranquil spot, and Lori took a
few moments to dwell on the little she could remember of
them. *Where were they now?* Sat on a fluffy cloud above, or
standing near her always? She hoped they watched over her
and her sisters in some way at least. Would they be proud of
her? Lori remembered the day of the funeral, holding hands
with her sisters and watching people place tight bunches of
cold white flowers at the graveside. It had felt unreal, as
though she were in a dream, just waiting to wake up. The
whole village and the town over had come to pay their
respects. Lori had never seen the church packed full of
people before, every seat taken leaving some standing in the
side aisles, their heads bowed and hands clasped. Her
parents had touched so many people's lives. Her dad always
smiling and good-humoured, a gentle man to the core. And
her mother: warm, intelligent and graceful but with a
mischievous sense of adventure. They both had been there
for many of the townsfolk in their respective times of need.
Lori felt a tear roll down her cheek, and she wiped it away.

She hadn't expected to be confronted with vivid memories of the past that she rarely thought of in New York. Lost in her thoughts, a crack of a branch and the bang of a door startled her. She wiped away another tear and quickly spun around to catch a glimpse of the new arrival, but could see no one. The graveyard was empty, apart from the odd bird that fluttered in and out of the trees nearby. *Perhaps it was Father Angus going into the church to run through his sermon?* Lori hesitated, should she go inside and say hello? *It would be rude not to, surely?* She knew the friendly priest would happily detain her for hours if he could. In the end she decided otherwise; she knew her gran would surely drag her to mass on Sunday, as usual, so she could speak to the priest then. Lori placed her hand gently on the headstone, then slowly moved away, following the narrow path that continued under canopy and skirted up hill. The familiar track played into her memories - as a girl she would often run up towards the summit, to the old school house, which herself and her sisters had attended. The more she climbed, the more the timid young girl she had once been came into the light, taking the same steps she had trodden all those years ago. The rough path got higher and higher, and alarmingly steeper; something she hadn't remembered. Or had it always been this dangerous, and she had simply never paid attention?

Finally, reaching the top past the clearing of trees, Lori gasped for breath - the daily walks in New York not having prepared her for the Scottish hills. She bent over panting, allowing the sun to warm her back. After some moments spent composing herself, she took in the Victorian school building, with its newer extension at the front expanding onto a new playground. It looked closed-up for the day, no doubt the children all away home for their teas leaving only faint chalk marks on the black tarmac. Lori continued walking around the grounds, the heat from the sun warming her body gloriously after the cool cover of trees. She thought back on her time at school, and of endless summer nights, playing anywhere and everywhere with her sisters. She had enjoyed such freedom, a definite rarity for kids these days. Having spoken to some mothers who worked at Costners, she could see the difference in modern children. Their detailed accounts of picking up their children from school and taking them to various extra curriculum classes, just so they could say with certainty that they knew where their offspring were. Some had even told her that they'd never allow their kids to go to a 'sleep-over', for fear of some adverse happening or other. Lori knew the world could be a bad place, but the childhood she had had, though tainted by sorrow, was still a good one. She had been free, but safe along with it. Lori grinned thinking of her gran, who would often leave them playing in the woods, and would happily not see them until the end of the day. And when Lori and her sisters would come home later that evening, hair messy or with mucky legs from playing in the dirt, her gran would raise an eyebrow: "Did you enjoy the cycle to the beach?" or "I hope you were careful playing on Farmer MacAulay's hay stacks?" Lori chuckled to herself, she had never been fully alone, her cunning guardian must have had spies everywhere!

Lori continued further on past the school and out towards the end of a long field which stood high above the sea below. Her sandals struggled a little through the high grass as she glided through the ferns enjoying the view of the horizon beyond. In the quiet sea breeze, her thoughts settled on Michael, and her current life. She felt uneasy about concealing things from him for those few years. But she hadn't *really* been lying, had she? Lori bit her lip and continued walking through the high rushes. As soon as she got back to New York they would really start making the most of the weekends; have breakfast together, go hiking and just relish time alone. All Lori needed to do now was to get this wedding business sorted and she could go back to Michael, and back to their life. Lori breathed out as she reached the end of the field and near the edge of the cliff. The sea surrounded her with small isles dotted far out in the distance. She cast her eye back to where she had walked from, down below where Arlochy lay neatly, every road and larger building familiar to her. The church was hidden under the canopy of bushy trees, but the graveyard was in view, its path leading all the way along to the main street, where tiny blotches of people moved around unaware of their spectator on a faraway hill. Around the harbour, a few yachts and fishing boats were scattered, looking so perfect bathed in the early evening sun that Lori reached for her phone to take a photograph. Just as her hand clasped the device, it started to buzz, giving her a jolt of panic and joy at the same time: it was Michael, *finally*. Lori wasted no time in answering.

"Lori?" His voice was quiet.

"Yes? Is everything OK?"

"I just wanted-" His voice cut out.

Lori panicked, the signal was very weak, she scrambled, thrusting the phone high in the air and squinting at its screen. "What is wrong with these rural places... we need phone signal!" she roared out on the empty hill, pleading over the phone: "Michael, can you hear me?" She raised the device as high as she could, and walked backward in a distracted frenzy until she lost her footing, making her shriek as the phone flew up in the air. She stumbled, gasping, falling to her knees at a strange angle frighteningly close to the edge of the cliff. She peered out over the long grass, her heart beating like a galloping horse. Down below the sea moaned and roared, repeatedly drenching the rocks with the cold Atlantic. She could have fallen down the cliff! What a right idiot she would've looked; trying to get phone signal and falling to her death? She shivered at the prospect, and shuffled back on hands and feet to a safer distance, where her heart gradually regained its natural speed. After a few deep breaths, she heard a muffled voice calling her name in the distance.

"Lori?" Michael's deep tones faintly drifted towards her.

"What?" Lori looked about her. "Michael?" Then breaking out of her daydream, she pulled back the long grass to locate the small glowing screen. "Michael, keep talking!" she demanded, and slowly but surely followed his voice until she found it, by a large cluster of daises.

"Yes I'm here!" she shouted, "can you hear me darling?" She clutched the phone and sat on her bum in the high grass.

"What the hell happened? Did you fall off a bike?"

Lori smiled, "Well no, I'm on a hill. But I'm absolutely fine!" No response came, and she looked at her phone to see that the signal had once more disappeared. "Bugger it!" she screamed. Throwing herself flat on the grass, and unable to take out her fury on anything else, she tore up some weeds and threw them into the air. *The signal in this village was going to be a serious problem alright.* She would be forced to use Gran's phone, but the idea of having personal calls while her gran pretended not to listen in, didn't exactly thrill her. Lori got up slowly, patting down her dress and placed her useless phone back in her pocket. Catching something bright in the corner of her eye, she turned to her left slightly, and gasped. The tiniest little Highland calf sat in amongst the long grass too, sheltering from the warm sun. It licked its wet nose, peering up at Lori with wide dark eyes under fair eyelashes. It must have only been a couple of days old, with sticky tufts adorning every delicate joint, and a pale milky stomach.

"Well hello! I didn't see you there wee guy!" She fawned over the big eyes, and couldn't resist tentatively reaching out to touch its fuzzy red head. The calf flinched for a second, but after a moment began to look quite relaxed as Lori gently stroked its head. *What a cutey!* Lori thought, *but where's his....* As if reading her mind, a deep, piercing bellow sounded behind her, unlike anything she had heard before, shaking her to the core. Two huge cows marched towards her, with enormous shaggy shoulders, hooves like anvils and the exact same colouring as the calf. One animal was slightly smaller with upturned horns, the other was larger, with huge thick spikey antlers aimed menacingly at Lori. "Oh... holy shit!" Lori whispered to herself, tiptoeing around the calf and stumbling backwards. The bull and cow were approaching her from the school-side of the field, closing in towards the edge of the hill. The calf blinked at her with detached interest as its parents advanced with an imperious tread. "Oh holy shit!" Lori yelled again; the deranged animals were wanting to run her off the cliff! What could she do? Those horns looked like they could do some serious damage; if she ran at them they would impale her, surely? Her heart beat like a horse in canter, and she knew she had to make up her mind quickly before they came any closer. She took a deep breath, and without further delay, ran screaming like a mad woman towards the beasts, bobbing about in different directions and wildly waving her arms, hoping it would alarm them somehow. Remarkably, it did;

they scattered nervously as she darted past in the direction of the school. Lori couldn't believe what had happened, had she just escaped a mauling? Slowing down, she breathed out with relief, and craned her neck back to find that the cows were still after her, angry that she dared touch their baby. Lori was sure they had to be a particularly crazy breed left out on the hill on purpose to scare off any undesirable tourists. Her feet slipped and slid in her sandals, making it impossible to run fast. Her body perspired all over at the frightening prospect she may trip up and submit to an attack from the bull, which was fast approaching. Luckily, she wasn't far from the school's low wall, and was sure the animal wouldn't follow her over the wall, but she had to admit that this was a hope rather than a confidence in cattle behaviour. Lori heard the piercing parental cry again and turned around in panic to see how close her pursuers were, but suddenly to her relief both cows had stopped in their tracks; maybe they were tired, or had perhaps lost interest? Either way, a few moments later Lori reached the grounds of the school and bent double to recover. With her hands resting on her knees and gasping for breath, she couldn't believe the near misses she had experienced in the space of ten minutes on her fondly-remembered hill.

"Bloody hell!" she shouted back to the cows, but they paid her little interest, already returning back to their calf as if nothing had happened. "Insane cows! You'd better stay back!" She breathed in and out, wheezing; she hadn't run like that since she was a child, and she didn't remember it being such a ridiculous effort then.

"Lori... are you OK?" Callum ran out towards her from the tree line behind.

She put her hands on her waist trying to get her gasps under control. "Yes, I think so!"

"I saw what happened!"

"Why didn't you come out earlier then?"

He looked out at the cows in the distance and then back at her with a shrug. "I- well – I mean it looked like you had everything under control!"

Lori opened her mouth about to protest, but instead she started laughing hysterically. She was furious, but couldn't help her reaction, chortling so hard that she thought she might pee herself. She walked off in the direction of the church, eyes ahead, ignoring Callum's steps behind her.

"I could've used your help out there!" she called over her shoulder, still laughing maniacally.

"I only clocked that things had turned nasty when I saw you running towards the school, and then I came as fast as I could!"

"Well, I can't believe I didn't get killed, you should've seen the look in that daddy cow's eyes!" She continued keeping the distance between them.

"I don't know what you did to annoy them, but generally Highland cows are the most chilled-out animal!"

"Well, apparently these ones are not!" Lori snapped and walked even faster, trying to get away, but Callum managed to keep pace next to her, no matter how fast she walked. She stumbled on some uneven rocks and swayed a little, as Callum caught her elbow and held her up. He was like cast iron; Lori was sure nothing could knock him over, not even the cows, with his calm blue eyes shining back at her. But not even Macrae's baby-blues could distract her from wanting to get home safely and out of her uncomfortable sandals. "I'm fine, I don't need any help!" Lori said sullenly.

"I'm going this way too though; thought maybe you'd want to walk together?"

She sighed and slowed down her speed. "OK, sure."

Lori slowly descended the steep path with caution until Callum turned to her. "You know, you really need to wear suitable clothing for hiking. This time of year, you'll need to get some wellies for the long grass, because –"

"I don't think I need to take fashion lessons from you, Callum" She eyed him up and down. His look, which hadn't really changed in all the years she knew him was practical and relaxed – jeans, hiking boots and a faded navy blue Sea Shepherd t-shirt.

He shook his head. "OK, I'm just giving you a wee bit of advice."

"I am from here!" Lori groaned.

"Well it's been a long time, eh? You're quite different to the girl I knew all those years ago," he said quietly. "How's New York?"

"It's good, I'm enjoying it. I'm working as a buyer for Costners."

"Yes I heard, a very big and important fashion brand." His tone was edging towards sarcasm.

Some moments passed between them until Callum stopped abruptly. "Are you going to give me an apology at some stage? Or just pretend it didn't happen?"

Lori immediately bristled. "Are you kidding me? What do I need to apologise for? You keep popping up your head at the worst moments, Callum! Is that a super-power of yours? When I'm drunk, and stuck halfway up a dress in a changing room, or being chased by a mob of angry cows after a near-death experience at the edge of the hill, you come out and just say: 'Surprise!'" She had to admit how bizarre all those incidents sounded to her now. Neither were exactly Callum's fault, after all.

Callum raised his eyebrows at Lori's turned back. "You

don't feel that you owe me an apology at all? Or even a proper hello?"

Lori ignored him, stepping forwards to take the lead as they reached the church grounds.

Callum stopped as Lori continued walking. "Well you're a stuck-up cow if you're not going to apologise!"

"I've got nothing to be sorry about!" Lori raised her head high and walked on, then shouted over her shoulder. "You should be the one to apologise, for calling me a stuck-up cow! None of you even know me any more! How dare you, Callum Macrae!" And with that she marched off, leaving Callum standing alone in the graveyard, hands folded across his chest.

Lori stomped along the outskirts of the church yard in her sandals, which had already given her a blister on each big toe, and she screwed up her nose at the pain that jabbed with each step she took. Irritation bubbled inside her as she approached the village. She couldn't believe Callum wanted her to grovel in front of him. Hadn't he heard in the changing room that she used to watch him, *lust* after him when she thought no one was looking in high school? He had listened happily to all that until she had called him a bit of a bimbo. She may have spoken a little hastily, but she'd had most of a bottle of Prosecco, and had been deliberately humiliated by Tammy; on display in front of everyone, feeling always an outsider, as they made fun of her. She felt small, like the young girl she used to be, trying desperately to fit in, first in Melbourne, then in New York. *An apology?* Lori scoffed to herself, *he'd be waiting a long time to get one of those.*

∾

Once Lori got back to the house, she laid out all her notes and lists to discuss with Tammy, who she forgave all over again as she crammed one of the delicate pink French Fancies into her mouth, feeling the cool cream burst under her tongue, and the sugar soothe her temper.

"Right I've sent emails to these photographers." She pushed the papers in front of Tammy, wiping crumbs from the edge of her mouth. "Do you know any of these people?"

Tammy bent forward to peruse the names, as Gran quietly read the newspaper over on the sofa, with Bracken curled up motionless by her feet as usual. She had retreated to let the sisters discuss plans at the kitchen table, but Lori was very aware her gran was the queen of multitasking; keeping abreast of what Tammy requested, and to maintain the peace if she was needed.

"Aye, I've heard of them all, but I thought maybe we'd just get a friend to take photos. There's my boss at the bakery, his daughter wants to be a photographer, so she'd be a nice cheap option. Oh - and Alan's brother is good at taking photos. He did a wonderful job taking shots of the shinty boys at the last game."

Lori sighed and turned to her sister. "Yes, well, taking amateur photos of the shinty boys isn't like documenting a wedding. These are important Tam, you need a proper photographer. This is all you'll have to keep for memories."

Tammy frowned. "But it's difficult taking photos of people playing shinty, they're moving all the time, they- "

Lori put her hand on Tammy's shoulder. "Sis, you need a professional for this."

"OK, I don't mind then," Tammy said in a small voice.

"Right next is the catering, I wonder if we can get anyone this close to the wedding?" Lori ticked off each bullet point from her list and made notes for the following day. She had her work cut out for her, that was for sure! At this moment, Tam's plan seemed, essentially, to be: rock up at the church, and then onto the venue, and hope everything just miraculously comes together.

Lori itched her leg as Tammy spoke about getting various people baking for the wedding. Lori was amazed at how little Tammy knew about the practical side of such things. Especially given the amount of people coming, they needed someone who knew how to carry out a professional catering operation. If Lori allowed herself to hand over any planning to her sister, there would be approximately one scone for each person, and a photographer running around trying to capture action shots. Lori scratched her leg again, pulling a face, and Tammy looked at her quizzically.

"Lori, have you been out in the fields?"

"Yeah... why?... it's Bracken giving me fleas!" She grunted and pointed over to the dog who slept soundly on the floor by Gran. "Or I must be getting allergic to dogs."

Tammy bent down to look closer. "Oh my god! No, you are crawling with ticks! What were you doing? Rolling around in the long grass? Go for a shower this instant!" She pulled her arm with haste and Lori felt like a child again, but gave in to Tammy's orders.

Undressing in the bathroom she looked down in horror to see her legs covered in tiny black spots, all moving, and trying to burrow their way into her skin. She shrieked, and threw herself into the shower swiftly. It had been so long since she had had a tick bite, having forgotten all about the dangerous bloodsuckers that waited for their prey all over the Highlands in the long grass. She felt sick. Was that why Callum had warned her about what to wear? God, she *had* been a bit horrible to him. She washed herself, cringing and wincing as she removed the ticks one by one with a pair of tweezers Tammy handed to her. Never again would she get caught out like that.

That evening Lori rummaged around in the wardrobe and under the bed in her room for anything practical to replace her offending sandals. Her legs were now covered in angry red spots, so she dotted ointment on them all, but felt very sorry for herself indeed. Gran appeared at the door holding a few pairs of trousers and a pair of hiking boots.

"You never know who might visit, and who might need them!" She nodded.

"I guess they'll have to do!" Lori looked down at the battered old looking boots, that had an odour of smelly feet, and sighed. *Ah well, when in Scotland...*

9

L ori woke to the smell of freshly baked scones and padded out to the kitchen barefooted in her pyjamas to investigate. Gran was sitting at the kitchen table with the radio loudly booming, cup of tea in hand and reading the newspaper. Lori raised her eyebrows, her gran listened to the same radio show every morning since Lori was a girl. One which made her usually mellow gran very vexed by the current news of the day. She would no doubt rant about politics soon if she was indulged. Lori quietly passed her gran's concentrated stance and went to grab a warm scone from the cooling rack above the cooker.

"Lori Robertson, put down that scone this instant!" Gran ordered without looking up, turning the page of the newspaper cooly.

"But Gran, they're at their best just out of the oven!"

"Even so." She looked over her blue spectacles like a disapproving teacher. "I need to take them to the Produce Show this morning. And I want to win this year!"

Gran had been entering the Arlochy Produce Show every year with her scones, and much to her annoyance always came second to her long-standing nemesis Flora Smith. Gran had always used a recipe of her grandmother's, an old family secret that was peerless and delicious in Lori's opinion. But no matter how Gran tinkered with the ingredients or perfected her technique, every year the prize went to Flora.

"It's not the winning that matters Gran, it's the taking part!" Lori teased and sniggered at her gran's stern reaction.

"Don't I know that! But just this once I'd like to win!"

"Well you know I adore your scones! They are the best." Pushing her lips out innocently Lori sidled closer. "I've always missed them while I've been away, no other scone has ever come close to yours... And I'd love to taste one again..." Lori smiled hopefully at her gran.

"Thank you, but... no you can't!" She barked.

Lori turned to head back to bed, evidently sulking.

"OK, just one then!" Gran sighed, giving in. Lori quickly grabbed a scone and opened the warm fluffy inside letting out a thin trail of fragrant steam as she applied salted butter, which melted immediately.

"On one condition though" Gran's eyes never left the newspaper in front of her. "You come along with me!"

Lori inwardly groaned. "Well I guess I have no choice, do I?" She bit into the soft buttery cake, and contemplated how one might make sure at least one other scone didn't make it to the judging tables.

∽

The Produce Show was set up just outside the village on the grounds of the big estate house, which was owned by the Grant family. Hector Grant, head of the clan, as it were, was a middle-aged, wealthy, single man who would have been a rather attractive catch if he wasn't well-known as the local womaniser.

Lori and her gran walked to the show, basket of scones in hand and an umbrella at the ready. The clouds clustered above them threatening a downpour; not an unusual occurrence considering most years the Produce Show fell victim to the rain. Today Lori wore her new-old hiking boots, along with jeans and an anorak. She felt frumpy but decided it didn't matter; she wasn't strolling the charming streets of Manhattan, or at an executive meeting with models, but most importantly: Michael wasn't here to bear witness to her countrified attire. Today was really about showing support for her gran, no-one would even notice her, hopefully! They walked past the grand entrance to the estate. Ivy wrapped around the gigantic pillars on either side as the black ornate gate stood ajar welcoming everyone for the day. Cars were parked all along the treelined road before them, getting more tightly compact the further they walked. A short distance on and past the oak trees, they came within view of white tents bunched together, in-front of the grand estate house. Its dark grey stone looked somewhat ominous against the dark sky, as if they were walking straight into a Gothic romance. After the hill, Lori tried to stop to catch her breath and take in the scene, but her gran continued walking with grim determination. Lori was mortified, even though she was by far the younger party, her grandmother could still run rings around her in terms of agility and speed. So, hastily, she leaped back into step, close on her gran's heels, and just as stubborn, never showing her weaknesses.

Under cover at the baking tent, Lori helped set up a scrumptious pile of scones in their allocated spot. She glanced at the other tables; the displays of Victoria sponges, chocolate cakes, various loafs, tablet, jams, and marmalades made her stomach gurgle, and she sniffed appreciatively at the deliciousness all around her. Her gran placed a ticket number next to the plate, lifted out a small bag, and pulled out yellow petals and dried daisies; sprinkling a delicate smattering of colour around the dish. As if she knew what Lori was thinking, gran winked at her granddaughter, just as Flora Smith walked over to their table.

"Lovely to see you Mary!"

"And you Flora - entering scones this year?" Gran stood clutching her basket and Lori watched the two old ladies in awe, witnessing a rare side to her gran that she hadn't seen before. The women nodded and smiled at one another, but Lori could see under the tight smiles lurked hidden truths. She couldn't tear her eyes away, unsure of what might happen, like seeing two opposing cats frozen on the spot, unable to move, their spoken niceties barely concealing the passionate rivalry beneath.

"Of course I'm entering," Flora continued with volume, "I can't let people down. I know the judges love them so much, every year I send them off home with a few scones – they never let me leave without raiding the table! You know how it is Mary, we have to keep these people happy!" She gripped her own basket, smiling broadly.

"Well, I wish you the very best of luck, Flora!" Gran said through gritted teeth.

"And you, Mary!" Flora chuckled with confidence and strolled back to her display, rearranging her scones again with a backwards glance at her opponent. Gran grabbed Lori's arm and tugged her behind their section.

"A bit of a gloat!" Lori raised her eyebrows, still looking over to Flora, who began setting her scones down like a pyramid, and calculating the angle with her own measuring tape.

Her gran giggled. "She is that!" she whispered. "Ach, it's all just a bit of fun though!"

Lori and Gran passed the next half hour mooching around the tents, arm in arm, deciding on what delicious delights they would sample. The variety of produce on display amazed Lori, far more impressive an offering than any farmer's market she had seen in Union Square. Gran stopped to buy some vegetables from a local couple she knew, as Lori walked past more stalls of local businesses. She stopped at a stand with a kayak laid down on the grass in front of a huge banner which depicted highly attractive people paddling in similar vessels in turquoise waters under the words: "Adventurous Tours" in bold yellow font. A pretty blonde woman came out from behind the stall desk holding out her hands. "Hi Lori!"

"Hi...?" Lori squinted at the girl.

The blonde giggled. "You don't recognise me! I was a few years under you in high school. I'm Karen!"

Realisation hit Lori. "Yes, I do recognise you. Karen! You've certainly changed since high school! How are you?" Lori remembered a chubby, shy girl; the younger sister of one of her friends, certainly not one for platinum hair dye, or extreme sports.

"I'm good, busy with the business - it's really taken off!"

"That's great, it's lovely to see local companies thriving. And how's Rhona?" Lori hadn't thought of her old friend in a long time, but they had spent a good deal of their teenage years together.

"Rhona is over on Shiel island. She's got three kids now: two boys and a girl."

"Wow, she's been busy, too!" Lori laughed. "I'll need to contact her, though I'm only here for a wee while."

"She'd love that, I'll give you her number!" Karen went in search of a pen.

"Lori," came a stern greeting from behind her, making her jump. Callum walked past her, his light brown hair was scruffy today, and he looked tired. He wore a black t-shirt, also emblazoned with the words: *Adventurous Tours*. Lori noticed his strong tanned arms as he strode forwards, and for some reason she became a little tongue-tied.

"Karen's getting me something..." was the only reply that came to mind. She stood fiddling with the umbrella in her hand as Callum looked at his phone. An awkwardness settled between them, and Lori panicked trying to think of something to say; what could she say? Thankfully Karen came back, her hand outstretched holding a piece of paper. "Thanks very much!" Lori smiled and gave them a wave goodbye, glad to be away from the stale atmosphere that she and Callum seemed to perpetually generate. Despite the relief, she found herself glancing back to see Callum touch Karen's back gently, and mutter something in her ear.

Lori and Gran cheered the school children on during their egg and spoon race, watching their hopeful faces as they balanced their eggs towards the finish line. Lori remembered when she herself had taken part in the competitions, the Produce Show having always been an annual occurrence as long as she could remember. Her favourite had been the Coconut Shot, where she would throw a ball, trying to knock over one of the three hairy coconuts perched on their display-poles. She often won at least one coconut, only to spend her evenings trying to get into the shell with a screwdriver, much to her gran's concern. In some ways, looking back now, Lori saw that she had been what you might call a tomboy; always playing with the boys, and forever cutting her knees. Even now, the faint scars still showed on her legs, like medals from an active childhood. On the green, people sat on blankets watching the day's events, and munched on tasty treats from the food tent. Lori couldn't listen to her rumbling stomach anymore, and led Gran towards food. Since being back in Scotland her appetite had grown rapidly, and with all her gran's baking and cooking she knew she'd need to keep an eye on her figure if she wanted to fit into all her designer office-wear upon her return to the city. But right now, surrounded by familiar smells and tastes, she was determined to relish everything - the diet could begin tomorrow. In the food tent, Lori piled her plate high, taking samples of everything that was on offer. Her gran got talking to two ladies serving teas and coffees, as Lori went off in pursuit of a free table. Most of the tables were full, but as Lori scanned the room, she spotted the local laird who owned the estate and stunning manor house, sitting by himself. A thought jumped into her head, an idea that might possibly be the best contribution she'd had so far to the wedding. Lori saw that this could be her only chance, so she stood tall, and shimmied around the tables to the vacant chair.

"Hi there! It's Hector isn't it? May I sit down?" Lori smiled down at the man wearing a tweed jacket, a red tartan kilt, and a blue beret with a bobble perched on top. Lori couldn't help but think that his appearance looked rather eccentric even for a Produce Show, but he was an unusual man after all. He abruptly got to his feet and bowed slightly.

"Of course my dear, it would be a pleasure!" His accent

was different from the locals of Arlochy, and there was a faint courtliness to his movements that stood him apart from the rest of the fair-goers. Hector had spent his childhood away at private schools down in England, the usual tradition for lairds in the area Lori remembered. Abundantly apparent in his voice and manner were the marks of difference; he wasn't really part of the festivities, and they would never be a part of him either. Something about that made her feel a bit sorry for him: he would never be a local, he would always be the laird. But he was wealthy, much more than anyone else she knew in the area, and he certainly wasn't lonely, for all his uprooted schooling, so her sympathy could only run so deep. Lori sat down graciously, her gran still speaking with the serving ladies in the background.

"It's actually been a long time since I've been home - I'm Mary's grand-daughter." She pointed behind her towards her gran, who at that moment gave a hearty laugh.

Hector clocked who it was she had indicated, then an expression came over his face that Lori couldn't read.

"Oh - I see. Your parents died in that tragic boating accident?" He put his hand on hers and for a moment Lori felt distinctly uncomfortable at his directness.

"Erm...yes...it was a long time ago. We've... all come to terms with it now." Lori wondered how to change the subject, there was no way she wanted to discuss her parents with this man who she didn't even know. She bit into a buttered pancake from the top of her plate as Hector took his hand away and awkwardly sipped his tea. "You have a beautiful house and the gardens are so neat and tidy as well as picturesque!"

"Thank you, I have a very attentive gardener."

"Dougie?" Lori smiled as she swallowed a chunk of an

egg sandwich, she was ravenous. "I know him, he's a friend of Grans. He's getting on a bit, I mean...to handle all of this himself isn't he?"

"He is a little older than most, but he does the job very well. No complaints from me!"

Lori smiled, the old man had worked most of his life for the estate, spending the majority of his time outside in all weathers, just to keep the beautiful garden in order. He probably knew a lot better than her of what it took to manage things effectively, thought Lori laughing at herself – after all, *Gran hardly let her age get in the way of anything!*

"Do you have weddings here?" She could hear her grandmother start to bring her own conversation to a close, and knew she would be coming to look for her soon.

"Yes yes, it's a busy time of year for weddings. We have most weekends fully booked now." He held his cup up as a serving lady holding a teapot weaved in and out of the tables. "We usually put a large tent in the gardens and hold the main event there, but sometimes we have the whole wedding - from service and dinner to ceilidh - in the big house. Mainly if the party is blessed with torrential rain!"

"You know, I haven't actually ever been in the big house." Lori smiled over her cup; if she could get this place for Tammy's wedding, her sister would be over the moon, she just knew it. Most brides would kill to have a wedding here, she just needed to get Hector on her side.

"Really?" He smiled "Well I could give you a private tour?" He looked at her intently.

"Erm...yeah, that ...would be lovely!" Lori was happy to jump on this rare chance, if she could secure this venue then everything would fall into place.

He looked at his gold watch, then moved his plate away from him. "I'm afraid I must go; I'm booked to dish out some prizes. But you could come back tomorrow, say midday? I can show you around then." With that he got up from his chair with a slight wince rubbing his left leg, and walked away.

Gran came over. "Talking to the laird?"

"Hmmm... yes." Lori pushed her lips together tightly. "Just between us: I want to try and have the wedding here!"

Gran raised her eyebrows, and took a sip from her cup of tea. "Have you asked Tammy?"

"I won't until I know we can. He's said it's booked out, but it's last minute - there might be an opening. I have a good feeling about this!" She mentally made a note in her head to contact tent-hire companies; if there was to be a wedding here, they'd most certainly need a beautiful marquee.

10

The next day Lori arrived at the big house earlier than arranged so she could take a look at the grounds more clearly. The tents from the previous day's show were sitting empty, the whole space quiet and still in contrast to the day before. Lori walked across the short grass and headed in the direction of the apple orchard she could see on the far side of the house. The trees were heavy with white blossom, promising an abundance of apples to come. Lori walked through the trees, which trailed all round one side of the large stone building. From the front garden she could see the silver bay on the far horizon. She breathed in the sea air, mingled with the heady perfume of blossom. She continued around the building to a stone shed, with rose bushes trailing up its front walls. The gardens were flourishing with springtime now passing into summer, and nature was coming alive across the county. Twittering birds fluttered in and out of the apple branches behind, and out beyond the shed in front of her. She looked at her watch, and seeing she had some minutes before their meeting, decided to walk further on, hoping her invitation from yesterday included a little independent exploration. She felt a little guilty somehow, but told herself there was no such thing as private land in Scotland, *freedom to roam and all that,* and she did have a few minutes after all; Hector wouldn't mind. She continued on a grassy path behind the shed, and strolled beneath some giant oak trees, which were so large they blocked out the sunlight. It was so tranquil: just her, the birds and the gentle rustling of the wind. Lori breathed out, she felt calm just being here. Then a thought popped into her head; work hadn't crossed her mind until now. She had forgotten to even check her phone for updates. Lori shook her head, today she had woke to birdsong and read some pages of a book she'd been trying to start for over a year now. A wholesome breakfast of avocado on toast had been consumed and then she slowly made her way to the estate house. A simple day, of just being in the moment. No panic attacks, no anxious thoughts of being out of her depth, or of being an imposter in the wrong crowd. She squirmed a little inwardly; she hadn't even missed Michael. Her family had taken up her thoughts almost entirely, and she had barely considered his caseload or his strange mood at their parting. Lori was just about to turn back to the house to keep her original appointment, when she saw an opening in the trees ahead, and some kind of stone statue at the end of the path, standing in the gap as though waiting for her. Curious to see more, she walked briskly, and as the trees that lined the pathway stopped, she was hit by bright sunlight. She squinted to see in front of her was a statue of a naked lady, with a thin layer of cloth draped over her shoulder and one breast, chiseled to almost-sheerness by the skill of the sculptor. The girl covered herself with one hand and with the other raised hand, she held the rippling cloth. To Lori, she looked to be half-temptress, half-innocent – not quite caught unawares, but still concealing most of her charms from the onlooker. Behind this figure, tall bushes were tightly bunched together, too high for Lori to see over. She walked past the statue, and saw that a small tunnel lay ahead between the bushes, which looked enticing, but dark with the chance of getting lost. Lori glanced at her watch again, she was already running late for her appointment with Hector, so she quickly left the slender young woman with the knowing expression, and ran back to the house. Within a few minutes, she stood at the front door catching her breath from the run, and wafting her t-shirt to filter cool air back over her body. The door opened and Hector's ruddy face beamed back at her, welcoming her in. He wore smart jeans and a green checkered shirt, with the top buttons open to expose a little greying chest hair. Lori followed him into a light room, with a large tartan sofa in one corner, and a dining table on the far side. The window on the west side of the room was huge, and opened out onto the islands in the distance, the view almost like a painting in Lori's appreciative gaze.

"I've never seen the grounds from this angle before; it's incredible!"

Hector chuckled, standing beside her. "Yes it's a nice spot - I usually sit here every morning for breakfast."

"God, I'd love to have breakfast here every morning!"

Hector gave a little smirk and gestured to the table. "Would you care for tea?"

Lori accepted, but all she really wanted to do was look around the house. *That would have to wait though,* she grimaced, *until all the niceties were over.*

"I've not seen you in the village yet, Lori?" Hector asked as a small plump woman appeared from a door behind them. She was carrying a tray, and laid out an elegant teapot alongside a plate of sandwiches and cakes.

"Thank you, Mrs. MacPhail," Hector nodded as the woman poured out the tea.

"Yes, thank you Mrs. MacPhail!" Lori smiled, recognising the woman; the problem with being from a small village was everyone knowing everyone. Living away for so many years, Lori annoyingly couldn't remember several names. Luckily, people tended to know hers, which kept her right – or in this case, Hector had provided an aide-memoire.

"You're welcome Lori, I heard you were home! I hope you're looking after your gran, she's a good woman."

"Oh, you know gran; she doesn't want *anyone* looking after her!" Lori picked up her china teacup. "But she's well, thank you – and as young as ever!"

"Good, I'm glad. Well I'll leave you both to it." She bustled away with tea towel over her shoulder, carrying the empty tray with her.

"You know my cook?" Hector placed a napkin on his lap and offered Lori the plate of sandwiches, all perfectly cut in triangles with crusts removed.

"Yes, she has sons around my age." Lori placed a few salmon pieces on her plate.

"So - as I was asking previously, you don't live here in the village now?"

"No I live in New York actually, I'm just home for a visit."

"Oh New York! I do enjoy the city. I try and go there once a year. I have some investments there, so I like to go and check up on things now and then. I have some family there too actually, so I try to kill two birds with one stone and all that." He winked at her, and continued working his way through the plate before them.

"That's interesting! Yeah it's fabulous there. I work for a

fashion label in Manhattan."

He looked impressed. "Well done you! Lovely place, that's where I stay when I go over there."

Of course it is, Lori thought.

Hector spoke a little about people he knew in New York, and then what he planned to do with the Arlochy estate house in the near future. "I think I might rent it out to people, like that Air BnB company – remote online bookings, you know. It's a bit big for just me now - well, unless I get married and have kids!" He scoffed.

"So you don't have any weddings here at the moment? It seems quiet."

"No, I leave the area at the start of July every year, then my house manager comes in and takes over the running of things. That's when I allow the wedding season to commence; I like to be away from all that business. So I'm in London for the next few months, then onto New York." His eyes flashed up to meet hers: "Perhaps we could arrange a meet up when I'm over there?"

"Um, yeah sure!" At this moment Lori thought she really should mention her boyfriend Michael, but time was passing and she wanted to talk about the wedding. "Hector, I wonder if it might be possible to have a wedding here on say the 1st June? I know it's last minute, but we'd appreciate it and would work to any conditions you have"

His facial expression suddenly changed to one of cold confusion. "Oh, you are getting married? You're here just to see the house for a booking?" He stood up abruptly, making Lori stand too, in response.

"No no, it's my sister who is getting married, I'm just helping organise it all."

Hector put his hand on the table, steadying himself slightly, and looked at her coyly. "Ah - that is good news then. It's your *sister* who is getting married. Well well, a local girl." He crossed his arms and then put one hand to his mouth, considering the situation. "I will still be here at the house, but I'm sure I could make myself scarce for the day. But I will need to consult with my manager briefly, to see if it's possible."

"Oh please, that would be just amazing Hector." Lori clasped her hands together with relief. "We'll take anything you can do, because at this rate she'll be using the local hall unless someone takes pity. And I think this would be the perfect venue!"

His eyes lit up at her enthusiasm. "Well of course, let me check. Would you like to see around the place?"

"Yes please!" Lori felt a rush of excitement as she looked around the exquisitely luxurious house. Each room surpassed her expectations. There was a large study, library, dining room and an even bigger lounge. The spaces were exceptional, and Lori saw that whoever Hector's estate manager was, they had done well in utilising such a dramatic household as a commercial venue. Her sister and gran would be so pleased with her after hearing what she had been up to today, and she was equally satisfied knowing that she would be helping make the wedding a more confirmed success. Hector had taken down her number, and promised to message her with details and confirm dates, and to Lori's delight after minutes of walking back to her gran's house her phone beeped:

> *"Manager says date is available for wedding. He*
> *will be in touch in the next few days. Perhaps*
> *we could meet to discuss, I could show you a*
> *few romantic spots for the photographs."*

Lori almost jumped with joy. *Still got it*, she grinned to herself. Feeling triumphant and ever so proud of her productivity, she knew who she must tell immediately. Leaning against a tree, and keeping phone within signal, she dialled Michael's number with slight anticipation. He answered, bright and breezy on the phone, much to Lori's surprise after their last conversation.

"Michael darling, I am so thrilled!" She announced dramatically.

"Hi Lori, how are you? What happened?"

Lori gave an inward sigh of relief at his usual phone manner, *things were good between them after all.* "I've just booked a beautiful manor house for Tammy's wedding. You should see it, it is stunning! It reminds me of that weekend we spent on Lake George, at that luxury château, remember? Well this place is *even* better - I wish you could see it!" Lori rambled, still excited from the news.

"Well done Lori. Well if anyone can make things happen, it's you" He said warmly "I'm actually having coffee with Matthew and Veronica."

Lori could hear his companions say hello in unison. Michael had often arranged catchups with the pair, a power couple who he had liked to bounce ideas with. Lori enjoyed their company, they were fun, lively and always interested in Michael's opinion. They would take them to the new and exclusive restaurants that the city boasted, and be on the guest list for every event. But as much as Lori liked their company, she often felt a subtle rivalry between them, as if she were taking part in some competition that she was continually losing.

She bid farewell to Michael, Matthew and Veronica,

while she headed home feeling altogether satisfied with her day so far.

Gran had made dinner preparations that evening inviting the family over again to eat in the back garden. Large-stemmed candles and small tea-lights trailed down the middle of the dining table, creating a soft glow as the pink sky above faded to dusk. Lori was excited to tell everyone the news; how she'd bagged the most beautiful wedding venue in Scotland in the space of a few minutes. But in the meantime, she tried her best to keep it as a surprise until she felt the moment was just right. Tammy and Alan arrived, holding hands as they stood out on the veranda and sipping at bubbling glasses. Lori saw that Tammy's glass was filled with sparkling water, and wondered if anyone else had noticed that detail too. Lori topped up Jean's glass and made sure her nieces had a fruit juice each. Gran clattered pots and pans in the kitchen as everyone began chatting in earnest, and then the doorbell rang.

"I'll get it!" Lori shouted, and ran to the door, grinning as she caught her gran swearing under her breath, hoping no-one had heard. Standing on the porch was Callum, in a fitted black shirt and light trousers. He was effortlessly handsome, though clearly he didn't know it. Lori swallowed a small lump in her throat.

"Hi." He seemed nervous, and Lori noticed a tremble in his voice. "Your gran invited me tonight," he looked down to Lori's hand, "but it seems I might've already missed the party?" He chuckled a little as Lori blushed slightly, remembering her hand was clasped firmly around an extra-large champagne bottle.

"No no, I'm just serving this now. You're just in time actually. Come in." She let Callum walk in front to the kitchen as she got him a glass. Why had no one told her Callum was coming? It's like everyone forgot the fact that he was her ex! He presented her gran with a box of chocolates and laid a bottle of red wine on the counter, giving the old lady a kiss on the cheek and a hug. Even Bracken walked right past Lori and waddled over, tongue out in delight to welcome their new guest.

"Can I help, Mary?" Callum asked.

"Call me Gran," she insisted "No, everything is under control, you both just go through and enjoy the evening. I'm sure you've got a lot to catch up on." She shooed them away and Lori caught the smallest of smirks on her grandmother's face.

They both ventured out onto the veranda, where Alan, Tammy and Jean were all in a deep conversation about politics. Alan casually saluted Callum, and Lori decided it best to leave the three to finish their discussion.

"How are you Callum?" Lori asked. After the chilliness between them the day before, she was unsure what else to say. Her heart beat so fast, she hoped he couldn't hear it. What was wrong with her? She felt her cheeks warming, and she didn't know why. Callum took a sip of his drink, taking his time to answer the question. His shirt clung tightly around his chest, making Lori imagine for a split second what he looked like without it on. It had been well over ten years since they had been together, but Callum looked just the same as he had in high school. Compared to many other local men who spent their weekends in the pub, he still looked athletic, and his brown skin showed he was to be found outside whenever possible.

"Uh, good. And you?"

Oh jeez, thought Lori. *This was going to be a slow night.*

11

Callum glanced over at Alan who had his arm around Tammy, both in an in-depth conversation with Jean. The two small girls hovered around their mother's legs, until Bracken shuffled past and immediately distracted them. Callum knew this family well; after spending time with Lori all those years ago, he had developed a close relationship with them after she had left. Gran had always been a stable, reliable figure in his life, someone from whom he could ask advice, which he did from time to time. He had never known his own grandparents, as his parents had been older than most when they had had him and his sister. Mary Robertson had always been there when he needed her, giving him objective support and encouragement when he first started *Adventurous Tours*. Now with Lori back home, he didn't feel as welcome here as he once had. *But it was her home,* he told himself. All he could do now was to take a step back and wait until he was included in the conversation, offering any small contribution he could. He looked at Lori; she wore a light blue dress that clung to her beautiful curves. He loved her curves, so much nicer than the stark angles women were supposed to inhabit nowadays. He always thought she suited blue, making her piercing eyes stand out from under her deep auburn hair. Her hair was a shorter length than when he knew her in high school. But he liked the change; she looked sophisticated and elegant, and, as he reflected to himself, sipping slowly at his champagne, she was just as pretty as she had been all those years ago. This was going to be tough, spending personal time with Lori after what she had done to him. But he needed to get over it, he thought, as she called over to her nieces who were lying on the grass nearby. If only they could be civil to one another, then he could get through this. But as Lori had been snooty and rude to him on all three occasions since her return - he sensed he was going to struggle. Callum found himself hostile towards her, unsure how to accept her, and he hated himself for it. This was not him, but each time they met his insides felt like they had been ripped open a little. By just seeing her inflicted the wounds all over again. She had set him up for a fall; besides, after the whole terrible business with Jennifer, Callum couldn't see himself being with anyone again. But as Lori's eyes met his, memories flashed before him of summer nights together out in wild open spaces, something he thought would continue on and to the other side of the world. But his hopes of going to Australia had fallen flat on their face. He had been so sure Lori had felt the same, but something had changed as soon as her feet left the Highland soil, leaving him to a dead-end job and a cold bed, alone and confused. After much discussion with her gran, he had almost been encouraged to go out to her with the daft idea of proposing, but after her total lack of response to any of his letters or his calls, he had decided to let her go. How wrong he had been, and what a lucky escape too, he thought to himself. The woman before him now was selfish, and thought herself superior to everyone around her. Whatever had happened to her in the city had made her into an entirely different person, one he liked considerably less. Or, he thought, maybe she was always this way and he had been too young and love-struck to see it. Shaking his head a little he tried to block out his unhelpful thoughts, and drank more deeply of his champagne.

Gran announced that the food was ready, and everyone eagerly sat around the table among the aromas of chicken, garlic and roast vegetables. Maggie and Anne squabbled with one another of who would sit next to Lori, so to calm them both Lori sat in between the sisters. Gran tapped her glass with her knife and all the murmurs quietened.

"I'd just like to welcome everyone here tonight. This house hasn't seen this many people since my son used to have parties here after the pub! I tell you I have never seen so many musicians in one house!" She chuckled and looked over to Tammy. "Your father would be so proud of you my dear, as he would of all his daughters." She smiled at Jean, and winked at Lori. "Now, I'm not one for speeches - but here's to a special summer and a special wedding for our youngest, Tammy, and her lad Alan - I'm sure you'll both be very happy. To Tammy and Alan!" She raised her glass, and the table cheered as the couple kissed.

The evening went on at a relaxed, gentle pace. Maggie and Anne told everyone what they had done at school that day, with Maggie the youngest, speaking out ever-louder to get the whole table to laugh. She spotted her mother, who was looking at her phone, preoccupied, and spoke up: "Mummy, didn't you hear my story? Why aren't ya laughing?"

Jean sighed, taking her eyes away from her device. "I

heard, toots. You were being a cheeky so-and-so today to the teacher, so I shall be having a wee chat with her to be more tough on you!"

Maggie's reaction was a perfect pout as she pushed potatoes around her plate.

"I learned about the war and all the men who left Arlochy to fight." Anne said in a quiet voice in-between mouthfuls.

"Well done dear, good on you," Gran declared. "Please help yourselves to more wine - Lori, please can you keep everyone topped up?" Gran glanced at her own empty glass, and Lori diligently obliged.

"So, seeing as I'm on my feet - I have some news for you Tammy – for you all! Pretty exciting news!" Lori smiled broadly. "I went up to the big house today and met Hector. Now, as you might know, he doesn't usually open his estate to weddings before July, and it's booked up anyway from then until October. Well..." She breathed in, pausing for dramatic suspense. "I have secured the big house and the grounds for your wedding, Tam! And before you go and say it's too expensive: this is my present to you both." Lori stood excitedly, with the bottle of wine in her hand, waiting for Tammy's response. But to her surprise, her sister stared down at her glass of orange juice, and then across to Alan in silence.

"That's great news!" Alan said, looking to his bride to be. "Are you sure Lori? That's very generous. What do you think Tam?" He put his arm around her but she remained still and rigid.

"Very fancy, it's normally all the London people who hire it out!" Jean remarked, and nodded to Lori, but her younger sister was still quiet, and shifted in her chair.

"Lori that's very kind, but we've booked the hall already.

It's a bit late to be changing our plans." Tammy ran her fingers up the stem of her glass. "Thanks so much, but it's.. too much..."

"Nonsense, I'm happy to do it! I can make all the preparations - think of me as your personal wedding assistant. I can meet with Hector and his manager, and get things all in place ASAP."

Alan squeezed Tammy's shoulder. "Well hun, what do you think?"

The suspense was killing Lori, and she was a little irritated too; there was no way anyone would turn down this offer. This was a generous and timely gift, and she had hoped for a more enthusiastic response.

"OK... Yes OK... If you're sure?" Tammy smiled, and Lori sat down feeling triumphant.

"Of course! It's going to be a bloody great wedding!" Lori squeaked with delight and downed the last dregs of her champagne.

Later that evening Lori walked with Callum into the village, mainly in order to contact Michael and her assistant in New York. They strolled down the main street on the side of the water. The sky was a hazy mix of pinks and oranges all swirling into one another. It was very late, but the day still did not want to relinquish its hold and fade into night. Lori squinted at her phone and held it up high to find signal.

"This is ridiculous, I've found signal at this exact spot before. Now I have nothing!" she groaned as Callum stood still beside her.

"Lori, you're really missing what's important here. Look at that view." He nudged her, and she reluctantly looked out at the horizon. The water was so still, reflecting the sky's hues, and the only sound that could be heard was a flock of geese flying in formation far in the distance. She saw a heron near them next to the pier, standing on a rock, its feet submerged underwater. It stood patiently, unmoving, like a statue waiting for dinner to swim its way.

"Bet you don't get *this* in the city," Callum whispered, and Lori felt his breath so close to her neck that it made her whole body stand to attention.

"No... but they have a lot that we don't have here."

"Oh aye?" He rolled his eyes.

"Yeah," she bristled. "Like galleries and museums, bars and cinemas. Our closest cinema is a two-hour drive away!"

He continued to gaze at the horizon, and Lori noticed the colour spilling onto his face as his brown eyes focused on the islands ahead. "No, we've no cinema. But I can make the journey if I want to see one of the new DC or Marvel movies. We can choose around here - to do those things when we want, and escape the rest of the time. What we have here is so precious. I realised how lucky I was, almost as soon as I left to go traveling."

"You left to go traveling?"

"Aye. You think you're the only one who upped sticks? That year you went to Australia, I moved away a few months after. New Zealand, Asia, and Nepal. It was incredible, seeing those huge landscapes, and the many different ways to live life. But it made me appreciate what a beautiful place we're from. That's when I thought, if I wanted to live here permanently, then I had to start my own business, instead of working for others."

Lori was shocked, but she tried to hide it from her face, and hoped Callum didn't see. "You were in New Zealand?

But I was in Australia!" She turned to him, hurt that at one stage he had been so near her, and she had never known.

"Yeah I know, Lori. I was writing to you. It seemed as soon as you left you just decided to ignore me, remember? I sent several letters, but you never responded."

Lori bit her lip, she knew she really should have an excuse for that fact by now, but nothing came to her. She was aware Callum had been trying to get in touch, but why hadn't she responded? Maybe she just hadn't been that interested in being with him? No, that wasn't it. She had really liked him; she had seen herself being happy with him at one point. But a part of her had feared that he would never achieve anything. One of those good-looking boys from high school who would stay in the area - never leaving, or making much of his life. That was the exact opposite of what she had been looking for. How could she say that to him? It was horrible to even think it.

"I couldn't find you on any social media, why didn't you email me?" Lori changed the subject.

"Lori, I hate all that bullshit, I thought you knew that? Even if I did email after I'd sent all those letters, I thought it was obvious you didn't want to see me - why would I lower myself to then send you emails that you would never reply to either?" He ruffled his hair with irritation, his calm composure gone. "I can walk myself the rest of the way. Goodnight." He marched off down the road, to then stop abruptly and turn back to face her. "By the way; when I asked if you were going to apologise that day at the church... It was for *then* - when I waited for you. The least you could've done was let me know you weren't interested in me. That's why I didn't go to Australia - you were there, and I didn't want to have you in my thoughts any more than you already were." He left her standing speechless on the road, phone hanging by her side, mouth open.

Lori crawled into bed, exhausted from her busy day but mainly from speaking with Callum. What could she say? She was with Michael now. She didn't want to spend too much time with Callum, partly because, as she hated to admit, she didn't trust herself not to fall for him all over again, just a little. But she did owe him an apology, and especially now that he was Alan's best man they both needed to be on good terms. Lori rolled over and removed the letters that were under her pillow. She slowly opened a discoloured envelope and propped herself up to read:

> *Dear Lori,*
> *Just checking you received my last letter?*
>> *Sometimes these things get lost, especially*
>> *covering all that distance. Your sister Tammy*
>> *said you've been busy in your new job*
>> *working in an office. I have to say I can't*
>> *imagine you in an office! – I thought you'd be*
>> *picking fruit or working on a farm? I'm still at*
>> *the fish farm, it's been a really harsh winter –*
>> *the snow has been on and off for weeks and*
>> *I'm forever cold. I've been exploring the idea*
>> *of traveling too, I'm going to stash the cash*
>> *and make a plan soon. Have you seen any*
>> *kangaroos or koalas? I love the idea of*
>> *stumbling across all those animals in the*
>> *wild, day in day out!*

*I've been playing with the idea of starting my
own business, but not sure what exactly right
now. It's been floating around in my head, so
I'm looking around for inspiration.*
I hope you're well Lori.
From Scotland with love.
Callum

12

The following morning, Lori was on a mission to find her sister and nut out the final details of the wedding. Since she had announced the wedding venue at supper, Tammy had been nowhere to be seen, and the big day was fast approaching. Lori was beginning to panic. She had done a lot of homework, and had contacted various people, she just needed her sister to pick out the specifics of what she wanted. Lori called into the bakery, but instead of her cheery sister, she was greeted by a man with a moustache and a big belly under his white apron. He didn't know where Tammy was; she had called in sick that morning. Lori couldn't find her sister at her gran's either, where she had been sleeping lately while Alan's parents were at his almost everyday, checking on wedding preparations. Since they kept her living with him as a secret, she would spread her time between Gran's and Alan's, a role which Lori was glad she wouldn't have to play for much longer. Lori drove along the coastline in the direction of Morvaig and knocked on Alan's door but no answer, so she gave up, and walked down to the Morvaig harbour. The town was a hub of activity, particularly after a large car ferry had come in from the Isle of Skye and unloaded a continuous stream of cars onto the mainland. Lori wandered around the lively shops, just in case Tammy was roaming the streets looking for last-minute wedding favours. Tourists walked around munching fish and chips or licking ice-creams to the cries of gulls above which swooped and dived for any morsel. The bustling town was once where Lori went to high school, and the transformation from domestic port to diverse tourist town left Lori stunned. She passed craft shops, delicatessens, pubs and of course, fish and chip cafes. She peered into The Isles Café where she would often go with Callum. In those days the tables were mostly empty, as the loved-up couple snuggled together in their usual booth. Now the booths were gone, to be replaced by wooden benches and communal tables, something Lori had seen in very hipster cafes in New York, but never imagined that the town of Morvaig would also exhibit. She continued along the street and came across the familiar yellow sign for 'Adventurous Tours'. She walked in without thinking, before she could talk herself out of it. Callum stood at a desk on the far wall talking on the phone, and nodded with a small smile as she entered. Lori busied herself looking at brochures and photographs on the wall, mostly displaying previous customers in hardhats, rock climbing and kayaking.

"I remember you used to be a bit of an adrenaline junky," Callum remarked as he placed down the receiver.

"That was a long time ago," Lori chuckled and looked at the delighted faces on the wall, full of exhilaration after climbing some epic rock-face or other.

"Not *that* long ago!" Callum walked towards Lori. "Are you in to book a lesson? I could put you down for diving off the coast?"

Lori shook her head. She looked down at the floor, and then forced herself to meet Callum's gaze. "I came here to apologise actually. You were right, I did ignore you. I don't know where my head was then, the least I could have done was to write or call. And the other day, what I said about you." She paused trying to find the words. "That day in the changing room. It was a horrible thing to say, and I want you to know I didn't mean it. I'm sorry if I hurt you - again."

Callum waved his hand, his cheeks flushing slightly. "It's fine Lori, I shouldn't have been so sensitive."

"No, really. I have been pretty awful to you. I don't know why. It stops here." She put out her hand. "Friends?"

He smiled and grasped her hand firmly, shaking it slowly. "Friends"

"Phew! I'm glad that's over!" Lori quickly let go of his hand and scratched the back of her neck.

"What? Were you nervous about seeing me? I don't believe that! Lori Robertson isn't scared of anything!" They both laughed in nervous relief as a small group of people entered the premises.

"Well, I've changed now, haven't I?"

"Did I say that?" He looked down at her with a playful smile. "Maybe I was a bit hasty, and if we're apologising, I shouldn't have talked to you the way I did either."

Lori put up her hand. "All forgiven, all forgotten!" She smiled, feeling like a huge weight had been lifted from her shoulders, as though an anchor around her waist had been cut loose, down into that harbour of Morvaig. She felt giddy at the light sensation flowing through her, and if she was being honest with herself, at the way Callum was looking at her this very moment. Suddenly, both of them became aware of the three potential customers hovering by the desk, and Lori forced herself back to reality. "Right, well – I need to get going and find that young sister of mine, before she misses her own wedding!" she joked. "And I think you might have just hooked some interested folks to throw off a cliff at the desk there!" She whispered. Callum grinned, and gave her arm a light touch as he turned to engage with the group of tourists.

She almost skipped out of *Adventurous Tours*, and smiled at the tinkle of the bell when the door swung shut behind her. Heading back up the high-street she felt on top of the world, with renewed energy and a much brighter smile.

Lori quickly decided to head over to Hector's to scope out where the ceremony should be. If Tammy was nowhere to be seen, then Lori was still determined to plan the wedding, with or without her sister. She drove on the wide open road, enjoying the crystal clear waters on one side and the sloping hills on the other, her windows rolled down, letting in the salty air from the sea, which pulsed through her curly hair. She turned off at the sign for the estate house, and drove up the long winding road, lined either side with old oaks. Behind the trees, she saw glimpses of cows happily munching on grass and laying side by side dozing in the lazy afternoon sun. The scene was so calming that Lori slowed the car to a crawl, watching the happy animals. *Maybe Callum was right about living in the country,* Lori thought, *it did have it's own special perks.* She parked by the front lawn on the pebbled road and turned to walk up to the house, but noticed Tammy's little Fiat beside the shed. *That's odd.* Then it occurred to her that perhaps Tammy wanted to start planning things immediately; maybe she had been looking for Lori this whole time, instead of the other way round! She marched through the orchard, and spent some time ringing the side-doorbell. There was no answer. And no sign of Tammy. She strolled around the grounds, but encountered no-one, not even a member of staff from Hector's large estate. It was silent, apart from the usual twittering birds fluttering to and fro around her. Then Lori considered for a moment, perhaps Tammy was viewing the maze that she stumbled on the other day – that, if anywhere, would be a great spot for photos. Lori slipped behind the garden shed and under the canopy of trees, taking the way she had been before, until she came to the opening where the seductive figure of the smiling young lady stood. As she approached the foot of the statue, she heard familiar voices coming from behind the hedge to her right.

"Call it off!" Tammy said in a desperate tone. "I won't ask again Hector!"

"My darling, we can talk about all that later. You must see, the important thing here is: it's me you should be with" came Hector's confident purr.

"No, we've been through this!"

Lori couldn't believe what she was hearing. *Hector and Tammy? But she was getting married to kind, loving Alan!*

"You could have so much more with me! The little one would have more opportunities too."

Lori gasped and covered her mouth.

"What was that noise?" Tammy demanded in panic. "Hector, get off me! I've told you, just tell Lori you've over-booked or something! I'm not getting married here."

"Of course not darling, because you can't get married to him! What can he give you? You'd be penniless and struggling for the rest of your lives."

"Hector, keep your hands to yourself! We're not like that

any more!" Tammy shouted. "Whatever happens with me and Alan...all I know is he loves me. I don't know what I am to you, I doubt I'm much more than a distraction – just like you were for me! Don't pretend you want more because I know you don't - it's over! Please, call Lori and cancel this ridiculous notion of using the house as a venue!"

"Tam, please!" Hector cried out passionately, and Lori hid behind a corner of the maze as she heard her sister stomp off into the trees, back towards the drive. She quickly followed suit, after making sure Hector had headed in the opposite direction, and was mentally preparing to confront her sister about the revelation she had just witnessed, when she heard the sound of a car starting, and saw Tammy speed off down the road.

Lori followed her sister a little way behind, and hoped Hector, being preoccupied with other things, had not heard her leave. She needed time to get her head around what she had just heard, her sister had all this time been deceiving everyone around her. Lori turned a corner, her head swimming, distracted she lost sight of the Fiat as she arrived outside the church in Arlochy. She parked next to the iron gates, but instead of entering the graveyard, she walked back along the path towards the main street, and ventured down another track to the bay, where a handful of craggy rocks lay in the shallow tide. Lori stretched out on a flat slab and looked out over the harbour. She was in serious need of advice just now, but the people she would usually have asked were Gran or Jean, both of whom didn't even know about Tammy's pregnancy. So she was well and truly stuck. *Oh god... is the baby Hectors?* Lori put her head in her hands.

"What a bloody mess!" she said to herself as the water gently lapped against the large stones. Lori looked out to the horizon, trying to find any answers that might be hiding in the depths of the water. What should she do? Pretend to know nothing and let things go on as planned? Lori grimaced, her stomach tightened and she bit her lip at the scale of Tammy's secret. *How many people would be affected? And there was the child to think of too. Maybe it would work out, Alan need never know. But if the baby is Hector's, surely that will always be a problem, Alan needs to be aware of what that means! But Tammy loves him, and it's her secret...* Lori had just happened to stumble on things by chance after all, maybe she could just pretend that she had never seen anything? But even after considering all the many options and solutions, it didn't look good, not good at all.

"Penny for your thoughts?" Tammy walked over towards Lori from behind the largest rock in the group, and perched next to her on the cool stone.

"Tam." Lori looked at her sister with sympathy.

"So... I saw your car..."

"Aye?"

"What did you see?" Tammy picked at her fingernails.

"Erm...basically everything. What were you thinking Tam, Hector of all people! A known womaniser!"

"I know I know, don't you think I've already punished myself?"

"But why?"

"I wasn't thinking straight. Alan was away for weeks. We had a huge fight about the usual things, money, work, not seeing each other, just before he left."

"But you love each other don't you?"

Tammy turned to face her sister, her expression filled with hurt and surprise at the question. "I love him completely." She paused and picked at her fingernails again. "The thought of losing him would... it would just destroy me, Lo. He's the best man I know, the best man I'll ever know."

"But why Hector?"

"I was sad and lonely after Alan left for that last trip, and Hector started coming to the pub pretty often lately. He walked me home after my shift one night when I'd locked up. He was a gentleman. At least, it felt like it at the time. Then... we started sleeping together."

Lori put her head in her hands. "Oh my god, Tam is the baby Hectors?"

"No, no it's not! Things ended with us as soon as they started. We... about two or three times, and then I came to my senses. It was just an argument I had with Alan; you know I have a bit of a temper; I just thought there was some-thing wrong between us, he was away a lot – I thought there was something wrong with *me*. But it turned out he was saving up to buy me a ring, and he proposed when he came back on land." Tears sprung from her eyes and she looked down at her engagement ring. "Oh Lori, I've made such a terrible mistake. I can't lose him!"

Lori put her arm around her sister and kissed her head. "Shhhh. Just let it out. We'll come up with something." *What an utter mess,* she thought inwardly. They were due to get married in just over a week, and at this rate it looked like the wedding really wasn't going to go ahead.

After some time sitting in silence, with only the distant sounds of seagulls and waves to intrude on their thoughts. Lori asked her sister the question she most needed to know.

"Will you tell Alan?"

Tammy's blotched tear-stained face looked at Lori in alarm. "Oh no, I couldn't bear him to think badly of me!"

"Do you want to cancel the wedding?" Lori pressed.

"No, I want to marry him. He's the father of my child. I love him!"

"Doesn't he deserve the chance to make the decision himself, before you..." Lori bit her lip as Tammy shrugged off her sister's arm from her shoulder.

"How dare you, it's not like I'm trapping him into some sort of lie! He's the one I want!"

Lori looked at Tammy with genuine love, and with pity. "You need to tell him."

13

L ori left Tammy alone on the beach to think things over, after all it was not her decision to make. She offered her sister the best advice she could, but there was nothing more that could be done. It was up to Tammy to decide what she wanted.

She went back to Gran's, hoping to spend the rest of her day with some comforting company, but found yet another note stuck to the fridge saying that Mary was having dinner over at a friend's that night, and not to wait up. Lori felt a little depressed. The fact that her Gran, who was over forty years her senior, had a far more exciting social life than her it seemed. She resisted contacting Jean, as it was a school night, her sister would also likely be occupied, marking homework or taking the girls to some exciting activity until evening set in. Lori sat on the sofa in the lounge, cooling off from her day. Bracken appeared and placed his heavy head on her lap.

"Oh Bracken, you need some exercise!" She stroked his silky head and he sighed, as though he had spent a busy day running about outside, rather than the reality of sleeping for the entirety of it. She continued to pat his fur. "OK, enough! We both could do with some walkies!" Bracken lifted his head slowly and looked at her, to then drop back down on her lap, stating his thoughts on the matter. Lori laughed and shook him off. "Come on lazy lump!" She rummaged in the kitchen cupboard for some dog biscuits as a bribe, which miraculously worked, and she and Bracken set out together in the evening sun towards the village hall. The street was quiet, which was strange for this time of year, but Lori wasn't complaining. She enjoyed the peace, a welcome solace from the twists and turns of the day. She strolled along the waterfront, with Bracken plodding along quietly by her side. Her thoughts drifted to Tammy and Alan. *Would Tammy tell him tonight? Would she ever tell him?* She breathed in and out, and mused to herself in mild surprise: *Another day without thinking of work! How was that possible?* She reached for her phone in her back pocket, but lost interest as soon as she touched the device, leaving it tucked away where it was. Bracken startled her by barking happily and wagging his tail, tongue dangling from his mouth. Lori looked up to see Callum walking towards them, smiling as the affectionate collie waddled up to him. He patted his old flanks, laughing.

"He loves you," Lori declared dryly.

"I know Bracken well, don't I wee man?" He briefly crouched, patted him on the head and stood up to face Lori. "What you up to?"

"Nothing much, just having a stroll. Beautiful night!"

"It is." He nodded and looked over to the water. "There's been some sightings today of a pod of porpoises. A few of the boat tours got some great photos."

"Oh wow, that would be incredible to see!"

He grinned at her with a mischievous glint in his eye.

"You fell into that trap Miss Robertson! Why don't I take you out tonight? We'll get in a kayak and who knows - we might see something."

"Oh no, I couldn't. It's been such a long time since I've been in a kayak or any boat for that matter!" Lori raised her hands and looked around for support from Bracken but he had already started walking back to the house.

"Come on, it's a perfect night for it. Plus you're with a professional guide, what's the worst that could happen?"

"Well something terrible now I'm sure, since you've said those words!" Lori laughed, and then gave in.

They met later that evening down at the small beach on the outskirts of the village. Callum's yellow van was parked in a nearby lay-by, and he was darting back and forth to grab various pieces of equipment when Lori arrived. She wore an old pair of trainers that Gran had kept for her since high school, and a tiny pair of sports shorts on, which she now regretted wearing, and self-consciously kept pulling down with each step. In no time Callum had fitted her out with a spray skirt, which drooped around her like a damp tutu, then he fixed over her a bulky vest-like life-jacket, and handed her a paddle. The water lapped rhythmically against the kayaks as they glided from the beach. Almost immediately Lori remembered a time when she had done this once before with Callum; it had been a summer night much like this when they had paddled around the bay to a tiny secluded island. They had camped there, lit a fire on the beach and had made love all through the night, surrounded by the sounds of the water, and the breeze sweeping into shore. Lori had all but forgotten this memory, but as it came back to her now she blushed brightly thinking of their tender moments together, and hoping Callum didn't notice, or remember the occasion himself.

The evening sun sparkled as it hit the shimmering water, and slowly descended into the horizon, melting from yellow tints to a dreamy pink, the shades growing deeper with each passing minute.

"I just never get sick of this," Callum said as he paddled next to her.

"I mean... it is amazing."

"It's very still tonight, hardly a breath of wind." Callum had his sunglasses on, and smiled over at Lori.

"What made you decide to do this? I mean apart from traveling and seeing that you wanted to start your business - why kayaking?"

"Hey, it's not just about the kayaking, Robertson! You know me, I love being outdoors."

"I do know that about you!" Lori chuckled and felt her face grow hot again. What was the matter with her tonight? She clenched her hands around the paddle, willing herself to keep calm.

"I really couldn't sit tight at the fish farm all my life. And just, well - working for others was making me go mad. I wanted to set my own rules, so after being in New Zealand, I realised that there was a market for extreme sports around here. In some ways the Highlands and Islands really are like New Zealand. Don't get me wrong, I don't do every extreme sport - we don't offer skydiving!"

"Have you done it before?" Lori breathed out, becoming comfortable just listening to Callum's familiar voice, and felt her hands loosen on the paddle.

"Oh aye. Done it twice, there's nothing like it!"

"Not bungee?"

"That's completely different! Have you done it? I would've thought you'd be doing all that well before me!"

"I never got round to it. I started a good job in Brisbane,

which got transferred to Melbourne, which then got moved to New York! I didn't really have time to explore the actual place itself."

"Well, I'm sure you crammed in a lot of worthwhile-" Callum abruptly stopped talking and put his finger to his lips, pointing over to an area a short distance in front of them. "Follow me," he whispered.

Lori diligently followed until Callum suddenly pointed over to a patch of water that was marked by ripples, Lori saw a pair of fins emerging slowly. She gasped: "Porpoises?" Callum nodded, and paddled further out, following the movement. Lori kept up as best she could, but couldn't match Callum's fast paddling. He glanced back to her and opened his mouth:

"Lori... stay still... "

"What?" Lori froze in fear, staring at Callum's silhouette ahead; was there a shark? *No you dumbo, that's only Australia and America!* Lori's heart pounded. *But what if by some freak of nature a great white shark had managed to adapt to the cold waters of Scotland and...*

"Look around you!"

Lori lifted her paddle above her head and looked around. What she was confronted with was not what she had perilously imagined. Fins rose above the water on either side of her kayak; there must have been about twenty Porpoises circling and twisting all around her; their grey curves rising gently above the surface, and their backs shining bright in the setting sun. Lori's fear disappeared immediately, and was replaced by an unfamiliar pleasant tightness in her chest.

"Oh my god, that is... the most beautiful thing-!" The words caught in her throat and to her utter surprise she began to cry.

Callum moved back to her. "What's wrong?"

Lori did not want him to see her like this, what was wrong with her? She was behaving like a silly emotional wreck, unable to be around Callum without crying or seizing up in panic or anger. "No, I- I'm fine! D-don't come any closer!" She tried to wipe her tears away, and in her confusion let go of her paddle, which floated away on the water out of her hands. Panicking, she somehow managed to lose her balance, and just as suddenly, before she realised what was happening, her kayak capsized and spun her upside-down underneath the water. Frightened and dazed, she pushed herself, moving her body desperately to try to escape the boat, but she was fixed tightly inside. Terror seized her as she gulped in water, unable to breathe, she panicked again: *Oh god, is this what it was like for Mum and Dad?* But then, coming to her senses, she reminded herself that it was only the slim rubber ring around her waist that was securing her in, so she felt around the opening of the kayak, and pulled her spray skirt open. Lori was plunged immediately into the cold sea, and kicked hard to reach the surface. She shook her head like a dog, clearing her eyes and breathing in the fresh air as Callum called down to her.

"OK Lori, I'm holding your kayak, I've got you!" Her kayak was upright again in it's proper position, and Callum had his arms wrapped around the nose. "Can you try to get yourself back in?"

Lori looked around deliriously, and wondered how the hell she had managed to almost drown herself. She tried to scrabble up the smooth side and grip the rubber rim again, but her body was so heavy, and her hands so cold that she struggled to get over the seat opening, and the kayak began to rock violently.

"It's too heavy! I can't!" she shouted, and Callum came closer in to the kayak, tightening his grip.

"I'm here, I'm holding it, you just focus about getting back in. I've got you!"

Lori closed her eyes, muttered something to herself and pushed her whole body out of the water with one huge effort, very ungracefully scrambling her body over the back of the kayak, and finally pushing and pulling herself into the seat again.

"Are you OK?" Callum had his hand on her kayak and waited for her response.

"Yes" She coughed out the salty water that she'd swallowed earlier.

Callum manoeuvred around her and went to fetch her paddle before it floated away for good.

Lori tried to smile "What a bloody fool I am"

Callum kept close "It happens, don't worry. I should have told you the safety precautions, some guide I am! I just presumed you had done this a lot. I'm sorry Lori. Let's get you on dry land, that's quite enough excitement for one night"

Once back at the beach, Lori sat down on the sand, exhausted. Callum, pulled the kayaks away and went to his van, to return moments later with a big towel and a flask. He wrapped the fluffy white towel around her shoulders and gave her a cup of hot tea.

"You're prepared!" She sipped the sweet tea gratefully. "It's like you knew I was going to fall in the water?"

Callum sat down next to her on the sand, wearing his shorts and t-shirt. "I'm a guide, I need to be prepared for every scenario!" He shook his head and buried it in his hands momentarily. "But I didn't prepare you for capsizing – I should have reminded you what to do if that happens!"

"I can't believe I did. I'm mortified!" Lori found herself cringing at the spectacle she had made of herself earlier.

"Hey, why are you so hard on yourself. Stop it!" Callum frowned at her. "But you're OK now, right?"

"Yes, thank you. The tea is good." Lori drank deeply, realising she hadn't drank much at all that day.

Callum nodded, slightly distracted "I think I was wrong about them being Porpoises. They looked like white beaked dolphins."

Lori looked up at him, wide-eyed, and then lay down on the sand with head resting on her hand.

"They're actually pretty rare to see, especially around here." He poured himself some tea from the flask, adding: "this is great news, I can mention it on our website!" He kicked the sand with enthusiasm and lay back, propped up on his elbow.

"Thank you, Callum, that was just so amazing."

He looked at her. "A special moment."

"Until I fell in!"

"Well that made it an especially funny moment!"

She playfully shoved him, almost spilling his tea.

"Hey!" He steadied his cup, chuckling at Lori's reaction.

She took off her wet trainers and let her feet feel the grains of cool sand beneath them. The sun was now setting and the sky was ablaze with vibrant pinks. They lay together in relaxed silence, Lori comfortable just being there with Callum, glad that a rather horrible day had turned into a wonderful evening. Callum placed his hand in the sand and moved it around carefully creating patterns. Lori watched quietly.

"Have you been with Karen long? You make a good team," Lori ventured, hoping to elicit an answer to the question that had been niggling at her for the last week now.

"Yeah she's a great worker, so good with people. Some days I can't face dealing with human beings, but she's always on an even keel and takes everything in her stride."

"What, you're moody? Jeez I would've never thought that...!" Lori chuckled to herself and it was Callum's turn to push her.

"OK OK, sometimes I may not always be 'on form'." He made speech marks with his fingers. "But she's great." He paused. "She works for me though, that's all." He took another sip from his cup. "Have you ever been married?"

"Oh god no, I've been married to my work for ten years!" Lori spoke the words and realised there and then that she *had* been married to her work. It had been her sole focus all these years, and she hadn't really noticed – only when the panic attacks came along did she have the urge to step back, to fight her way out and retrain her way of thinking. Callum had gone off on adventures, adventures that she had planned to do herself. But instead she'd got caught up in the nine to five - the promotions, the luxury clothes, and all those experiences she had wanted to have had never actually happened. "Did you get married?"

Callum nodded. "Yes, I was married for about seven years. She worked along with me for a bit. I actually met her in New Zealand."

"Oh?" Lori tried to sound unaffected by the news, though for some reason she felt like her gut had received a sharp punch. She hadn't realised he had been married; no-one had told her, why had no one told her?

"Yeah, turns out I wasn't enough though. She left me." He looked down at his hands that were submerged in the sand.

"I'm sorry Callum."

"Hey, it was a long time ago. In reality, it was me that left, but she had cheated, you see. I couldn't forgive her in the end."

"Oh, I'm sorry. You don't need to tell me anymore," Lori said softly, unsure of what the best response might be. She thought for a second of Tammy, and sighed. There were two sides to every story.

"It's actually good to say it aloud. I've struggled for some time with it. But she's back in New Zealand. I think it worked out for the best in some ways."

"Do you have children?"

"No, thankfully. That would have complicated things!"

Lori nodded, wondering how to change the conversation, but nothing came to mind. Instead they both lay there watching the last of the sun leave and dusk start to settle in, the sound of the waves sloshing impassively up and over the edges of the shore.

14

L ori spent the next morning baking with Gran, who had promised to take some shortbread to the community centre for their habitual tea morning, and a batch of red velvet cakes for a Whist drive later that evening.

"I swear Gran, I have no idea where you get all your energy. You don't need to bake this much, aren't there any other locals who can do it?" Lori poured the last of the red cake batter into paper cases, while Gran fiddled with the knobs on the cooker, which, she never could master and forgot how to work almost every time she used it.

"Nonsense! There's lots of others baking. It's a community, Lori. The leftovers certainly won't go to waste! This is just how things are in rural life, did you forget that?"

Lori smirked; she knew her Gran was in one of those moods which meant if Lori really wanted to, she could wind up the old lady very easily.

"Now - you'll be coming tonight, yes? Oh my goodness, where is my head! Mass! It's Sunday!" Gran suddenly marched off into her bedroom, towel flung over her shoulder. Minutes later she emerged wearing a respectable long navy skirt, and a white shirt covered in bluebell flowers.

"Very nice Gran!" Lori spun around after watching the cakes rising in the oven.

Gran accepted the compliment and ordered her granddaughter to follow suit.

"Gran, do I really have to go? It's just a bunch of old people listening to a man wearing a dress!" Lori groaned.

"Lass, do you or do you not want roast beef, Yorkshire puddings and fluffy potatoes from the garden roasted to perfection for your dinner?" Gran gave Lori a very direct sort of a look, and Lori caved immediately at the promise of home cooking.

"OK" She stomped off to her room, throwing on anything that looked clean, which ended up being jeans, a t-shirt and a smart linen jacket.

"Very nice," her Gran remarked, and took out the cakes and shortbread to cool on top of the counter.

"Let's get this over with, shall we?" Lori grumbled. It had been years since she had stepped into a church. She usually relished the Sundays she wasn't working, which typically consisted of a long sleep in, and then trotting out for brunch with Kim, or a visit to her favourite bakery for chocolate croissants and the best coffee in the whole of Manhattan. The remainder of her day would be spent catching up on the news of the week, touching base with friends, and eating through the highly-anticipated box of buttery treats. Now, looking back on her free time fondly, it had been such a luxury to do whatever she wanted, whenever she wanted. But now, under Gran's roof, if Gran wanted Lori to go to church, there was no way in hell she'd have the courage to refuse. Gran possessed the very useful talent of making people feel a lingering and pervasive sense of guilt as and when she required it. It was a skill to which Lori had never quite managed to raise sufficient defence.

They walked together to the church. The air smelled of summer; its sticky sweetness of freshly cut grass along with the odd hovering dragonfly, made the stroll down to the iron gates all the more pleasant. The sound of the waves in the distance crashed along the big rocks Lori had sat near the day before. *Quite a contrast to last night's still waters,* she pondered, when she had glided over mirror-like water as if gliding on the evening sky above them. She hadn't mentioned to Gran that Callum and her had spent the evening together, mainly because it felt strange to be out with another man who wasn't Michael, even if it had just been to explore the - *Michael!* Lori could scream at herself, where was her head these days? She needed to contact her boyfriend! But he hadn't been calling her either, was it really down to her to be the one who made the effort?

Lori sat down with Gran at the back of the church and counted ten other people in pews ahead, most of whom sported a grey head of hair; she was the youngest person there by thirty years at least. The priest marched up the aisle as the organ suddenly bellowed loudly and everyone stood to sing the first hymn. The noise of which was atrocious. Lori looked around for anyone else who might have thought the scene as bizarre as she did, but all present had their heads dipped over their hymn books singing to the out-of-tune blasts like some horror movie. She felt like Dracula or Frankenstein was going to pop out from behind the altar at any second. Her Gran had her blue spectacles on, with hymn book in hand, singing aloud with the rest of the congregation. The priest sang the loudest, in fairly good voice, as if trying to drown out the organ, or at least keeping it in time. Lori joined in when Gran nudged her and held out the book before her. The large old church echoed at the racket everyone made and Lori's gaze fell back over the other parishioners, surely there was a much more interesting way to spend their time than in a dusty old church? As if proving her right, a cobweb floated down from a high rafter, twisting and unfurling to land right down on top of the only non grey haired person in the room - a bald man. The cobweb sprawled across his head as if it had always been there. Lori bit her lip trying not to laugh, just as the man glanced back at her with suspicion. His eyes narrowed and he scratched the side of his head, missing the cobweb completely.

The priest spoke aloud in a welcoming speech once the singing stopped and everyone had stiffly retaken their seats: "Hello everyone. It's lovely to see ye all on this beautiful day. I hope ye all had a good week. It's nice to see new members in the stalls too!" He squinted in Lori's direction and she slide down her seat trying to hide. "Is that your grand daugh'er, Mary?" Father Angus asked loudly in his Glaswegian accent.

Gran grabbed Lori's elbow and hoisted her up. "It is Father, it's Lori! Back from New York."

The bespectacled man with a protruding belly under his white and green gown, beamed down at them. Lori noticed that he was wearing sandals, exposing rather long feet under his garment as he moved gently from side to side.

"Well that's lovely! From the Big Apple indeed! Somewhere I've always wanted to go!" He clasped his hands together. "Ye'll be here for the wedding?" His jolly manner was seemingly unaffected by Lori's silence, and to her alarm, a few of the other parishioners turned around to look at her. What did they want? For her to stand up and give a speech on why she was home? In the end all she could do was nod.

"Welcome Lori!" Father Angus smiled again, then closed his eyes, breathed deeply for a moment, and started his sermon. Lori quietly exhaled, and noticed all the while that Gran had been chuckling quietly to herself.

After what felt like at least three hours, the mass was finally over and they huddled at the back of the church where tea and coffee miraculously appeared, and cups and saucers were given out. Gran introduced Lori to other church-goers, although the conversation soon steered towards local news and church doings, and Lori casually edged towards the door.

The priest came over to her holding a cup of tea and munching on a biscuit, unwilling to let her go so easily. "Would you like a coffee or tea, Lori?"

"Um, yeah OK. Coffee please, thanks Father." She stood awkwardly as the priest poured her a coffee, then proffered a box of biscuits, out of which Lori gratefully chose a chocolate one, in the hopes that the energy might carry her through the rest of the morning.

The priest gestured to a couple who hovered nearby. "Lori do you know Mr and Mrs Mackenzie?" The couple appeared shy, but nodded at Lori, smiling. The husband was very tall, and the wife incredibly short; complete opposites, Lori mused.

"Hello Lori. We're Alan's parents!" The woman held out a slim hand which Lori took.

"Oh yes, it's so nice to finally meet you!" Lori shook the tall Mr Mackenzie's hand too, noticing that he was holding his own bible in the other. *I see what Tam meant.*

"We're so looking forward to the wedding! Although they're leaving it all last minute! I've told Alan to give us any jobs that need doing, but he says he doesn't know just yet!"

the small woman said, looking both proud and anxious at the same time.

"They *are* being a bit late in their planning!" Lori didn't know what to say at this point. So far she knew too many secrets to engage in any conversation too seriously. "I'm sure you don't need to do a thing; let us girls handle it!"

Mrs Mackenzie tapped Lori's hand with affection. "We're so happy Alan found someone like Tammy, she's a lovely girl."

"She is," Lori smiled, wondering if only they knew the details of the current situation, would they think the same way about her sister?

One coffee drunk, one priest spoken to, and one couple lied to, Lori was all set and ready to go back home with Gran. It was only when they finally reached the kitchen again, with its array of cooling cakes, that they found Tammy sitting on the sofa, biting her nails.

"Well you got off scot-free!" Lori rolled her eyes "Gran made me go to church!" The sulky teenager in her shone through.

Her sister looked so wild eyed, that Lori immediately excused them both and led Tammy outside into the garden as Gran busied herself in preparing lunch.

"He's gone!" Tammy bit her lip and paced about the garden.

Lori tried to take in an accurate picture of what was going on. "Who?"

"Alan!" Tammy shouted.

"Shh!" Lori led Tammy to the garden shed, well out of earshot.

"Did you tell him?" Lori placed her hand on Tammy's shoulder, and her sister nodded solemnly. "OK, he might just need time to think. Let him do that."

Tammy shook her head. "He's been gone since I told him last night. He walked out and drove away. He's not answering his phone!" Tammy looked just about on the verge of tears, and bit her lip again.

"But Tammy, he needs time. You were sleeping with Hector. It's big news for Alan. He'll be unsure if he can trust you again. He needs space to process that, honey."

"But it's him I want. It's his baby. I can't lose him Lori!"

"I'm sorry Tam, I know this isn't nice but you need to go through this so that Alan can have some time to sort his head out. You need to leave him be."

Tammy's eyes darted back and forth from the kitchen door to Lori. "I know! You don't think I've been punishing myself enough without having you give me the third degree!" She paused and sighed. "Sorry... I just need to know he's OK, that's all. I'm just worried he's... he's hurt himself, or done something stupid!"

"Like what? Do you think he's gone to Hector?"

"I've been, he's not there."

Lori took a moment thinking of the possible scenarios. If she was in Alan's shoes, and had just found out this news, where would she go? Then she thought of the one person who might know.

"Tam, I will need help from the best man – can I tell Callum what's going on?"

Tammy's eyes met Lori's with certainty. "Whatever it is, do it – I need to know Al is okay!"

15

L ori walked into Callum's empty shop, glad that the only pair of eyes looking back at her were his.

"Have you seen Alan?"

Callum stepped around his desk and came up to her, sensing her panic, he placed a hand on her wrist. The action left tingling sensations rushing up her arm like crackling fireworks on a cold winter's night.

"No, not since yesterday morning. How?" His concerned eyes penetrated Lori, making her feel naked and exposed.

She sighed at how dreadful things had turned out, one minute everything was going well, great even, the next all came crashing down around her ears again. But right now she needed to focus, so she told Callum what had happened, the whole sorry story with Hector and how Alan had disappeared, skipping over the detail of Tammy's pregnancy, feeling that was one detail too many to divulge.

He locked up the shop and placed his hand on Lori's back leading her to his yellow van, which was parked next to the harbour. He moved away spare life jackets, helmets and other equipment that was crammed into the passenger seat to allow her to squeeze into the space.

"Have you any idea where he might be?" Lori fastened her seatbelt as Callum speed off down the busy street.

"How about that bastard Hector's joint?" Callum grabbed the gearstick, pushing it hard as he revved the van.

"No, Tammy said she checked there." Lori scratched her head in irritation. Callum looked over at her with a set jaw.

"She went to see Hector? Jesus, hasn't she done enough of that already!" he shouted.

Lori closed her eyes with a sinking feeling in the pit of her stomach. She had hoped Callum would refrain from making any judgements, at least until they had found Alan. But now she doubted her first instinct to confide in him - perhaps it wasn't a good idea after all? Without further discussion Callum zipped down the road in the direction of the Grant house, as they both sat in anxious silence. The large van took up the whole road on approach to the estate and finally skidded to a halt in the parking area around the back of the big house. No other cars were visible.

"Looks like the bastard has done a runner. Wimp!" He spat the words.

It did indeed look as if the house was closed, with everything locked up, and not a soul in sight. Lori thought it likely that Hector had left to go to New York, or wherever it was he had said he spent half the year.

Callum shook his head and slowly drove the van behind the stone shed and a little further down the lane that led to the garden maze. "Maybe best if we hide the van, just in case," he grimaced.

Lori hopped out of the van and leaned against the shed door, a large padlock tightly secured its opening, blocking anyone from entering. Callum stood near her, leaning against the stone wall. Lori tried not to look at him for too long, but couldn't help notice his skin was a deeper shade of brown compared to their last meeting; a golden sun kiss, the perks of working outside in nature.

"What do we do now?" Lori kicked a loose stone and watched it tumble across the driveway.

"We wait" Callum sighed.

The pair moved around, changing position often, from the step at the back door, to the van, until they found a comfortable patch of green grass up the lane towards the maze. They had propped themselves under the oak trees and waited there in the gentle dappled sunlight for some time before Lori dared ask the question.

"You really think Alan will come? Surely Hector's long gone by now."

"Maybe, but Alan will definitely come. If he didn't turn up yesterday when he found out the news, then he'll be here today – I know him well enough to be sure of that. Alan takes his time, but he can make a rash decision as well as the next lad."

Lori watched the magpies dart back and forth above, hoping for the best possible outcome for everyone. The sound of an engine in the distance interrupted her daydream, and both friends exchanged a look then quickly made their way back to see who was arriving. A BMW Convertible skidded to a stop at the edge of the car park, and Hector got out. His face was flushed as he made his way to the back door with keys out, shouting over his shoulder.

"Can you please leave, this is private property!"

"I'd say you'll want us to be here when Alan arrives, Hector!" Callum called over, Lori at his side.

Hector stopped and turned around "Well well, Callum.

I've been seeing you a lot recently. Though I thought you wanted to keep a good distance nowadays. Was that not the agreement?" Hector began to smirk slightly, but his expression changed as a vehicle came up the driveway. It was Alan, red-faced and eyes bright with fury. He leaped out of his small car, slammed the door behind him and walked straight up to Hector. Callum and Lori rushed over.

"Get off my land!" Hector yelled, turning back to the door. Still rattling with the keys, he dropped them on the ground as Alan closed the gap at an alarming pace, but Callum jumped forward and grabbed his friend firmly at the shoulder with both hands.

"How dare you," Alan said quietly to Hector. Hector ignored him, picking up the keys once again. Alan grabbed them from his hand in an instant and threw them away into the grass. Hector pushed past him.

"I'm not telling you again, I'll call the police!" Hector bellowed.

"You think you can control us? You think you have any power here? Like you had power over Tammy?"

Hector laughed harshly. "I didn't have power over Tam, she all but came looking for it. I can't help it if she wasn't happy at home!"

"You leech, you dirty pathetic -!" Alan tried to shake himself free and take after the retreating Hector, but Callum quickly pulled him back.

"Alan, come on man! He's not worth it!" He urged his friend.

Hector retrieved his keys and went to his car, abandoning any further attempt to enter his house. "Listen to your friend Alan Mackenzie - if you come near me, I'll press charges!"

Alan's face was crimson, ready to attack. "I don't give a damn what you'll do, Grant! You're not even sorry, are you?"

Callum pulled his friend back. He was smaller in size compared to Alan, but as he pulled his friend away Lori could see his strength was immense.

Hector opened the car door. "Callum, take your friend away. There's no need for violence here, there's a good lad. It's not my fault you both can't keep your women."

"What did you say?" Alan screamed.

Hector started the engine, appearing more confident now he was back in his vehicle. "As I say, I can't help it. Your women just needed something that you could never give them. They're all the same in the end - I wouldn't get so het up about it, boys."

With that comment, Hector lost his one-time ally. Callum released Alan, spun his head round and walked up to the convertible, opening the door in a flash and pulling Hector out. "I can't believe you would gloat about what happened all those years ago!"

Hector pushed him off "You still think about her, Callum? About her with me? We had some crazy times in this house, even at your own place too! Hector laughed and Callum glared at him for a second, then swiftly and sharply punched him on the nose, without hesitation. Lori heard a disgusting dull snap, and ran over, finally finding her voice.

"That's enough!" she screamed, pulling Callum away, which he let her do with ease. Lori led him away to the van. "Come on Alan, we need to leave now!" she shouted.

Hector lay against his car door, cupping his bleeding face and crying out: "You broke my bloody nose!"

Alan walked past him seeing the blood staining his crisp white shirt, and kicked a handful of gravel over the older man's expensive boots. "You're pathetic." He walked to his car without giving him another glance, and took off quickly down the drive.

That afternoon Lori let herself and Callum into his small flat. He had been pretty quiet in the van, and Lori didn't know what to say, so she merely let the silence surround them, without acknowledging the temptation for small talk. She rummaged around in his box freezer and found a bag of frozen peas. She guided him to the worn leather sofa and placed the cold bag on top of his red right hand. He sighed, lying back.

"Nice place you have...?" Lori couldn't stay silent anymore.

"Thanks.... Can... can you get me a whisky?" He said gesturing to the cabinet next to the television. Lori got straight to work, and pulled out a bottle of malt and two glasses. She poured a large dram for them both and sat down beside him, sinking down onto the cool fabric.

"Well, that was quite a day," Lori offered through gritted teeth.

"I shouldn't have punched him."

Lori nodded, but stayed silent.

"Now you know why Hector and I have history, anyway." He took a gulp of whisky and groaned.

"I'm sorry," Lori sipped her drink, feeling the hot spicy liquid spread all the way to her belly.

Callum stared ahead with hand resting under the bag of peas. "She really hurt me. I just didn't understand why she did it. I was so besotted with her. She made me able to love again." He looked down and Lori felt the whisky tingling all through her, wondering if he was referring to her as being his first love. She pushed down the ache inside her; this was not about her. Callum continued. "And then she went with him, that smarmy rich vulgar man." Lori kept quiet beside him, nursing her glass of whisky, not meeting his eyes, just staring ahead too. "She could never offer me a reason why she did it. She just said she lost her mind and he flattered her. I think she thought she was in a bloody novel or movie. The laird taking a fancy to a normal girl like her!" He took another sip, shaking his head. "I just never could understand, so - ".

Lori sat there thinking of Alan and Tammy. "I wonder what's going to happen now?"

"Well if that creep does go to the police, at least it's me and not Alan who did it." He sighed, "I should check up on Alan." He moved in his seat just as a knock came at the front door, and Alan walked in.

"How are you mate?" Alan grimaced standing above them both.

Callum laid his head back. "I'm sorry Al. I let that get out of hand."

Alan shook his head. "You did me a favour, honestly - I don't know if I would've stopped had I got my hands on him." Lori noticed Alan's fists clench and she quickly handed her glass to him. He took the glass, sniffed it then downed it's contents with a cough. "I know you were protecting me. That's why I asked you to be my best man." Alan crouched on the floor, and nudged Callum's knee with his empty glass. "But just tell me one thing will you? Tell me that felt as good as it looked?"

Callum smiled broadly. "Bloody amazing!" Both men started laughing uncontrollably and Lori watched the mad spectacle before her; the line between love, hate and maybe forgiveness. Lori hoped that things would work out; for Alan and Tammy, and for Callum. She shook her head, and shivered a little, *what a day! What intense feelings people in love endure?* She reflected, considering her own experiences with her heart. What would she do for love? She watched the two friends together, and soon gave in too, laughing, wholly and completely with her body.

16

Tammy called around to the house where Lori and Gran were having a cup of tea and a slice of Gran's special elderflower cake in the kitchen, running through the door and up to Lori in mid-bite of cake, she wrapped her arms around her sister with an excited squeal.

"What's all this?" Gran said, already cutting a slice of cake for Tammy.

"Can't a sister hug another sister?" She kissed Lori on the cheek, whispering, "Thank you."

Over the day Tammy divulged the news to Lori, that after much soul searching with Alan, they decided to have the wedding, but with some fundamental changes.

"If we're going to start our lives together, then we've both agreed - no debt," Tammy stated firmly, and opened the bag with her wedding dress. "Which means, I'm returning this expensive article, and the two bridesmaids dresses here." She huffed nervously at Lori's concerned expression.

"Tam, you don't need to do that. I'm happy to loan you the money, hell - I'll pay for it!" Lori pushed the bag back into Tammy's hands. "You deserve the wedding dress you want".

Tammy shook her head "I actually feel good about this. Why don't I just wear a dress I like and already look good in? And same with you girls, you can wear what you want!" She showed Lori her wedding list, with recent alterations "I've gone through it with Alan, the money we don't spend will be for the baby and for our life afterwards."

"No, you need a bloody wedding dress!" Lori insisted.

"I don't want your money Lori; we've been through this!" Tammy sighed.

Gran appeared in her usual timely manner "It may not be in great condition, or particularly in fashion, but there's been a wedding dress waiting upstairs in the attic for one of you girls for a good thirty years!"

After much rummaging and raking through bags upstairs, Lori found an old brown suitcase with faded black letters "D.M" on the outside.

Gran looked on proudly. "Donalda MacIntosh, she was your grannie. Your mum's mum, - I think she taught your mum how to sew from a young age before she passed away.."

"Hey, I remember grannie-Mac, we would visit her in hospital," Lori mused and peeked inside the case to see various old dress patterns and sewing equipment. Underneath it all, was a slightly stiff package swaddled in tissue paper. Lori carefully unwrapped the item and found an ivory dress inside. She lifted it out gently, but Tammy immediately screwed up her nose at the piece, perhaps not as fashionable a design as either of them had hoped; a 1970s voluminous style, with ruffles and trimming covering almost every inch of the cloth.

"Ew. Mum had no taste!" Tammy declared looking at the

article as if it had committed some disgusting crime. "I don't think it'll fit anyway, look at that tiny waist!" She pointed to the small waistband, which underneath held multiple gathers of pleated fabric.

"Hmmm," Gran tapped her mouth with her index finger, looking thoughtful. "It's a shame we don't know anyone who can jazz it up, maybe let it out a bit..." Her eyes met Lori's with a knowing look.

"No Gran, I wouldn't even know where to start!" Lori hastily put the dress back into its bag.

"You'd know more than any of us!" Gran tilted her head at Tammy, whose eyes had opened wide.

"Oh yes, Lori! That's a great idea! You used to make things!" Tammy bounced and clapped her hands.

"That was a long time ago Tam. This is a *wedding* dress!" Lori could not imagine the work involved in salvaging such a garment within the limited time given. It was true that she had spent her younger years making clothes for her teddy bears and dolls, which then transitioned into summer dresses for herself. But she had not touched a sewing machine since leaving for Australia. Instead, she packed those creative notions away in order to focus on her career.

"A wedding dress that no one will wear unless you lend us your skills!" Her gran smiled and linked arms with Tammy in excited camaraderie.

"I love this idea, please please please!" She looked at Lori, big eyes shining like a puppy dog, to which Lori found herself caving in almost immediately; Tammy was the bride after all, and she had promised to help out.

"OK...!" she muttered, and Tammy bounced on the spot.

Luckily for Lori, Tammy accepted the help of Gran, Jean and Alan to organise the remainder of the wedding, leaving her second sister to the task of making her mother's dress wearable, and somehow coming up with an idea for the bridesmaid's dresses that would fit in with the new theme. She only had days to accomplish the job, and every second mattered. Gran pulled down Lori's old sewing machine, once also her mother's, and made the large kitchen table available for use. Lori went through some old dress patterns in the box, and adapted them to Tammy's size, using as much of the dress's original fabric as possible. Around her as she worked, wedding preparations continued and as far as Lori's attentions could measure, it was turning into a very cheap, though undeniably decent, country affair. Women from Gran's circle all promised to donate cooking and baking to feed the guests, and Tammy and Jean handmade the invitations, with help from Maggie and Anne, who insisted on dressing up as princesses to deliver the envelopes by hand. Alan organised his musician friends to form a band for the night, promising them all sorts of freshly caught shellfish in payment for their efforts. All wedding plans continued on as Lori spent each waking hour working on the dress. A sense of mild dread consumed her, making her feel a little sick with nerves about how the dress would actually turn out for the Cinderella-type transformation, but after a couple of days she had made enough solid progress to relax and let the stress melt away. She even found herself enjoying the process. Each stitch gave her motivation, and inspired her to keep going. She was so immersed in her work that she didn't think of Michael much, and the fact that he hadn't been in touch. *Perhaps he was incredibly busy at work?* she thought, but then launched back into more sewing. The days before the wedding were a blur and as Lori worked into the small hours every night, she became aware of the tedious long hours she would often spend working in New York. It was clear however that the two jobs were beyond comparison. She stitched another seam and inspected her work carefully - somehow sewing seemed to give her energy, rather than take it away.

The last day before the wedding was a frantic haze of fitting and refitting the dress to Tammy, triple checking it didn't fall apart, and then sighing with utter relief and pleasure at the result. Tammy beamed at her reflection as she stood by her sisters in front of the mirror, both of whom had donned their new dresses too. Lori had re-fashioned two older, slightly more expensive items of Gran's own wardrobe, happily donated to the cause. One was in a pale heather-purple, the other a rich mossy green. Lori marvelled at the successful outcome – and congratulated herself, responding to urgency was a main aspect of her role at Costner's, which she needed to get her through the last few days! But rather than watch others design and manufacture the garments, she now felt elated at producing something so elegant with her own hands.

The day of the wedding was a bright and sunny one. The wedding party walked to the church with the guests trailing behind them. Father Angus remarked with a smile that showed every tooth in his head at how full the church was, and that he hoped more people would come to next Sunday's service as a consequence. The whole affair was informal, relaxed and very happy. Lori couldn't help but think of the wedding she had originally planned for her sister. It would have been beautiful too, but not like this; this wedding was completely and utterly Alan and Tam's, from the home-baking in the local hall, and the fact that Tam and Alan had everyone taking part and contributing some kind of job for the day, which resulted in a buzz of community spirit that Lori hadn't felt before. She gave an internal sigh of relief and bit into her third slightly knobbly but delicious raspberry-and-rose macaron. Now, as the newly married couple slow-danced to their wedding song, and the evening fell around them, Lori felt full of emotion at the resilient and intimate love they clearly had for one another. Luckily Hector had left the area several days previously, possibly now somewhere in New York, prowling the cafes and bars for another Tammy, Lori suspected. She hoped he wouldn't come back anytime soon, especially after Callum's actions the week before. She knew that there might be bumps down the line for the newly-weds, as it would be hard to avoid Hector completely, but overcoming these hurdles, as she knew they would, would serve as Alan and Tam's testament to their love. Lori watched them swaying slowly, wrapped gently around one another and knew they could achieve anything. In some ways they were stronger now more than ever.

Many drinks and embraces later, Tammy hugged her two sisters and pulled them onto the dance floor for a Dolly Parton number. The three sisters held hands, singing to one another as little Maggie and Anne skipped in and around them, exhausted and full of cake, but still giggling uproariously. Lori suddenly felt eyes on her, and looked round to find Callum standing at the edge of the floor, drinking a whisky and watching the sisters intently. He had removed his dress jacket and now looked stronger than ever in his fitted white shirt and kilt. Lori had always loved men in kilts, and how Callum looked just now, admiring her from afar, made her feel like she was dancing there just for him. Aware of her heart pounding inside her, she knew with a sinking feeling that she couldn't stop the attraction, but she could stop anything from happening between them that she might regret. The song finished, and Lori edged away outside to call Michael, conscious again of how ridiculous it was that he had not been in touch almost the whole time she had been away. Miraculously, for once the signal was strong and the line rang out.

"Hi Michael."

"Hi Lori." Michael yawned down the phone.

"So... I don't hear... from you much!" Lori stuttered, not really the best way to start a conversation, but she was annoyed, and this time she wanted answers.

"I don't hear from you either," Michael sighed. "How was the wedding?"

"It's still going, I've just come out to call you."

"You should get back in then, go and enjoy yourself." Michael's tone was unreadable.

"What? You don't want to talk? I feel like you've been punishing me all this time!" Lori couldn't understand anything about him any more.

"Of course I haven't. But as I said before you left, we need time apart to think, not to talk. Things have changed, for me." He paused, his voice muffled like he was speaking to someone else in the background.

"No... you said time apart would be good for me to spend with my family?" Lori felt her heart beat faster.

He sighed again. "Lori, no. After discovering that you had hidden so much from me about your childhood, and where you were from, we needed time to reflect on everything. Running off halfway across the world was also rather uncharacteristic of you, but in this instance I think it was a fortunate move."

"A move...? It wasn't a move, Michael, it was to be there for my family – because they needed me – because I owed them some time. God knows I've spent enough of the last few years working on my career and having dinner with you, I would have thought anyone could understand taking time out for a sibling's wedding! This is all about you, *you* need time to think! That's what you really mean. Or did you just want to dump me anyway and you've decided to use all this as an excuse?" Lori's temper flared.

"There's no need for that tone. You were the one lying to me. You even sound different now, your accent for Christ's sake! I don't know you any more. And no, I wasn't going to *dump you*, as you so maturely put it, I was going to – You know what, never mind, I doubt you'd be ready for that anyway now. I'm certainly not. I need some time - "

"Yeah, yeah I heard about how you needed some time! Dammit, Michael...! I've never lied to you, I just left out the most painful part of my story because I decided I didn't want it to dictate my life; of who I wanted to be in America. But maybe I should have been more honest with myself. Hey, you know what? How about I make this super easy for you!" Lori hung up, glared at her phone and threw it with gusto far into the darkness, hearing a distant splash seconds later. She swore loudly at the sound, and held her hands to her head; why had she thrown her phone into the sea...?

At that moment, Callum came out of the hall with two drinks, and handed one to Lori, which she necked back without taking a breath, and coughed in surprise.

"Jeez girl, that's whisky!" He laughed.

"I needed it!" Lori winced at the strong fiery taste filling her throat.

"Everything OK?"

"Yes fine, just a bit of bother at work." She looked out to the blackness to wherever her phone now lay; most likely at the bottom of the sea, and knowing her luck, being eaten by the local legend, Sheila the sea-monster.

"You look great Lori, you all do. I can't believe you made three dresses within the week!" He raised his glass, saluting her achievement.

Lori looked down at her dress. It had held up well during the course of the evening, considering she had stitched in the back zip by hand last minute. Her bodice had an embroidery feature that she had filched from another of Gran's dresses and stitched on. It all pieced together beautifully and she had to admit that she did have an eye for details. She let her hands fall by her side over the gentle folds of emerald green satin that skimmed around her thighs and fell to the floor.

"Thanks. But really all I did was alterations; although I have to say, I'm amazed the wedding dress is still in one piece! My nieces have already put in orders for fairy dresses before I leave!" She screwed her face and laughed, forcing herself to forget her phone conversation, and put it to the back of her mind. The whisky had relaxed her into a delicious confidence. "You look really good too, Callum." She sighed, then covered her mouth with her hand. *Damn that whisky.*

Callum leaned forward and gently touched a lock of hair that had come loose from her hairpin, tucking it behind her ear. His finger ever so lightly brushed the side of her neck, making her quiver softly, and her spine straighten. "Thanks." His focus locked onto her one curl, then his eyes moved to hers slowly, and Lori swallowed hard. "You are one bonny lass. I don't think you realise just how bonny you really are." He smiled at her, and Lori couldn't help but smile too. She felt like she was slowly melting in his hands. He edged closer to her and Lori felt her mouth open, wanting, needing a taste of him before she melted away altogether. But before anything could happen, the door banged open and Alan bounded out along with some other shinty boys, all of whom cheered and hooted at Callum and Lori's cosy position, which immediately broke any spell between them. Alan pulled Callum by the arm.

"Come on best man. My wife -" He stopped and hooted again. "My wife!" The men around him cheered with abandon. "...My wife wants us on the dance floor, but we need to do shots first!" He pulled a reluctant Callum away, and Lori was frozen to the same spot, watching him re-enter the hall with the boys, his head turning back to look at her as the door closed behind them.

She shivered in the cool evening air, not trusting herself to go back in just yet for fear of not resisting the desire to pull Callum to her and have her way with him there on the dance floor in front of everyone. She thought about Michael and the life they had together. *What is our relationship to him?* He was using the excuse that she had been lying to him, and for some reason that meant for him a straightforward conclusion – things were no longer the same, and they needed to readjust their parameters. Weren't relationships by their very nature supposed to be difficult, full of the unexpected, and requiring flexibility from both sides? What was she to do, she had already apologised, what more did he want? For the last three years it had been her who had fitted in with his take on life, with his schedule and his social circles. But had that been, underneath it all, to further her own ambitions? *Was Michael just convenient?* Lori let down her hair and breathed out. A part of her felt sad, seeing so many flaws in their relationship for the first time, as though examining a favourite painting at close range, and discovering the perspective was all wrong. Michael and her were different, too different. For him, they had been on a break all this time - free to re-evaluate their lives, and he didn't seem to see the issue in this, he didn't even have the courtesy to make it clear to her, leaving her wondering and hesitating. It was all so confusing. *Well screw him.* She didn't need Michael; all she was to him was someone to have dinner with from time to time. Everything was planned, appointments were made and kept to. They would never meet spontaneously, and the sex and the passion had dwindled away as the months had passed, as she now recounted their intimate moments together. Lori decided to take a step back from her thoughts, and resist making any big decisions. Tonight was Tam and Alan's night.

Once she had felt sufficiently cooler and somewhat more sober, she walked back into the hall, making sure to steer clear from Callum the rest of the evening. Just in case.

17

Lori was due to go back to New York in the coming days, and she was determined to leave whatever feelings Callum stirred in her to one side, and devote her remaining time to her nieces. She crammed in as many activities as possible, like baking overstuffed butterfly cakes, swimming in the sea, endless Disney movies and spilling popcorn all over Bracken, then venturing out into the nearby woods in search of fairies. The woods held special memories for Lori. As a girl she would explore the mossy banks with her sisters, and make dens out of fallen leaves and branches, living in their own fairytale. It was in these magical places that she wanted her nieces to know. As the afternoon light shone through the cracks of the old forest branches, they played hide and seek together, darting behind trees and trying not to stand on the newly sprouted mushrooms that were sprinkled across the mossy grass. Lori's heart soared with each giggle, but with the passing moments she knew this would be over all too soon. The little girls were changing, growing up, and these times together would not last forever. Lori led the two girls up further past the forest to where she would often go as a young girl. The trees thinned, as they walked over a stone bridge and further up a grassy path, which took them onto an exposed landscape surrounded by hills.

"Why are there clumps of rocks dotted about?" Anne panted, staring up at her auntie. They looked out over old ruins in-between the green bracken that carpeted the hillsides.

"This was an old settlement. People lived here many years ago, these rocks were once homes."

Maggie grabbed Lori's hand. "Like, families would be here?"

"Yes, many families. A community lived here, they would work the land with sheep and cows, and eat porridge and sleep by fires to keep warm at night." She looked down at their grave faces. "Has your mum never taken you here before?"

The two girls shook their heads quietly.

"It's OK, there's nothing to be afraid of! It's a peaceful place." Lori regarded the remains of an old existence, imagining what it was like when people were here before they were cleared off the land and the clans were broken up. Another sad episode of the Highlands, haunting the hills with a whisper. "The people from here were moved away, or had to leave. Many of them left their homes forever, going to Canada, America and Australia."

"Like you, auntie Lori?" Anne asked, taking Lori's other hand.

"Yes, like me." Lori looked out and took a breath of the fresh mountain air. "But I *had* a choice." Suddenly Lori felt a pain in her chest. The people that once called this place home had been dragged away, their villages torched, starved into loyalty to the Crown, or driven away through rifts between their native peoples, and here she was, never appreciating her background, her upbringing, even feeling ashamed of it. Michael and his opinions could go to hell, he did not understand her at all. Lori bit her lip and took her nieces back down the hill, before her emotions betrayed her.

～

"Did you have a nice time on the hill?" Gran cuddled her two great-granddaughters on the front porch, welcoming them home. "If you go into the kitchen there's some of the fairy cakes still on the table". Maggie and Anne clamoured past Gran without needing any further encouragement. Gran turned to Lori "You OK?"

"Yeah, course!" Lori smiled stepping inside. "Why d'you ask?"

"You just look a wee bit sad." Gran didn't wait for an answer, but led Lori to the kitchen where Maggie and Anne were licking the icing off their cupcakes.

A knock came at the door behind them. "Hello!" Callum stepped inside, carrying several large bunches of flowers. "I'm sorry for being such a crap best man, I was meant to give the bridesmaids and the grandmother these flowers yesterday! I'm a bit slow!" He approached Gran and Lori with a bunch of roses, mingled with wildflowers each, then left another bundle on the kitchen table for Jean.

"Aw thank you, aren't they beautiful Lori?" Gran nudged her and Lori nodded shyly.

Maggie pulled Callum's arm "Do you want a cupcake?" She pointed to the stack in the middle of the counter, Anne having just nicked another one thinking no one had seen.

"Yes please!" Callum opened his hand as Maggie picked

one for him, dusted in pink glitter and laid it in his palm reverently.

"Auntie Lori took us up to the fairy wood and then a creepy glen," Maggie announced to their guest.

"It's not a creepy glen!" Lori retorted, "it was up High Arlour, the old clearance village."

Callum nodded. "We used to go there a lot when we were kids," he confirmed, looking a little solemn.

"You knew Auntie Lori as a kid? Like when she was our age?" Anne devoured her cake, yellow icing still left on her upper lip. She went in optimistically for another, but not before Gran slapped away her hand from the tray of delights.

"Ah uh, you'll have no room for your tea!" She winked.

Callum glanced at Lori. "I did, we didn't know each other too well though as children. We didn't play together at school you see. But we knew each other very well as teenagers." He chuckled, and Lori's face went red.

"OK, what shall we do the rest of the day!" She clapped her hands, eagerly changing the subject. "Shall we go into town, maybe see the ferry boats come in?" The two girls expressions showed less enthusiasm than Lori had hoped. "Maybe if you're good and have a run around, we might get you both an ice cream...!" Maggie and Anne nodded far more vigorously at the promise of treats, and ran to get their coats again.

At the insistence of Maggie, Callum came along with them, and spent the rest of the day walking beside Lori while the girls ran along the harbour, and tried spotting whales and ferries simultaneously. Lori didn't want to inwardly acknowledge what pleasant company Callum was, but it was difficult. They drifted in and out of the crowds and popped into some of the shops with the girls. The day had started out with a hearty dose of sun, but now the sky had grown darker and before they knew it, torrential rain began to flood the town and everyone scattered for cover. Lori had parked on the outskirts of the town, now regretting her decision as they remained in a craft shop, watching the rain slamming into the windows from outside.

"Bugger!" Lori said under her breath. "How long will this last?" she looked up at the dark sky. Callum stood near, his arm lightly grazing hers.

"You know my place is around the corner, why don't we go there until the rain stops?"

Lori turned around to see the two girls picking up some very expensive ceramic cups and saucers to her horror, and the decision was made for her instantly. Callum's small apartment was across the road, and up a few flights of stairs. They all ran through streams of water that flooded the street and dried off on a couple of clean tea-towels in his warm home. The girls sat on the sofa, damp from the rain as Callum fiddled with the electric heater to warm them all up further.

"Now girls, would you like a cup of cocoa?" Callum knelt down by the TV and switched it on, handing Anne the remote control. "Put on whatever you like, I have Netflix there."

"As long as it's for kids!" Lori said in an authoritative voice.

Their two innocent faces nodded and expertly selected yet another Disney film. Lori was always astounded at how easily children took to technology; it was instinctive for them in ways she would never understand.

She followed Callum into his small kitchen and watched him heat up milk in a saucepan. He searched around in the cupboards, opening up every last one until he found an old tin of cocoa. Lori smiled and stayed quiet, observing him. She peered over to the next room to see her nieces engrossed, Anne sat on the sofa and Maggie lay on the floor next to the heater, with head in hands, both watching the movie in appreciative silence.

"They're great girls." Callum pulled out four cups and spooned a little cocoa into each one.

"They are." Lori smiled. "Jean has done a good job raising them. It's not been easy for her."

"She has. And she's back to school the day after the wedding? That sister of yours is a hard worker all right." Callum shook his head in amazement.

"Have you recovered from last night?" Lori grinned.

"Well... a lot better than your new brother-in-law, I'll give myself that! I gave him a call this morning and let's just say he was a bit short with me!"

Lori watched Callum carefully pour steaming milk into each cup, mixing and stirring each one with concentration.

"Tammy wanted to have the day to themselves to recover, she was probably right to suggest it!" Lori offered, thinking that besides a husband with a hangover, her sister had gone through quite a lot recently and needed the rest, particularly in her condition.

Callum took the cups through to the girls, warning them to blow on the cocoa carefully before taking their first sips. Lori grinned; he had quite a way with kids, a natural. *It must come from working on tours with all those families.* They both leaned against the kitchen counter and drank their cocoa, talking about each other's work, and the various contributing factors to their current lives. Callum confided in her about ideas of eventually selling up and having a new adventure elsewhere.

"I wouldn't say no to some more traveling," he ended, draining his cup. "What about you?"

"I don't know." She sighed, looking over at her nieces who were laughing at a funny moment in the film. "I honestly don't know what I want." She looked down at her feet "I'm going back to New York the day after tomorrow."

"Oh?" Callum folded his arms nodding.

"Yeah, I need to get back to work. I hate to think what I've been missing and what I'm going back to." She gritted her teeth. "I think we need a bit of a revamp with our collection. It seems our sales are deteriorating, though no one is really talking about it in the office - but I overheard my boss Frankie on the phone."

"I'm sorry to hear that." Callum spoke quietly. "Do you think it's that bad? Isn't that just how things are in fashion?" He laughed. "Not that I know *anything* about fashion!"

She smiled warmly at his standard t-shirt and jeans ensemble. "Yeah, some years can be better than others, but according to Frankie it's gone downwards consistently over the last five years."

They both stood in silence as the girls continued giggling at the TV, both wishing secretly that life could be that simple once again, and feeling the weight of the knowledge that it never would be.

Lori drove the girls back to Jean's, and spent some quality time with her big sister when the girls were tucked up in bed fast sleep.

"Out like a light, they're jiggered! Whatever did you do to them, Maggie always asks for a story, but tonight she ordered me out of her room, announcing: "'I need to sleep mummy!'" Jean chuckled, looking relieved to be sipping wine on the sofa instead of trudging through another chapter of Harry Potter.

"Gran and I baked with them, then we went to look for fairies in the wood, up to the old clearance village, and then Callum came into town with us, and we narrowly escaped being washed out to sea in that downpour!" Lori listed their activities and breathless, lay back on Jean's sofa. She scanned the cheese platter on the glass coffee table near them and wasted no time in tasting.

"Oh aye?" Jean pouted her lips and nodded.

"Oh aye what?"

"Callum again? You've been seeing a lot of each other recently. And I couldn't help but notice you were making eyes at the wedding... most of the night!" Jean moved the stem of her glass a little, swirling the wine around in a circle, giving her sister a suspicious look.

"Oh don't be daft!" Lori sighed. "Nothing's happened - besides, I'm going back to New York in two days!"

"Well anything can happen in that time!" Jean pressed. "You both seem a bit smitten".

Lori shushed her sister, and soon diverted their conversation to the Maggie and Anne and Jean's ex. Jean shifted in her seat and chewed her lip as she asked Lori to look after the girls the next day. "It's just... Douglas wants to meet up..."

"Of course, I'll mind the girls, it would be my pleasure! What does Douglas want?"

"I'm not too sure. I just hope it's nothing to do with taking the girls out of school. They still have weeks before the summer holidays start." Jean knocked back the rest of her wine. "Anyway, take me off the topic, I feel sick about what could happen with Doug." She filled her glass with a top-up. "Now, I want to know more about Callum. Did you kiss?"

"No we didn't, nothing's happened Jean!" Lori yelled, exasperated by her sister's nagging.

"Are you still with Michael? You've not spoken about him once since the first night!" Jean got up and closed the door, fearing her sister's protests would wake up the girls, then she *really* wouldn't be able to get any of the saucy details.

"No, actually. At least, I don't think so. He called me up, basically to say we were on a break, and he was taking some time out. Can you believe it? He just decided this himself! Bloody men! So, I decided to end it. At least... I told him I was going to make it a really easy decision for him, and threw my cell phone in the sea...? What's the point? If a man who's as steady and logically-orientated as anyone can get, thinks you need to be on a break, then something is terribly off! We all know 'a break' is one bus stop away from a breakup!"

"You've split up?" Jean leaned closer over the platter listening intently to every word.

"Yip. Well, unless he flies in tomorrow morning on a helicopter with a rose clenched between his teeth and a diamond ring, I'm not sure how we're coming back from this. I just don't really know who I am anymore. Michael, and our life together – it seems so far away. Like a distant dream, I just can't imagine it moving forwards anymore. Oh, I don't know what I'm saying... just that New York...and so much that I was sure about... is not certain any more." Lori looked down at her empty glass. "More importantly... what does a girl have to do to get a drink around here!"

18

With an extremely sore head the next day, Lori found herself clambering out of Jean's bed just as her nieces jumped onto the duvet shouting ,"Auntie Lori stayed over!" She shushed the girls as best she could, feeling as if a giant Clydesdale horse had been kicking her in the head continually the night before. Lori grimaced at the whisky and gin concoctions she and Jean had made, believing they had come up with the crème de la crème of cocktails, one that the world deserved to see. But now, with how Lori's stomach felt this morning, she was sure *she'd* be the one seeing those cocktails again very soon.

Jean walked into the room, fresh faced and already dressed. She perched on the edge of the bed and brushed her hair. Catching Lori's eye in the mirror, she winked. "Wakey wakey, lazy lump!"

Lori squinted in disbelief at her sister.

"Remember, you have the girls today!" She applied some lipstick, and with her leather jacket and skinny jeans, looked altogether gorgeous, Lori thought groggily.

"You're still meeting Douglas?" Lori stood by the bed wearing a long grey t-shirt she had never seen before.

"Yes, I am," Jean whispered, giving Lori the wide eye as the girls continued jumping on the bed.

"Oh god stop moving girls, you're making me ill!" Lori pushed past Jean and ran to the bathroom.

Jean turned to the girls. "Now remember girls, it's *you* who are looking after Lori today, OK?" She put the lipstick in her hand bag, kissed the nodding children, and left.

After what felt like hours to Lori, she finally emerged shaken and very pale. She had put her head under the shower and raked around Jean's cupboards for something to wear. Since Jean was more petite than herself, she had managed to only find a loose t-shirt and yoga pants. If she could just get through these next few hours, then she should be able to get back home to Gran's, and sleep the remainder of the day until it was time to return to New York. Lori burped and to her horror felt ill all over again, dashing back to the bathroom as Anne and Maggie looked at each other with a shrug.

Lori and the girls ended up watching a movie together, lying on the sofa and eating buttered toast. Lori cuddled up with them, drinking her third cup of tea; she was definitely beginning to feel better. That meant, however, she couldn't ignore her fidgety nieces, and their pleas of going outside into the sunshine any longer, something she would have happily forgone, and returned to bed. But she willed herself against the lethargy, thinking that in no time she would be back in New York and missing them terribly. She looked at their pleading faces and said something inadvisable for any hung-over adult to communicate to a child:

"OK girls, what do you want to do? Whatever you want, we'll do it!"

The two girls looked excitedly at each other and shouted in unison: "Cycling!"

A modest lunch and two strong coffees later, Lori managed to summon up the energy to take the girls out on their Sunday ride. Jean lived on the outskirts of the main town, so they ventured through Morvaig and in the direction of Gran's. Lori kept as focused as she could, with her nieces trailing behind her. Feeling a bit more like herself, the wind blew through her hair bringing fresh smells of the sea to her. She turned around to check on her nieces, to find two energised and content little girls; oh how Lori missed those days! She hoped her nieces would at least remember this small pocket of time she had spent with them, absorbing it as yet another loving part of their wonderful childhood. Lori smiled to herself and thought of all the bike rides of her past; cycling to primary school, then high school with her sisters, and occasionally to the shops to pick up supplies for the odd outing or sleepover. She could see her nieces were having a similar childhood to her own, and loved that she was able to be a part of it again, even if it was only for a few short days. Lost in her rose-tinted memories, Lori didn't realise that the chain on her bike had come off several meters behind her, and almost crashed into a parked car at the side of the road.

Lori looked down at the chain which hung off the pedals, completely broken. "What the?"

Anne gritted her teeth. "Mum hasn't used that bike in a while!"

"Yeah, looks like she hasn't been giving it any upkeep either!" Lori looked back at the big hill they had come down; it would take them about forty minutes to walk home if they went back. Cars passed by but no one stopped; luckily, they were still in the town of Morvaig so they weren't completely stranded. She groaned inside; going back up the steep hill was something Lori couldn't face in her current state. If only she hadn't thrown her cell phone into the sea...! Her insides tightened at the thought, but she knew Callum would be her best bet for help. So, with the girls trailing behind, she walked the defunct bicycle to Callum's shop, which fortunately was open. Callum was standing over Karen, staring at a computer screen and when Lori walked in, Karen's face beamed in welcome.

"Well well, I didn't think I'd see you again so soon!" Callum nodded, with hands shoved into his pockets.

"I'm really sorry to ask you Callum, but my chain broke – are you able to fix it for me?"

He tutted looking down at pedals. "What do you think I am? A repair man?" he scoffed.

"No," Lori said through gritted teeth, "it just happened, out there, and I thought you wouldn't leave a damsel in her distress?"

"Well I'm not sure you're that distressed!" He squinted at her with a playful smile, "or for that matter... a damsel!" He chuckled as Lori rolled her eyes. "Karen, will you be OK with these rascals for a few minutes?"

Karen had already befriended the girls, and showed them something on the computer. "Of course, they can help me!" she announced.

Callum led Lori to his apartment, but instead of going up the stairs he took her around the back where a couple of wooden sheds stood. He opened the door to the closest one, obviously not locked, thought Lori wryly, and started rummaging around looking for tools. Lori placed the bike against a wall and snooped around a little, seeing all manner of things – kayaks, tents, gardening equipment and endless odd wellington boots dotted about. The shed was packed with so much stuff, Lori wondered if Callum was a bit of a secret hoarder, and whether he managed to ever find what he was looking for! He searched, lifting up boxes and throwing them down, as jangling metal-upon-metal noises and thuds sounded.

Distracted by the commotion, Lori bumped into an iron structure. "Ouch!" There was a jaggy-out part that had caught her hip, and she wanted to kick it in frustration, but whatever it was felt incredibly heavy. A stiff, dirty blanket lay over the top, but something about the shape intrigued her. "What's this?" She peeked under the blanket to find an old-looking machine, with polished knobs, a multitude of shafts, and several small pedals. Callum pulled off the blanket, fully exposing a magnificent machine.

"It's a loom, you know, for weaving?" He put his hands on his hips and turned his head this way and that looking for something, then tossed a bag of fabric scraps to Lori. She peered inside to see wool fabrics in all sorts of colours and patterns.

"Are you saying you weave these?" She gazed at Callum, opened mouthed. "This... machine-loom-thing can do these? You're a weaver?" Her excitement shone through and Callum laughed.

"Well I've helped from time to time, but haven't done anything in a year or two. This is my aunt's loom." He sat on the chair by it and put his feet on pedals, like he was about to play some strange piano. "You see, you arrange the yarns along the front there then you pedal away, which sort of criss-crosses and weaves the yarns together - making those." He gestured to the bag that was still in Lori's hands.

"I had no idea! This is incredible!" She looked in the bag and touched the soft cloth. "I can't believe you can weave these; these tartans and checks look so complicated."

"Well *those* I don't, I only help my aunt with the plain weaves." He got up off the seat and continued looking for tools. Lori walked around the loom and touched its strong fixtures, ideas were spinning around in her head, but she didn't know which one to listen to first. The tweed fabric was so unique, nothing like she had seen before, and woven by one person with one machine. She examined the solid structure until a cough came from behind her.

"You want to hold this bike while I fix it then?" He waved her over and momentarily Lori put the weaving apparatus out of her mind.

Lori took her newly repaired bike and the girls to the nearest beach. Since their plans to go to Gran's had been somewhat derailed after the bike fell apart, she wanted to make the most of the little time they had left. To her relief, her nieces raved about Karen and had spent the time drawing their favourite outdoor activities, with Karen promising to display their art on the shop wall.

"She said to go over tomorrow to see them!" Anne announced proudly as she peddled in front of the group and led them down the path to the beach.

"Well that sounds lovely, perhaps you can go with your mum after school?"

They left their bikes by a clump of bushes and ran out onto the sand. The tide was out, exposing the pearly expanse that stretched on and on before them.

"Are you not going to come?" Maggie sat down and started scooping up sand.

Lori lay down beside them both, happy for the rest. "No, I can't, I'm going back to the US tomorrow." She ran her fingers over the sand, making zigzag shapes just as Callum had done the night they kayaked together. The girls started to construct a sandcastle mound with their hands, but Lori noticed their usual chatter had stopped, and they both pushed and patted the sand quietly. "Hey now, I'll be back again soon. Or perhaps your mum could take you out to me?"

Anne's face lit up. "We can go to the zoo? And Disneyland?"

"Well I'm not sure about Disneyland, but I'm sure we can do the zoo..." Lori wondered if she should've spoken to Jean about this first before promising anything to the kids. She took a breath of sea air and lay back as the girls ran back and forth dripping sea water over the sand. She thought of the dusty loom sitting in Callum's shed. Was she onto something - *woven fabric from Scotland*, it sounded romantic, and may give them an advantage over their competitors? Lori considered the pros and cons, but couldn't stop the excitement that bubbled within her.

"A tweed fabric?" Frankie asked in a distracted manner over a babble of voices whispering in the background.

"Yes," Lori enthused, "they weave it here, by hand, and the quality is out of this world!" Lori had tried to make a fast-pitched sell to Frankie, but couldn't tell how it was going over the telephone. "I've done a quick search, and all our competitors seem to use either mass produced wool from China, or they use well-known commercial wool from other areas."

"But... I mean, Scottish tweed is a thing...? People have

heard of it, but..." Frankie began in a flat voice that Lori breezily ignored.

"Not everyone has heard of tweed; and if they have, they just see it as a type of fabric. What we have is a family brand, made with the finest natural wools and local resources. They even have a special breed of sheep, it's such quality Frankie, honestly it would be incredible in the men's range, and just think of all the various colours and patterns we could use in our autumn and winter collections. These people have been weaving for centuries - we could take all that heritage and make a limited-edition collection, using tweed especially designed for us!" Lori ended her delivery in triumph, but was greeted with silence. Some moments passed, and Lori began to think the worst; that her efforts were wasted, and Frankie hated the idea and wanted to fire her that very minute.

"I can't commit to anything just now," Frankie said slowly.

"But Frankie - " Lori started.

"Lori will you let me speak!" Frankie cut in and Lori bit her tongue, feeling she had overstepped the mark. "What I mean is, I want more information. I want samples. I want to see the story - their story, their branding. I want photos. Do you think you can get all this for me and present it at our designers meeting?"

Lori panicked. "But... I'm due to come back tomorrow!" There was no way she could compile everything within a day; she was passionate about her pitch, but a day was realistically unachievable.

"Can you change your flight? I think this is an intriguing idea, I want to get as much knowledge of this concept as I can, I want to feel immersed in it, like I'm there with you."

Lori resisted jumping in the air out of pure excitement

and tried to stay calm. "Well, I can take a trip to visit them, but they live in the Outer Hebrides!"

"What does that mean?" Frankie shushed someone in the background, and Lori wondered if she was on loud speaker.

"It means it's... a bit further away..."

"Further away from you? But you're the furthest from everything!" Frankie said hotly, and Lori decided that she could definitely hear a difference in her boss. She sounded stressed, hesitant, and unlike her usual calm self.

"I know I am, but this will take time." Lori bit her lip waiting for the reaction.

"OK... two weeks then?" Frankie sighed, and now spoke to the person in the background, Lori wasn't on loud speaker, thankfully.

"Yes two weeks, I'll see you then!" Lori rang off call and whooped. She had reached the foot of the pier, using her gran's cell-phone and as people passed by they began to avoid eye-contact. She didn't care if she looked a bit mad, she was over the moon. With another two weeks at home, and the chance of a wee adventure, she tingled all over with hope. She looked out to the familiar horizon as a fishing boat sailed across, her stomach knotting with nerves and excitement at the prospect before her. Then she smiled suddenly – she would need to ask Callum for even more help.

19

That next morning Lori sat with Gran in the garden, drinking tea and enjoying the gentle summer breeze. Gran had been equally excited about Lori's chance of staying another two weeks; so much so in fact that she planned to have a dinner party to celebrate. Lori cringed at the idea; being the cause of yet another celebration, but Gran refused to listen to her objections.

"You'll be here for the Highland games!" Gran clapped her hands together, laughing at Lori's expression.

"Oh Gran, those games are so silly. Men showing off by throwing bits of tree around, while the women are expected to cheer? It's primitive!" Lori groaned.

"I'll have you know there's history in Highland games, it's your heritage!" Gran gave Lori a sharp eye.

"Even so, it's a bit ridiculous!" Lori shook her head, the thought of sitting in a damp field watching the games - *well, there were so many other interesting ways of catching a cold!*

"How are things in New York?" Gran changed the subject with ease.

"I'm not sure, Frankie didn't seem overly anxious to get me back there. I'm assuming things are going well enough."

Her gran held her mug of coffee in both hands and glanced down at a stretched-out Bracken under her chair, making gentle snoring noises. "I hope you don't mind me saying, but -" Gran paused. "But, I always thought you would be a great designer yourself. Remember all those sewing projects you'd undertake? You made me a beautiful skirt once, which I still have." Gran nodded at Bracken, who had tilted his head at the tone of her voice. "You have that skill, just like your mother did. You might think about using it more, perhaps."

Lori looked down at the grass to see daisies had already started sprouting. She wondered if Gran still cut the grass herself, or whether she needed help with the garden nowadays. She was getting older after all, something Lori never really thought about, for various reasons. If she was honest, she hadn't given her family too much serious thought during those years abroad. She had missed them however, and so blocking them out of her mind, probably more than most might have done, had given her the excuse not to act on her feelings. She gave a half-smile, and leaned over to squeeze Gran's hand, unable to find what words to say. The days before the wedding had been hugely enjoyable, the hours spent at the sewing machine had felt like meditation, calming her with each stitch. But a dressmaker was not the most profitable way to make a living, even if she did have the talent for it like her mother. No, she would return to New York, save up some more money, and see if she could progress as far in the company as Frankie had implied she might. If she could manage to retire early, then she might consider a career change, but right now she knew she hadn't spent all those years in retail to just throw it all away on a nice hobby.

Gran ushered Callum into the kitchen later that evening, after promptly answering Lori's earlier invitation. Mary offered food and wine, fussing over him like a royal prince. Lori had noticed early on during her stay that whenever Gran saw Callum she lit up, admiring him proudly as if he was another member of the family. Lori rolled her eyes at the spectacle; she had planned to give Callum refreshments anyway, but Gran immediately started opening and closing cupboard doors, bringing out such a large number of delectable treats that Lori resigned herself to just sit and let her grandmother do what she needed to do. Wine was topped up and after Callum had worked his way through one bowl of pudding and cream, Lori noticed Gran had produced a fresh bottle of wine for the table, and was lighting a small cluster of candles on the oak sideboard. Thoughts of her cocktail night with Jean resurfaced, but she shook them off. One bottle between two was not the same as a cabinet of gin. *Wait a minute... one bottle between two? Candles?*

"Right, I'm off to bed!" Gran slowly stepped back from the table, as though admiring a work of art she had just finished.

"It's only 8pm Gran?" Lori looked at the bright yellow kitchen clock above her, now definitely suspicious of her gran's motives.

"Don't I need my beauty sleep!" She called over her shoulder and left the room, Bracken shuffling behind her.

Lori and Callum looked at each other for a few bewildering moments, then burst out laughing.

Callum scooped up another piece of gran's bread and butter pudding from the dish in front of them. "Subtle!" he said with his mouth full.

Lori refilled his glass, shaking her head. "So, you got my text?" She gritted her teeth, hoping that all this treatment would merely encourage Callum to help her.

"Yes, so you want me to take you to my aunts? It's quite a trek Lori!"

"Well I'm not expecting to walk there!" She rolled her eyes.

"Aye, but still. You know I do have work; I can't just drop everything for you!" He looked at her intently. "What's in it for me?"

Lori sat back speechless. What did he want from her? She felt her cheeks blush at the undertone to his question, and couldn't stop her own inappropriate thoughts now surfacing.

Callum drummed his fingers on the table quietly. "Come on Lori, you think I don't see what you're up to. Buttering me up with all this" He gestured to the now almost empty plates of baking and wine glasses. "You are a bit conniving; I see that trait hasn't left you entirely!" He laughed at her outraged look.

"That was Gran who gave you the special treatment!" Lori protested.

"Oh dear, throwing your gran under the bus, after everything she's done for you!" He shook his head with mock disapproval. "Hey, I know you. Even if Mary hadn't been here, you would've still buttered me up. You always try to get things your way."

"That's not true..." Lori muttered sulkily, pulling the

plate of the pudding towards her, determined to eat the last piece herself.

Callum laughed heartily and thumped the table, groaning dramatically. "Oh here we go, you can be a petulant child sometimes Lori Robertson!" He shook his head, still laughing. "OK OK, anything but a moody Lori!"

"Hey!" Lori objected.

"If I come with you, I'd like to do something other than just follow you around the tweed mill."

"Of course! You can do whatever you want once we get there!"

"No, I mean do something *with* you, not *for* you." He sipped his wine, eyes fixed on hers.

"Like what?" Lori squinted at him in suspicion.

"Never you mind that now. I just need a promise."

Lori bit her lip, unsure of what she was signing herself up for, but whatever it was, it was worth the gamble. "Sure," she nodded, and held out her hand.

"And.." Callum playfully hit her hand away. "You have to do the tug of war at the Highland games!"

"What? Why? Have you been talking to Gran?"

"Hey, one question at a time!" Callum laughed raising his hands.

"Why do you want me to do tug of war?" Lori rolled her eyes again. "I mean, it's the men who do that one isn't it?"

"Now where's the feminist in you? Plus, I think you need to get your hands dirty while you're here, just this once. You've spent a wee bit too long in the city."

Lori sighed, unenthused about the prospect.

"Come on, too afraid to break a nail?" Callum teased, making Lori bristle. He knew he had her, she needed him to introduce her to his aunt; after all this could be the start of a very lucrative business deal. Against Lori's better judgment,

and the stubbornness within her, she held out her hand and
they shook on it.

"Are you sure you have everything?" Gran asked, placing a
packed lunch on Lori's lap. Lori sat in the van, with arms
crossed while her gran flapped around them. The longer
Lori stayed at the house, the more she reverted back to the
sulky teenager she used to be. It didn't help that Gran still
saw her as that girl, hopeless and unorganised. Never mind
that Lori was a worldly woman who had been living alone
very successfully for over ten years now! She shuffled in her
seat as Callum sat patiently behind the wheel.

"You two have a good time now!" Gran winked, and Lori
squirmed inside. She had stipulated very clearly that this
was a business trip, and Callum was there specifically and
exclusively to introduce her to a potential business partner.

They left Arlochy and headed to Morvaig for the ferry,
which would take them onto one island, from which they
would catch another ferry, or so Callum had explained. The
waters were rough but Lori walked outside to the front of
the ferry, feeling the wind push and pull her as she looked
out across the sea. She breathed in the salty air, looking for
any dolphins, which would occasionally follow the boats on
their trips, playing delightedly around the swell. She felt
light, with no worries or stresses, on the edge of the world,
hidden away and off to a remote island. She closed her eyes
and let the wind wrap around her.

Callum ordered their coffees and walked to the window, to see on the other side, an open-armed Lori. Her messy hair whipped across her face as the ferry rocked back and forth, her nose and cheeks had turned rosy pink from the cold sea spray. Callum was about to knock on the window, but decided to leave her be; he didn't want to interrupt whatever happy thoughts she was enjoying. Instead he watched her staring out to the distant islands, her whole body embracing the physical torrent of nature swirling around them. He couldn't have imagined a week ago that they'd be spending this much time together. As enjoyable as it was to spend time with Lori, he wasn't under any illusion. He knew he was there to "seal the deal" with his aunt. Yes he was helping Lori out, but he was also helping his aunt's business. His aunt had cheered down the phone after his tentative call to her; she had been working so hard to keep the mill going amidst low sales and staff shortages. He just hoped Lori wouldn't muck her about. Would she do that? *Had New York really turned her into a ruthless, money-grabbing business-woman?* he sipped his coffee and reflected on their first encounter in the bridal shop, she had seemed so dismissive, but now.. He let his mind wander onto Alan and Tammy's wedding. They were in Spain now on their honeymoon, likely sipping cocktails and walking hand in hand across pristine white beaches. Callum sincerely hoped they would be happy. After punching Hector that awful day before the ceremony, something had changed in him. He felt free, and happier, dare he say it, dare he even think it! Could it be possible that punching someone could make a usually mild-mannered person feel this way? His thoughts sprang organically to his ex-wife Jennifer. He wished in some ways he had confronted Hector all those years ago, but would it have saved his marriage? There was no point regretting things now, it was in the past. Now was the time to think about what he wanted for the future. If he spent his life wondering about the what-ifs, he'd still be asking himself what might have happened if he had just taken Mary's advice and gone to Australia, demanding to see Lori. *Then things might have been very different.* Callum removed the thought from his head almost as soon as it had appeared, and relaxed back into his happy replay of punching Hector. A week had passed now since the incident, and he still hadn't heard from the police. That was a surprise, since Callum had been sure Hector was the type of guy who would certainly press charges, just as he was the type of guy to pursue other people's women. Callum hoped Alan had forgiven Tammy entirely, so that they could both move forward together. But was it that easy? Did he really forgive Jennifer? Even now, her betrayal made his stomach churn automatically, but he had moved on. He wasn't that person anymore, he wanted to be happy and he *was* happy. He had built up his business from scratch, and was now able to take on staff. Soon he might even be able to sell it - if he wanted to. Karen had a good head on her shoulders, perhaps in some ways he knew he was already training her to eventually take the business from him. The shop had been pretty busy with bookings for the following month, and Karen continued to keep the pace for the next season. People were always popping in to say hi, and Karen without fail took advantage of every opportunity – such as when she had welcomed Lori's sister and her two kids to the shop, pinning up their drawings on the wall and later suggesting the whole school get involved. Showcasing a whole wall dedicated to favourite activities, encouraging locals to take part instead of simply being a tourist-focussed game. Callum was happy to let her take the reins and welcomed anything that would give them more exposure as a business. Jean had loved the idea too, so he had left them to discuss things, and told Karen his trip away was a great chance to see how she fared at the helm. No sooner had he left the two women - Jean had tapped him on the shoulder, and told some very surprising news. He was taken aback slightly just speaking to Jean in such a close manner; she was the sister he knew the least, and the most they would exchange would be a salute or a quick catch-up if they bumped into each other in the local shops.

"I really shouldn't be saying this, my sister will kill me," she whispered as Karen distracted the girls showing them photos of some recent dolphin sightings. "But, well I thought you should know, that Lori..." she moved side to side a little, uneasily, "she's pretty much single!"

Callum squinted, unsure what to say. "I um... OK?"

Jean glanced back at the girls then continued. "I think she likes you. And my sister is very proud and very stubborn, so to prove a point she'd never act on something. Even if she actually... wants to act on that thing..." Jean's blue eyes, the same depth and shape as Lori's, looked up at Callum. He had never particularly noticed the resemblance between them until this moment, but the way Jean Robertson had looked intensely into him with those penetrating eyes, had made Callum feel cornered, and under pressure. He found himself a little confused, which must have shown on his face as Jean then groaned, "Callum, man! She really likes you. She might not think she does, but I *know* she does. Call it sister's intuition."

"I... uh... Has she said something?"

"Not in so many words, but she is single. She as much told us that her fella had taken her coming over here as some kind of a break, and she seemed pretty okay with that! And I know she likes you!" Jean pulled up the strap of her handbag over her shoulder smartly, and left promptly with the kids, after having set Callum's head spinning. Should he do something with this newfound information? But Lori was going back to New York... He had thought of nothing else that day, evidently Karen had noticed and told him to go home, thinking he was under the weather. He hadn't protested too much, and instead had walked along the harbour until he was alone. Just him and the sea, watching the fishing boats rock in the rough water. He had begun to feel stressed over his attitude towards Lori, and the news he had heard. Did Jean expect him to go over and persuade her to stay? Was he supposed to sweep her off her feet or was the implication to simply make the most, so to speak, of the days they had left on the same continent? But she had a life in New York... it was all so rushed, and Callum hated impulsive decisions. Maybe he could stay in touch with her, properly this time, and see what happened further down the road? But he knew how much Lori was consumed by her work, and that once she was back in New York, she would be impossible to get hold of... just like last time. After hours of wandering aimlessly and thinking over the confusing array of possibilities now at stake, he had decided to not make any rash decisions: if Lori wanted to stay then she would, and he wasn't going to make things complicated for her only days after she'd gone through a break-up.

It was then that he had received a grovelling phone message from Lori informing him that she would be staying a while longer after all, and would be eternally grateful for his help with a new venture for her company, in the Hebrides, no less. Callum couldn't believe it, so much had been altered for him in a day. He supposed he should start enjoying that side of life instead of constantly reverting to the familiar whenever change loomed its head. Standing on that ferry, two cups of instant coffee cooling in his hands and looking out at the woman who left him all those years ago, he was fizzing with so many different emotions. He didn't know which to lean to. For now, he took a breath, and knocked on the window to a startled Lori, holding up the paper cups and smiling.

20

When they first drove off the ferry, they were greeted by sparkling beaches along the coast. As they continued along twisting bumpy roads they reached the flat peatland stretching out as far as the eye could see, with little houses dotted here and there as though tossed across the earth like bleached pebbles. They pulled into their destination, and Callum finally turned off the engine. Aunt Betty walked out to meet them as they stretched their limbs out by the side of the van. Lori didn't know what she had necessarily expected to see, but next to the house stood a barn structure that she presumed was the mill, and along the road sheep grazed, walking about freely, paying no heed to approaching vehicles. It was all a little shabbier than she had imagined, and the signs of a harder kind of life, that generations of people from these parts had known, she supposed, were still very apparent. Lori had changed into her smart business clothes en-route, to make a good professional first impression that a potential business deal demanded. But now, as she saw Aunt Betty approaching them in a ripped jumper and scuffed jeans, she wondered if she had made a terrible mistake. She had envisaged a clean-cut figure of a woman, wearing her own tweeds, but the ripped clothing and wild wiry grey hair left Lori confused. Betty hugged Callum warmly, and ruffled his hair playfully. *Just like Gran,* Lori reflected. Callum introduced them and Lori extended her hand, only for it to be pushed away by the woman who instead leaned in for a hug also.

"It's lovely to meet you Lori!" Betty said, pulling out of their embrace suddenly as two black Labradors came bounding out to greet the new guests, their inquisitive noses moving wetly over Lori's legs until Betty shooed them away.

"Thank you so much for allowing me to come visit, I'm sure Callum has told you my background?"

"Oh that you broke his heart when he was a teenager? I remember that, that was the first time he came over to help. Such a glum face the whole holiday!" She patted his reddening cheek, chuckling.

"Auntie!" He pushed her hand away, looking mortified, something Lori hadn't seen before. She had thought Callum was unmovable.

Lori coughed and decided to ignore the teasing jibes. "I meant, um... who I work for, and what we do?"

"Sorry pet, I'm just playing. Yes he did, it sounds very interesting. Come in for a cuppa tea and we'll chat!" Betty turned back, leading them into the traditional farmhouse. It was cool inside compared to the warm afternoon air, and as they walked in Lori noticed Callum ducking his head to get through the kitchen door. A wooden table was set up with teacups, a teapot and some cakes and sandwiches on a big plate. Lori spent little time on chitchat, and launched into business, asking Betty about their brand and stock management. Callum happily worked through the supper on display as the two women each went through their own plans, and what they'd both like from a collaboration. After Lori's first uncertain impression of Betty, she warmed to the woman greatly; she was a determined, strong and motivated woman that Lori could relate to very easily. Betty, clearly proud of their weaving business, showed her the mill which was indeed the barn next to the house as she had suspected. She found herself walking around in amazement, the modest metal barn was deceiving from outside, as she discovered once inside, where huge weaving machinery greeted her. It was more than Lori had hoped for, and she tried to suppress the urge to jump on Betty, arms open on the spot, so thankful was she that her gut feeling had been right. As well as the equipment, the mill's infrastructure could produce more fabric to the kind of scale Frankie would be requiring. Betty took her on a tour and showed her the washing of the wool, how they dyed it, then how it was spun into yarn. After all yarns were prepared, they were transported out to the locals who would weave the cloth in their own garden sheds.

"People have their own jobs, some are crofters, some work in the nearby town. We want them to weave when it's convenient for them, that's why every house along this road has a loom in their shed." Betty put her hands on her hips and beamed proudly as they walked around the quiet mill. Lori inspected samples of previous tweeds and couldn't believe the luxurious feel of each unique piece. Betty grabbed a square, Lori was admiring. "It's the breed of sheep we use that makes the fabric this soft, but it's durable too, I guarantee you!"

Lori took photographs, videos and collected samples of cloth, compiling a collection for Frankie to peruse on her return. She loved the idea of supporting a community like this one and to nurture something that was part of their heritage. She felt elated after spending the evening with Betty and had noticed Callum seemed very relaxed too. He was different somehow in the company of his aunt than behind the Adventure Tours desk, or even in kilt and sporran amongst the other shinty boys.

The early morning sun streamed through the small kitchen window to an already wide awake Lori. She had been up hours before and sat at the table jotting down ideas in her notepad. The previous day had proved so informative for her. She had learned so much about a process and a fabric that she had never really paid much attention to before now. It had stoked up her imagination and she was eager to put her plans into motion. There was a fire in her belly; she wanted Costner's to use this material, and the ideas poured out of her, as well as sketches for the new collection that she would pass onto the design team...for inspiration.

Callum appeared at the door, bleary-eyed and yawned his way to the nearest cupboard, grabbing a bowl and cereal box. "OK: it's just us today. Auntie Betty is away sorting out something or other with deliveries. So..." he moved his head around surreptitiously to glance at Lori sideways. "Let's have a wee explore shall we?"

"What - around some more machinery? or maybe to the shops that sell some of this fabric? I could chat to -" Lori looked over her notes, excited at the prospect of more research.

"No, I think you've seen enough machines, and enough material! It's my turn for *my* end of the bargain." He leaned against the sink eating a bowl of coco pops.

"Sure - where were you thinking of kayaking?" She put her pen down and stretched out in her chair. She had to admit it, she had made good progress already and a little time away wouldn't hurt.

"Actually, no. Not kayaking. It's a surprise." He raised his eyes in a question, and Lori groaned inside.

"What is the surprise Callum?"

"Well it wouldn't be a surprise if you knew!" He shook his head quietly and munched happily on his cereal. Lori resigned herself to his mystery activity, but her stomach knotted thinking of all the various extreme ideas Callum might have indulged in.

Callum drove the van across the island until they reached a glen where the road gradually began to rise higher and higher. They slowly made their way up the steep gradient, winding around corners, all the while Lori gazed out onto the glen, with its small loch at the bottom, surrounded by hills, heather, and sparkling ferns. It was so magnificent that she remained in complete silence as Callum concentrated on getting the slow van up the hill, but absentmindedly switched on the radio. It buzzed loudly, the signal coming in waves, then through the crackling frequency, notes of a piano came on air, a pretty piece of traditional music that made Lori turn up the volume. As more instruments joined in she could hear it more clearly, she knew the music, but how? The music accompanied them uphill, with Callum gently humming along. It was only then that it hit her; the song held history between them. She had sang it as a girl, and once Callum had played it on guitar for her years ago on the beach in Arlochy. He had learnt the chords especially, and had proudly strummed the guitar to her utter surprise and delight. The night flooded back to her instantly. They had had a small gathering of friends on the beach by the harbour, with her sisters included, to celebrate her last day of high school. A fire had been made on the shores, and many gallons of cider consumed. Callum had brought out the guitar, and there in front of all their friends, played Lori's favourite piece of music. Whistles and shouts from the crowd had not distracted him as he watched Lori's face light up, then her sisters had begun to sing – standing and swaying near Callum - it had all been planned. He had wanted to give Lori something special to remember her last day as a high-schooler, and he certainly had.

Callum's eyes remained on the road ahead, gently tapping the steering wheel in time with the rhythm. That sensation in her body occurred, a tingling and fluttering like butterfly wings beating against her skin. So glorious were her feelings, that she wanted Callum to know they were there, even if it was all over now between them..

"OK, we're here!" Callum announced and Lori bit her tongue at whatever had been about to pour out of her. What was she thinking? Did she imagine such things could be openly said without any ramifications? She realised they were at the top of the glen, parked off-road next to some other cars. Once she stepped outside, the wind was so wild that Lori felt it would blow her away if she didn't hold onto something. Callum winked at her, but abruptly walked away to speak to some people on the other side of the hill.

"What the hell is going on?" Lori muttered to herself, watching him shake hands with a few men hovering around together, waiting for something, *but waiting for what?*

Callum laughed, clearly joking with the men, and patted one of them on the back. They walked off further across the hill until Lori couldn't quite see them anymore, as the hill dipped down into the skyline. Callum came back rubbing his hands together playfully.

"It's a bit cold, so make sure you wear a fleece under your jacket." He looked up, squinting at the sun glaring angrily behind thick clouds. "It shouldn't rain, I just wish it wasn't so gloomy-looking!" He opened the van's sliding door, and threw one of his fleeces to a startled Lori, who remained stuck to the spot.

"Callum, aren't you going to tell me what's going on?"

Callum put on an extra layer, then rummaged in the back of the van again until he pulled out two helmets. "Try this one on, let me know if it fits." He looked at her expectantly. "Come on Lori, we need to be there already!"

Lori, still in a state of unease, put the helmet on. "It fits, so... what are we doing Callum?"

Callum smiled and held out his hand. "Everything will be explained once we walk down there."

Lori hesitated, with her helmet on and her fleece half-zipped up, she looked over the hill, but nothing could be seen from the van. Without further protest, she placed her hand in his and slowly walked on ahead. They moved in silence, accompanied only by the sound of the rising wind and the harks of a buzzard overhead. Lori didn't know what to expect, but she was very aware of Callum's warm hand folded around hers, which tightened just as they reached the dip in the hill, over which Lori could now see what was happening beyond. Someone saluted Callum and he waved back, but the person was holding down what looked like a tent, observed a bemused Lori. There was also a handful of tents on the hill by the cliff edge. Two people, further down the hill suddenly detached themselves from the rest, and still attached to their own strange-looking tent, casually walked right off the edge of the cliff. Lori gasped in horror, and her hands went to her face.

"Hey hey," Callum said in soothing tones, gently bringing her hands away from her eyes. "Look, they are fine. It's just a bit of hang-gliding."

Lori saw that the people who she had been sure would fall to their death, were soaring through the air, away from the cliff edge, and heading further out, gently gliding over the glen. The next couple were behind them, and this time Lori could see the process more fully. They were harnessed together, underneath the hang-glider. Lori stood in awe as they took a run together, then launched themselves off the cliff, dipping gently off the hill and gliding through the air like a pair of kites.

"What do you think?" Callum grinned at her.

"Why didn't you tell me!" Lori couldn't control the sudden rage inside her, she didn't want to do this, not one part of her. Callum was trapping her into it and he knew it.

Callum pressed his lips together like an unapologetic naughty school child. "I knew if I told you, you would refuse! Come on Lori, it's safe – I do this when I come here, I've got a licence and everything." He reassured her, holding her hand still as she continued watching the next couple walk off the cliff edge.

Madness, pure madness! She shook her head, not looking at Callum.

"Look, I know you'll love this. It's a feeling that no one knows until they are up in the air. Trust me Lori. This is something you'll always remember, don't you want to experience more than just your bog-standard nine to five?" Lori bristled at this, which Callum noticed immediately. "I'm sorry, I don't mean that. I just thought this would be nice to do together. I will take care of you Lori, you don't need to worry. You're in safe hands." He tightened his grip once again. "Trust me?"

Lori shook her head again, and gave a shaky sigh. "Just let's get this over with, OK?"

Callum quickly led her over to their hang-glider, and the man who was keeping watch on them nodded to Callum, and gave Lori a thumbs up. Lori stared in horror at the flimsy-looking device that would be the only thing holding them aloft, and felt her stomach lurch. They were the last couple on the hilltop to launch, and Lori felt her whole body shake as Callum fastened a harness over them both. Ordinarily Lori would have secretly enjoyed how close he was, adjusting her belts and loops, making sure she was secure. But not today. He laughed aloud at her expression.

"Lori it's fine, I've done this a lot. Just breathe, try to relax your body. It'll be over sooner than you think – and you'll wish it wasn't!" He placed his hands on her shoulders, waiting for her approval, but all Lori could do was give a brief nod. Following Callum's lead, they retreated back up the gentle incline, turned back to face the cliff ahead, and paused for some moments while Callum looked out to the distance, pondering some unknown factors on which Lori hoped he was an expert. They took large steps at first, which eventually broke into a run, Lori keeping her steps in line with his as if they were tied in a potato sack race at a Highland games. Then they were off the cliff, Lori still running as the sensation of being in the air took over. She kept her eyes firmly shut, not daring to look at where they were, then quickly and seamlessly Callum manoeuvred the harness and a pole slid out of nowhere for Lori and himself to place their feet on. Their bodies tilted horizontally as the glider took them over the edge. Carried by a gust of air that caught the glider at just the right moment, they soared together like a bird. Lori opened her eyes and gasped at their height, the glen below vast and still like an epic painting, with the odd tiny car driving up the winding road underneath them. She could see past the glen and further out to the sea ahead; the view was spectacular. The perspective they had up there, almost a part of the clouds and moving with the sharp icy currents was unlike anything Lori had ever known. She felt free, gliding up high above the world, just her and Callum soaring through the sky. Callum nudged her and she laughed as the wind blew her hair over her face momentarily obscuring the magnificent scene below. He steered them towards the sea, and a beach appeared, stretching out for miles all along the coastline. Lori realised that this was the spot they were going to land. Callum gently spiralled them down towards a field next to the first dunes. They skimmed on their bellies and gently greeted the grass, lying face down together, recovering from the high of their few moments in the air.

"Good work Lori!" Callum congratulated her as applause from the other participants sounded out around them.

"I didn't do anything; you did all the work!" Lori slowly got up, with a helping hand from Callum.

"But you followed my instructions exactly - and calmly!" He waved to the others who were now packing up and one by one, getting onto a bus. "Come on – want the window seat?"

Once reunited with Callum's van, they sat on a woollen rug that Gran had helpfully packed, with a straw basket between them. Callum pulled out the picnic inside, placing down sandwiches, pastries and cakes.

"This is incredible!" Lori beamed at him as he handed her an Irn-Bru. "Oh my god, I haven't had one of these in ages!" She opened the can and let the neon-orange fizzy sweetness hit her. "Wow!"

"Classic drink for a classic bird!" He opened one himself and lay back looking at her.

"Ew, you did not just say that...!" Lori shook her head, giggling from the caffeine hit.

"You sound so American sometimes!" Callum bit into a ham and mustard sandwich.

"Well I do live there!"

"But sometimes you start talking and I swear you are American, then after a while your accent changes again, and I think, the local lass is back."

Lori shrugged. "I'm still adapting to being home, I've been in New York a long time."

The sun had finally managed to pierce the clouds, and a sharp shard of light spilled onto the beach next to them. The water was a dark murky green, and white waves lapped the shoreline. They were the only people on the beach, which still amazed Lori even now. If she had been anywhere else in the world, this beach would have been mobbed with people – dog-walkers, swimmers, sunbathers, anybody. But here, it lay untouched and unpopulated, and the peace that environment engendered was just heavenly. Lori lay her head back onto the soft blanket, feeling her eyes grow heavy. She had spent yet another day with Callum, without argument or awkwardness, and apart from the brief moments of anxiety near the cliff edge, she felt elated. The excitement she still felt around him was intense, but on the other hand she was so comfortable in his company that no words needed to be spoken. Before Lori could think of anything else, her body gave in to the rhythmic swell of the water, and soon fell into a light and delicious sleep.

21

Michael had been invited to his parents for dinner, a tradition he had tried to keep up every week, but had let slip once too often of late. His mother's tone on the phone had been a little more passive aggressive than usual, so Michael had accepted the invite graciously, though in truth the last thing he wanted was to go there this evening. It had been a long week already, and he had had an argument with a client earlier, and was convinced it was due to how he felt about Lori rather than anything to do with the case, or his workload. He had been undeniably out of sorts, and as he drove up the driveway to the lit up house he told himself sternly to perk up and enjoy the night. His parents wouldn't appreciate him moping, so he cast aside any negative thoughts and made his way in at the front door. The door opened and he was greeted by Marcie, his parent's maid. The old woman smiled warmly at Michael and touched his face, a gesture he was used to, and now fond of. He had known Marcie since he was a boy. She would allow him to sit in the warm kitchen with her as she cooked. He would play with his toys, making noises and voices to himself as she scrubbed, chopped and stirred the pots and pans. Those evenings were cosy, with a quiet sense of safety and love, and Michael closely guarded them in his collection of fuzzy childhood memories. One of the few real happy periods in his life. No matter where his mother was, which was on most occasions some college fundraiser or committee meeting, Marcie was always there in the kitchen, ready for a hug, a cookie and a kind smile. Without her, the house would have been cold and empty.

"Mio Caro, Michele!" Marcie clasped her hands, beaming at Michael like a proud mother.

"Hello Marcie!" Michael patted her shoulder warmly, and took her hand in his. It had been a couple of months since he had seen her but the old lady had changed even in that short space of time. Her hair was now entirely grey, and Michael found himself almost worried at her appearance. "How are you? How is the family?"

"Good, good." She nodded. Even after all the years working for his parents, she still spoke very little English, but she understood everything, particularly the things that were impossible to put into words, and her wonderful Italian accent was still as strong as ever. She led him through to the dining room with its large candelabras in a line over the table, and lights that twinkled all around, from the table, to the crystal chandelier suspended above.

"Michael, lovely to see you my dear!" His mother walked into the room welcoming him, wearing her usual designer two-piece. Her blonde hair pulled back in a French roll, the same style she had kept for years: *if it's not broken, darling, then don't fix it.* His father soon joined them, holding a glass of bourbon as he looked his son up and down.

"Michael." They shook hands, and stood awkwardly for a moment. Michael had a fairly good relationship with his parents, and they were proud of him, so he would make the effort to see them from time to time...although the occasions ended up more as informal business meetings than laughing reunions. They had never been one of those families who embraced every time they saw one another either, but that was fine by Michael. He hated those over-the-top people who couldn't end a conversation without saying, "I love you!" It made him cringe just thinking about it. No, a bit of familial indifference never did anyone any harm, he was sure of that.

"How's the firm?" His father poured him a glass of the dark liquid and Michael accepted.

"Very well, father. I've had a meeting with Daniel O'Brien this week. He's been happy with my work and sees a future for me there. He's going to start introducing me to the other partners in the fall."

"I know Daniel, he's a good man, head screwed on right." His father nodded, and refilled his own glass. "In fact, I was at the club the other day and Daniel was there. You should really think about coming along next week, I'll introduce you to more contacts. Good way to make connections."

Michael nodded. He had put off playing golf for some time, specifically wanting to make it on his own, without too much help from his father. But it was where all the CEO's and Directors played, and perhaps now was the time to accept some back-up, and start attending.

His mother sat down at one end of the table and gestured for the men to sit also. Marcie came out with a silver tray carrying a heavy deep dish, she walked around to his mother and stood as she helped herself to the meal. The old maid looked tired; Michael could see she was unsteady and watched anxiously as she shuffled over to his father with the tray. After a few more moments he decided he couldn't watch her struggle anymore. It was bad enough that she looked an old lady, but now to be walking like one, it was too much.

He stood up abruptly and took the tray from her. "Marcie, let me." He took the tray, which wasn't as heavy as he had thought, but a look of relief spread over the old lady's face, and he could see she had been struggling more than he had suspected. "If there's anything heavy tell me, and I'll bring it out," he smiled kindly, and offered the dish to his father. His mother was quiet at the head of the table, but she gently tutted when Marcie was out of the room and out of earshot.

"She is getting a bit old now," she whispered. "The Hudsons next-door have said their new Mexican housekeeper is very good. And cheap in comparison."

Michael gently put a finger to his lips as Marcie walked in again.

"Michele, you help please?"

Michael went through to see a large bowl of potato salad and a whole roast chicken ready to be carried through; much more than any of them would eat, but Marcie had always cooked for a large family, which his was not.

"Marcie, you don't need to cook this much. It's just us three!" Michael felt less than comfortable about this evening already. Now, seeing Marcie like this, her beaming smile broke his heart. He hoped his feelings were nothing more than unfounded concern, and that old Marcie would continue living at the house for a while longer, though perhaps with lighter duties. No matter how much he tried to avoid coming home, Marcie had always made it warm and welcoming, but he couldn't ignore the fact that the old woman would need to retire soon. He walked back to his parents, carrying the chicken, to find them looking at each other bewildered. "I've told Marcie to go and rest, we can manage ourselves mother".

"That wasn't your place to tell her that, Michael." His mother drank her wine, but remained on the edge of her seat, as if at any moment she was going to stand up and fetch Marcie out from her room to put her back in the kitchen where she belonged.

"It's fine, mother." Silence fell upon them and they began to eat. Michael didn't want the evening to end sourly, and tried to think of something lighthearted to talk about. His mother coughed and he continued looking at his food, aware that his parents were exchanging looks between them.

"How is Lori?" his mother suddenly asked, and it occurred to Michael he hadn't told them of their break-up. After his conversation with her the previous week he had been sure the right decision had been made, and had felt comfortable with it. He had already taken some of her things to her apartment, and had left his keys. But now, sitting there at the family table, he didn't know how to even answer the simple question.

"Is everything alright between you two?" His mother looked at him intently. "You've not spoken about her recently." She sipped her wine, waiting for a reply.

"We just -" He broke off trying to find the words, was it too early to let them know? He should have prepared his answer before that night, but seeing Marcie struggle had shaken him in a way too difficult to put into words. He laid down his knife and fork and looked up at his parents, who were chewing expectantly.

"You have haven't you? You've split!" his mother exclaimed.

"Now Katherine, let him speak." His father's look was

one of support, but his mother was almost beside herself, unable to wait for an answer.

"I knew it, I knew she wasn't the one for you! Oh darling, don't you worry!" She swirled her glass of wine. "It's just as well it happens now, you're still a catch, and -"

"Mother!" He hadn't meant to raise his voice, but this was just like her - to control the conversation, to control his life.

His mother continued on, unaffected by her son's tone: "I know some very fine ladies, who have delightful daughters. I will call and arrange a meet. It's really best it ended my darling. Lori was nice, but.." She stopped, trying to find the words politely. "She just wasn't one of us, our kind of person. Our way of life is different to that of so many people. You deserve the best of everything." She nodded meaningfully as her mouth curved upward.

Michael knew she was enjoying this. She held no loyalty to anyone, aside from herself, and her own way of life. Michael couldn't eat another bite. The rising irritation was such that he could no longer ignore it. He glanced over to his father for support, but he sat there, eyes carefully on his plate. Well, he would not give in to them. He needed to be himself. Create his own life, and make his own mistakes, away from the golf course, this house and the family name. This whole time they had merely pretended to *like* Lori, just to humour him! Michael didn't know if it was the alcohol, or the feelings of betrayal his mother had provoked. All he knew was that he didn't want to see that knowing smirk on her face ever again. He and Lori had been happy, he had been sure she would make a good wife, and maybe he *had* been too hasty in taking this break from her. When he thought of it now, he wondered what had made him so sure about ending things. Uncertainty, difference, and a change in direction? They were strong together before his hesitations got the better of him.

"Lori and I are still together mother. I'm sorry if that makes you unhappy, but there you have it. We are in love, and I don't want a girl of your choosing – I want her. And I don't want you to interfere again." Michael tried to keep his voice as calm as possible, but his hands were shaking slightly.

"Michael, you have no intention of marrying her. People will talk if you persevere with such a casual relationship. Our family does things properly." His mother tapped her index finger on the table, his father nodded in agreement.

"Well mother, if you must know - I am going over there to surprise her with an engagement ring next week. I thought a proposal with her family around might be a lovely idea." He almost bit his lip at the declaration, but his hands held his cutlery firmly now.

"Well... that's... good news! You're getting married!" His father raised his glass with a smile and looked over to his wife, who sat still.

"Mother?" Michael could actually feel the tables turning, the power returning to his side of the game. He tried hard not to smile at his victory.

She nodded in a daze. His father piped up again: "It'll take you a while to get to Australia son, when are you planning to go?"

Michael swallowed. Yes... this.

"It's not too far actually. She's from Scotland."

22

L ori had gone through all her notes and photographs she had taken at Aunt Betty's. She felt good about things, and couldn't wait to show Frankie and the team, she just needed to send over the videos to Julian ahead of schedule, so she decided to check in with him. When she eventually got hold of her assistant she couldn't believe the transformation.

"Hi Lori! Yeah sure I can compile the videos. Are you having a nice time at home?" he asked in a breezy manner, so unlike his usual panicked tones that Lori wondered where the ever-questioning, unsure young man had gone. "It'll be so nice to see you, Frankie has been telling us all about your adventure - discovering heritage weaving - sounds pretty exciting!" Julian rang off and Lori felt a wave of reassurance that things were running smoothly in her absence after all. She clearly didn't need to panic about cleaning up issues on her return to work, which was great, but in some ways, if she admitted it to herself, it also made her feel a little unwanted. Lori pushed the uneasiness away as she passed the bakery, where a queue of customers had formed out the door as usual. She popped her head in to see Tammy already run off her feet.

"Did you have a good honeymoon?" Lori hugged her, aware of hungry customers waiting for them to finish their meet.

"The best! We got home last night." Her face was covered in more freckles than usual, and she glowed, Lori wasn't sure if it was from the pregnancy or the sunshine.

Without any encouragement from Tammy, she slipped on an apron and started taking orders, then with ease began packing cakes and pastries for customers. Lori reflected about the beauty of this type of job. She was able to chat to all sorts of people, promote the bakery with every sale, and catch up with her sister before heading back to the city. In between customer orders she stole glances at Tammy, and could see a little bump now forming below her belly button. She hoped that she and Alan were going to be kind to one another, and thought to herself that if she ever did see Hector in New York, she'd give him a piece of her mind.

Tammy put a sign over the door to indicate an early closing time. "The games are on!" She announced to the alarmed-looking customers crammed inside the shop. "But don't worry - we'll serve you all first!" She chuckled but Lori groaned inwardly:

"I said I'd do tug of war today, can you believe?" She placed three iced buns into a bag for a woman with two small boys.

"That'll be fun, won't it?" The woman with smiling eyes nodded and then suddenly put on a higher-pitched, formal voice: "Well, Loretta Robertson I don't believe it, do I look so old that you don't recognise your old friend?"

"Oh my god, Rhona!" Lori ran around the counter, and the two women hugged and squealed together.

"You look so fancy! Look at that hair, look at those nails!" Rhona grabbed Lori's hand, cooed at her manicure and sighed, looking down at her boys. "Something I could only dream of!"

"You haven't changed one bit!" Lori laughed. "Well, no actually - you have kids! That is different!" Lori bent down to the small boys, handing them a couple of the sweets used to decorate the gingerbread men from a box on the counter.

"Yes - and they can be a handful, especially after sugar – so don't be fooled by their quiet innocent faces and give them any more of those jelly tots!" Rhona shook her head. "I have a daughter too, but she's fishing with her daddy today. These rascals are a wee bit young for that, so I have the pleasure of taking them to the Highland games instead!" She gave a mischievous giggle and a hoot. "Oh Lori, remember *all* the things we'd get up to!"

"Yes; you were a bad influence! Terrible." Lori tried to keep a straight face.

"That's like, so not true, missy!" Rhona flipped her hair nonchalantly. "*You* led me astray!"

Tammy saluted Rhona. "It's nice to see you Rhona, is Karen with you today?"

"Yes we're meeting my sis up there, I forgot she was in your class wasn't she Tam! Oh, and congratulations on your wedding, Alan is gorgeous!"

"He is that!" Tammy beamed, taking money from Rhona and giving her back change simultaneously. "He'll be playing in the shinty match at the games later."

"Oh yes, all the usual traditions each year, aye I'll be there to watch it. Looking forward to it, in fact. I'm sure Lori will be there in the front row, watching her old flame play!" Rhona nudged her friend playfully.

Lori walked up to the event with Tammy, Rhona and her two boys. The annual Highland games always took place near the old school, and the whole area converted, with the long grass now trimmed and, luckily, not a Highland cow in sight. Tents of local produce were dotted around a large space marked out for the day's activities. As soon as they arrived they bumped into Jean and Karen, who were eating ice-creams as Maggie and Anne ran around with chocolate-covered faces.

"Auntie Lori!" Maggie gave her a big sticky hug, with Anne running up behind and pinning Lori to the soft grass-land. This time Lori had been extra careful to make sure her legs were completely covered, in defence of any ticks. The sun shone brightly in the clear blue sky, which ensured constant queues outside the ice cream van and the large beer tent.

"Fancy a pint Lori?" Rhona let her two boys run off with Maggie and Anne, who had instantly made friends with them. Lori's eldest niece Anne was older, and fairly responsible; so she took the boys sun-hats and strolled off behind, keeping an eye on all three children.

"I can't, I need to do the tug of war...!" She looked at her friend's disappointed face. "Maybe afterwards?"

Over the loud speaker came a voice. "Good afternoon everyone, welcome to the 30th annual Arlochy Games! We are delighted to see some familiar, and some not so familiar faces ready to cheer on the action! We have quite a show lined up for you today, and we're going to start right in at the deep end with the Caber Tossing! So if you would like to make your way to the orange zone, we will commence play there in five minutes. Thank you!"

They spent time in the orange zone until a small group
of men wearing kilts appeared and waved to the crowds.
Lori was gobsmacked to see Callum among them. Bagpipes
sounded, adding to the spectacle as each man took his shot
at picking up a huge tree trunk. Callum was the smallest in
build compared to the others but Lori knew he was incredibly strong, and quietly watched him, feeling proud, excited
and nervous all at the same time. He picked up the smooth
trunk slowly, and then flipped it up from his arms into his
hands, slowly getting his balance. All the while Lori stood in
awe, alongside the other spectators. Calls of encouragement
came from already drunk people at the beer tent and
Callum stepped forwards slowly then faster until he tossed
up the trunk in the air. Lori didn't really know what she was
watching, *was he to throw it further than the last man?* She
wondered, but hated how she felt. Something primal and
instinctive bubbled within her, all she wanted was Callum.
She felt ridiculous for even thinking it! She had succumbed
to classic male bravado - wasn't this the whole point of the
games? Men wearing kilts, showing off in front of women?
She pushed the longing away and was now determined to
do the tug of war to prove a point...she just didn't know
what that point was right now. Lori removed herself from
watching anymore, took Rhona's offer of a drink and
promptly went to the busy beer tent as Jean and Karen
looked after the kids.

"Wow, I have to say Callum is looking mighty hot"
Rhona attempted to clink plastic glasses with Lori, which
made an unsatisfying dull tap.

"Oh really?" Lori sipped her drink and looked away.

"Like you haven't noticed? He looks just like he did in
high school, it's hard to believe."

"Yeah he looks after himself, I think he's pretty serious

about it. Involving one hundred squats, an ice bath and a clay mask every night, I would imagine!" Lori snorted.

"Well even so, I think it's good if men take care of themselves. It can't just be left up to the women-folk!"

Lori had to agree, and tried to focus on some of Callum's less defined, less likeable traits. "He's just a bit serious sometimes, moody, you know."

Rhona looked around and whispered. "Hmmm...maybe not. I know a secret on that score and you don't!"

"What do you know?" Lori took a gulp of her beer.

"Well... I know that he *does* have fun... apparently he's been out the last couple of nights with Francesca Campbell. I've been told they seemed quite cosy, actually!" Rhona smugly nodded and sipped her cider.

"I don't think he'd be interested in Francesca!" Lori dismissed the gossip almost immediately. "She's a bit too extra - a bit vain, a bit girly. He's not that kind of guy. No, I don't think so."

"Excuse me, he is a man isn't he?" Rhona's wide eyes met Lori's. "There has always been something that men love about Francesca! Remember in high school, how she was so popular? All that lush blonde hair and those big boobs - I'm sure *those* assets helped! I don't think everyone's out for her personality, you know!"

Lori's heart stopped, she hadn't seen Callum since their trip together. She had made it clear, to herself and to him, that it had just been a business trip, which of course had been the right thing to do. After her non-breakup with Michael - she didn't have space in her head for complicated just now. Callum had needs, didn't he? He could date or shag whoever he wanted, he didn't owe Lori any explanation. They were just... what were they? Friends? Ex's? Lori thought back to how Francesca had been in high school;

she'd certainly used her sexuality to get what she wanted. But was that really such a bad thing at sixteen? They had all grown up since then. Lori made herself face the reality of the situation: it was a small area; they must have slept together by now. They were two consenting adults. It was no big deal.

Two pints later, Lori made her way to the tug of war event that had just been announced over the speakers. She saw Callum waving at her from the other side of the rope and she ignored both him, and the feelings surging within her, deciding to take them out as soon as possible on that ridiculous rope. Her team was made up principally of athletic-looking middle-aged men, but on the other side, to her horror she noticed the illustrious Francesca standing, Lycra-clad, proudly part of Callum's team. What the hell was going on? Was he trying to have the two women play off each other? Wrestling in a mud fight to gain his attentions? Whatever he had imagined, Lori was going to make damn sure her team won. The gun-shot sounded and the game commenced. Lori threw her weight backwards, bracing her shoulders and forearms as she felt the rope snap into a taught iron line, and pulled as hard as she could, aware of the crowds around them cheering. She heard Rhona screaming at the top of her voice:

"Lori come on, pull girl pull!"

Lori's team started yelling and they gradually eased back behind the mid-line, bit by bit.

"Come on Lori!" bellowed Rhona with excitement. "Pull like you've never pulled before!"

It was working; they had a flow, and good coordination, and with each second that passed they edged further back-ward. But suddenly the pull behind Lori went, and the strain on her hands was unbearable, the rope was dragging her forwards, burning her palms. The other team's strength came like a wave and her team's momentum all but disappeared. There was a shout from behind her, a final pull, and then in one movement, Lori and her teammates fell like dominoes into the mud right in the middle of the circle of spectators. There were cheers all around as the winning team celebrated their triumph. Lori lay in the mud, exhausted, disorientated, and very annoyed. She got up gingerly, and Rhona and her sisters all ran out to her.

"Are you OK?" Jean asked, as Tammy tried to brush her down, but with the mud being so thick, wet, and everywhere, she grimaced, she didn't want to get mucky hands. So instead, she patted her sister's shoulder lightly.

"I'm fine. Well, that was a waste of time!" Lori threw up her hands, exasperated.

"Commiserations, Lori!" Callum came over and shook her hand, Francesca at his side. "You remember Fran?" He re-introduced them with a gesture of his free hand, and Lori almost looked the girl up and down, but stopped herself.

"Oh yes, from school?" Francesca flicked her ponytail. "What was your nickname again, oh I remember - Lori MacNori!" She laughed. "Been a long time! So lovely of you to come all the way over for the wedding! Shame you guys lost – but no hard feelings, huh!" Francesca gave a dazzling smile, and walked off.

Lori decided quite explicitly that she wanted to be far away from here, not covered in mud, and not witness to the girl she had despised in high school now flirting, and god knows what else, with Callum. *But that was fine, he could do whatever he wanted to, he was a free agent.* Lori followed Callum's gaze as he watched Francesca leave. Then after some moments clearly admiring her arse, he turned back to Lori a little dazed.

"Are you going to be around later?"

Lori shook her head. "I'm going home." She wiped her dirty hands on her jeans.

Callum turned around, Francesca was calling and waving at him "I've got to go, I have to get ready for the shinty match."

Lori had made her excuses and left the games early, she walked back home deflated, annoyed at Callum, and most of all, furious with herself. She was due back in New York in a few days and needed to focus on *that* instead of impossibilities and old memories. She marched down the lane by the church and into the village, and by the time she came to her gran's lane, there were no parked cars in the driveway. Lori took the opportunity to make the most of the free house, and ran a bath; the day was beautiful but she didn't care, wanting only comfort, and to forget everything that had happened in the last hour. She showered off the worst of the mud, and then spent a good time luxuriating in the hot soapy water, washing away the rest of the day's events. She then popped on her silk dressing gown and pulled out a bottle of white wine from the fridge. She had decided mid-bath that a bit of self-care was all she really needed, so she poured herself a glass and went out to lay on the lounger. The sky had turned a nasty grey, hiding the sunshine behind dark clouds and Lori sighed as the rain suddenly lashed down. A loud thump at the front door made her jump, just as a rumble of thunder sounded above. Assuming it would be Rhona or one of her sisters, she was surprised to see Callum standing on the porch wearing his shinty uniform; white and black t-shirt and shorts, and holding a shinty stick in one hand.

"Callum! Are you... OK?" Lori stood bemused. The rain fell on him, he stood without saying a word, breathing hard.

"Did you... run here?" Lori suddenly felt a bit exposed in her silk, making a mental note to put on something underneath at the earliest opportunity.

His eyes took her in, and that most definitely did not help matters. His t-shirt was soaked, she didn't know whether in sweat or rain, or perhaps both, but it meant she could make out the curves of his muscles even more clearly than usual. The tops of his arms and his chest stood rigid, and to Lori, he was breathtaking. There was no denying her attraction, but she didn't want to be distracted by another man, she couldn't be distracted from her life, or her career, not now.

"Callum, jeez! Come in!" Lori opened the door but he stayed on the spot just looking at her.

"Lori, I - I can't stop thinking about you. When you left the show - I thought you might have... well, thought maybe I was with Fran?" He spoke slowly, in between breaths.

Lori wrapped her arms tightly around herself. "I - Well... aren't you?"

"No. She's just a friend, that's all."

"OK..." Lori looked away, as he walked up the steps towards her. He smelled of nature, of wood and sweat, and Lori felt her legs would buckle beneath her if she didn't focus on what was at stake here. "Callum, I don't think this is a good idea... I'm going back to New York- "

He now was on the top step with her, looking down at her with an unfamiliar fierceness in his eyes, as though he was going to devour her. Lori felt herself unable to refuse, her body had wanted him for so long, and now he seemed to have let down his own remaining defences. He ran a finger down her cheek and took some of her wet hair in his hands.

"Do you really want me to go?" He moved forward again

and closed the door behind him, as Lori moved back, letting go of anymore thoughts. Drawing him to her without words, their bodies up close in a slow, sensual dance. He guided her down the hallway and around the corner, suddenly pinning her to the wall. His hands moved around her neck and slid around and down her back, lifting her up as Lori wrapped her legs around his waist. She could have him just now, all of him, and think about tomorrow... tomorrow. Panting, he grabbed her thighs and buttocks, and they locked eyes. Her body had turned to putty; there was something familiar yet new about him, and she wanted to know more. But just as his lips touched hers, the front door opened.

"Coo-ee!" Gran's voice sounded, and Callum quickly spun around and sat down awkwardly at the kitchen table while Lori retied her dressing gown and leaned in what she hoped was an entirely casual pose on the counter opposite. Gran's head peered around the corner. "Oh great, you've been chatting! Sorry I'm late Callum, thanks for letting him in Lori."

Lori and Callum exchanged confused looks.

"I have a wee visitor for you!" She smiled broadly and Michael walked into the kitchen, and marched straight up to hug a bewildered Lori.

"Darling! I've missed you!" He cast a brief glance at Callum, who sat there quietly, looking at Gran with a pleading expression.

"Well isn't that a picture! Now, why don't you lovebirds go and catch-up. I'll stay here and discuss my new bathroom ideas with Callum."

Michael took Lori's hand and led her into the garden. She was lost in a daze as they both stood undercover, raindrops still falling. She still felt numb even when Michael confessed his love for her, and presented her with an engagement ring.

Callum sat quietly as Gran murmured phrases like, "boyfriend from New York," and "been together a few years". He looked out to the veranda and saw the couple speaking, then Lori hugged the newcomer, and Callum felt like the floor had been ripped from under him. He didn't know what he said to Gran to excuse himself, but a jumble of words came out of his mouth and he walked out of the house, leaving Lori for good this time. He grabbed his shinty stick on the way out, and thought about the reason he had come to the house in the first place. There was to be a match over the next few days in the northern Highlands, to which he had intended to ask Lori to accompany him, and spend a weekend away in a romantic hotel, getting to know each other again. But when she had opened the door to him standing there like something from a dream, he hadn't been able to help himself; he had wanted her so badly. Now he felt nothing but an old-time fool. How could he let this happen all over again, women had played him all too often and he just seemed to let them get on with it. He ran out into the now misting rain, desperate to be away from Lori, the house, and all the memories. Angry tears spilled out as he thought back over all his mistakes; he had allowed Jennifer to treat him like shit, and now it was Lori's turn. Was he just a punch bag? Lori's face came to him then, after all those years he had honestly felt that there was something still strong between them. But now everything seemed so clear, Lori merely wanted to go back to New York, back to her shiny new life, and her boyfriend – or fiancé now. She had been using him all along; needing his help before the wedding, then wanting to use his aunt's business, all for her own gain. He really should've known better. She had exhibited a selfish and spoilt streak that he had presumed was a product of her way of living in the city, and the type of people who surrounded her. But now he saw she was just a snobby, greedy, egocentric girl after all. The fury rose up in him, beating to get out, and he was tempted to find something to punch again, preferably Michael or even Hector, to make him feel better. But instead he just walked on, hoping that the rain would wash away his feelings. *What an idiot,* he thought to himself. Well, he was not going to let this happen again, he would not see her anymore. He had spent his nights wondering how to win her back, after Jean's encouragement, he thought of little else. Jean clearly didn't know her sister after all, it seemed. Lori had merely been leading him on just to get ahead in her work and secure her latest business venture. Well, she could live whatever life she wanted, he wasn't going to waste anymore time thinking about her. Especially when he could see he had meant nothing to her all along.

23

L ori held up her hand to Gran, ring facing outwards, as Michael stood proudly behind her. Was she dreaming? Michael announced their engagement triumphantly and all she could do was smile and nod. He had taken her aside and apologised for the "brief" break they had taken, reassuring her that nothing had changed, and there was no one but her. The guilt she felt was consuming, making her feel paralysed and speechless. He passed his cell phone to her as his parents congratulated her, and gave their well-wishes to the newly engaged couple. Lori's life was now back on track, Michael was who she had always planned to be with. There would never be money problems, and she could pursue any career she wanted – as long as his family approved, of course. Lori would have financial freedom and a private independence, unlike anything she'd ever experience in Arlochy. She could have easily ended up like her sister, working in the local pub and bakery just to pay the bills. She knew that wasn't the life she wanted, just like she knew she wanted success and the ability to indulge in luxuries - she had never made any bones about that. Lori took in Michael's blue eyes and his familiar smile, and she took a deep breath. She would go back with him, and start the life they had both been working for. That was the right thing to do.

Gran invited Jean and Tammy over to meet Michael almost immediately, and they were so captivated by his good looks and expensive clothes, that they did little to hide their admiration. He smelled of endless possibilities, and wooed them all with his good manners.

"Let me cook us all a lovely meal!" Gran had gushed. "It's not everyday that a granddaughter of mine gets engaged!"

Michael gathered her hands in his. "My dear Mary, I wouldn't hear of it. Let me take you all out for dinner tonight. I have showed up here unannounced, and so it would be my pleasure to take you somewhere nice. Anywhere you'd like!"

Gran giggled like a schoolgirl, as Tammy swooned, watching him over her cup of tea.

"Is he a film star?" Jean whispered to Lori.

"No!" Lori couldn't help but laugh at the question, especially coming from her sensible big sister. "Why would you think that?"

Jean squinted her eyes at him as he discussed local restaurants with Gran. "Mmmm... he just looks like he stepped right out of 'Ocean's Eleven...'"

Michael had taken them out to a seafood restaurant in Morvaig, and Lori hoped with all her heart that they wouldn't run into Callum. She had no idea what happened earlier, but luckily nothing *really* had happened. She panicked briefly at the thought of being caught even another minute later, then forced the idea angrily out of her head. Michael wore his Armani suit, and she saw people looking over at him every few minutes. *Jean might have a point,* she thought, maybe people did think he was a movie star, showing up in a tiny fishing town in the Highlands of Scotland to make a new movie – *the new Local Hero, perhaps?* Gran and her sisters equally made every effort to pull out all the stops, and dressed up for the occasion. Jean sat, relaxed and delighted to be out on the town without her children. "Ex has got the kids tonight!" she beamed, and Lori thought with a small smile that she looked a lot happier than usual. She herself had worn one of the dresses she hadn't been able to find an occasion for until now, and she relished looking and feeling like her old self again. Black silk decorated with white lilies clung to her elegantly, as she sat proudly next to the most handsome man in the restaurant. The evening was a success, and Lori breathed an internal sigh of relief; she had made her decision. She would be going back to New York with Michael tomorrow night.

Michael woke up early next to Lori, and stroked her shoulders and neck, rousing her from sleep. Lori's eyes gently flickered open to find him watching her.

"Good morning..." She stretched her limbs in the cosy bed.

"Are you coming back with me today?" Michael drew circles with his fingers over her freckled shoulders.

"Yes," said Lori, knowing that she needed to go back to New York regardless, and now was the time, before she became any more confused.

"Good." He kissed her on the forehead and went for a shower.

Lori had planned to spend her last few precious hours with her nieces, but they were with their father. So she passed the time instead with Gran and Bracken, strolling along the seafront while Michael prepared the bags and arranged their flight. Gran put her arm through Lori's as they stood at the edge of the pier. Bracken leaned his warm furry body against her bare legs, and a quiet moment fell between them, with only the sounds of the water gently splashing and clapping against the wooden jetty.

"Well my dear, it was so very lovely having you home. I hope you will be wonderfully happy together, and get settled back in the city very quickly. Lord knows we spend so much time apart, but I want you to know, there's always a place for you here. This is home, remember that." She kissed Lori's cool hand, and they continued looking out to the islands in the distance. Lori thought of all the times she had spent at this spot: chasing her sisters in the dying light of the first warm spring afternoons; witnessing the dolphins rising and falling over the mirrored surface of the water; Tammy and Alan holding hands over on the green outside the village hall, toasting each other in front of a pink, cloudless sky. She now had new memories that intermingled with the ones from her childhood, but she had to move on from both. Michael and her job awaited her.

"Thanks Gran. You've been the best grandmother, and mother, and father, all rolled into one -" the words caught in her throat and she stopped herself from saying anymore.

Her gran smoothed Lori's hair, and lovingly kissed her on the cheek. "My Lolo. I know, it's OK. It's been my life's work, and you girls are my pride and joy."

The two women strolled back to the house, arriving just

as the farewell party turned up, with Maggie and Anne making their final affectionate appearance.

"We wanted to say bye to Auntie!" Anne ran to hug Lori, Maggie not far behind. Lori bent down and kept her two nieces close.

"We will see each other very soon."

"In Disneyland?" Maggie suggested.

Jean's face fell. "Disneyland..?"

Lori quickly sent them back to their mother and tried to hold back the tears. Since Michael and Lori had arrived in separate cars, he headed off first allowing her time to say a proper goodbye. She opened her car door and turned round to see them all on the front steps waving at her, love shining on every face. Maggie held onto Gran's hand, Anne cuddled into Jean, and Tammy wiped away a few stubborn tears. Lori drove off resolutely, only when she reached the main road did she allow the tears to stream down her face.

"Have you got everything?" Michael carried his briefcase onto the plane. "I'm looking forward to catching up on some emails before I get some sleep." He hitched up his suit trousers elegantly before taking his seat in their spacious business class cubicle. Lori reflected on Michael's strong work ethic, *but couldn't he have just one day away from work? After all it was the weekend!* Lori shook herself, there was nothing unusual in his attitude - this was their routine, they both worked hard to keep on top of things. Shouldn't she be grateful that Michael enjoyed his work, rather than be a failure and always anxious of how to pay the next bill? Her parents had struggled in that way, and Lori had always known she would never be caught in the same trap. If

Michael could, he would work every day. As admirable as that was, especially since he hoped to make partner eventually, Lori made the firm decision in her head that they would be spending more time together enjoying experiences. Treks, horse-riding, surfing - taking weekends away to explore other cities and other cultures. She smiled to herself; she would make certain of it by organising *both* their calendars well in advance.

The air steward came over with a tray of champagne, but Lori declined, preferring to wait until the plane was in the air before she tried to relax. She thought of her desk at the office, of Julian's nervous face, and the toilet cubicle she'd no doubt be going back to. She breathed in and out as her office came into her mind's eye, with all the well-known problems surrounding it. Suddenly she had the feeling that her breath had disappeared, and was caught somewhere in her throat as blood pumped loudly in her ears. The panic reared its head that very moment, embracing her on the plane. Lori gasped, and looked over to Michael in desperation, but he was preoccupied with his laptop. The familiar and aggressive hold flared up inside her, and she felt like the plane was moving already. She closed her eyes, willing the attack to subside, and faintly heard Michael calling her, as though from some distance away, like she were in a dream.

"Lori! Your phone!" He shook her by the shoulders.

How long had she been in this trance? Her trembling hands took the small device from him.

"Lori?" It was Jean, and Lori knew immediately that something was very wrong. "Lori are you there?"

Lori reminded herself: she was on the plane, she was in Inverness. "I'm here. Jean, what is it?"

"It's Gran. I'm sorry, I wouldn't call you otherwise, but... she's had a stroke!"

Lori stood up without a second thought, pulling her bag from under the seat. "I'm coming, where is she?"

Jean sniffed, talking to Tammy in the background for a moment, then she came back to the conversation on the phone. "I'm sorry, I wouldn't have called. But she's in the ambulance, we're driving behind it. Oh god, I've never seen her like that before!" Jean wept on the phone.

All Lori could say was, "I'm coming."

The stewardess's alarmed faces stared at Lori as she pleaded with them to open the door.

"Lori this is madness, we're about to take off!" Michael was still in his seat, with the seat-belt firmly fastened. "Why don't you quickly call them back, perhaps they've been caught up in the moment, and are just exaggerating things. Was it Tammy you spoke to?" He tried to placate her.

"No! I have to go! And it was Jean I spoke to!" She marched towards the stewards who were discussing with one another the dangers of opening the door at this late stage.

"Sit down Lori!" Michael ordered, and Lori turned back.

"It's my gran, Michael!" Tears streamed down her face and the other passengers were now watching the spectacle unfold in front of them, moments before the entertainment on their screens began.

"Yes Lori, it's your gran. Not your mum, not your dad - your gran. She's old, darling. This was always going to happen some day." He whispered the words soothingly, and at that moment everything made sense to Lori. She knew what mattered to her, and what mattered to Michael. He was not the man with whom she belonged. He had been brought up not to care, not to be vulnerable, or take risks, or accept change, and Lori did not want a life spent being his wife. She pulled off the diamond engagement ring and threw it at him.

"I can't believe you, Michael. She looked after me when my parents died! She looked after all of us! Please - go back to New York, to your simple, cold, clear-cut world and never call me again!" She marched up to the exit and was led out by a staff member. Michael picked up the ring in a daze. Staring at it, he tried to register what had just happened. He remained in his seat, seatbelt still fastened as the last voice-over for take-off blared out over the speakers and the cabin doors closed on Lori forever.

24

"Where is she?" Lori ran into the emergency unit to find Jean and Tammy sitting anxiously together under the stark bright light.

"They've taken her in to operate. Oh Lori what will we do without Gran?" Tammy cried, and Lori embraced her, stroking her hair.

"We don't know anything, no one will tell us *anything*." Jean chewed her fingernail and made a quick phone call to check on the girls.

"What happened?" Lori needed answers, anything right now to help her focus on what steps to take to help Gran.

"We were sitting down to dinner, not long after you left. Gran got up to get the salt and pepper, but she came back, without either, and started mumbling something about granddad, and the pickles, then... then she collapsed on the ground before she reached the table." Tammy choked on her tears, and Lori hugged her again, trying to soothe her.

Lori left Tammy perched on the chair beside Jean, and went looking for answers. The hospital was huge, and being the main establishment that everyone from the furthest

Highlands and Islands used, it was busy with people coming and going. She thought of the last words her gran had said to her. She couldn't lose the old lady now, she just couldn't bear it. Why had she spent all those years away from home, from Gran, and her family? And then to have to let her go forever after just two weeks together again? She had wasted years working, for what? Self-induced panic attacks and a boyfriend who didn't love the *real* her. Her gran was her home, and if she lost her - well she couldn't bear to think of it. Lori managed to get hold of a receptionist, a nurse, and then a doctor. All of whom told her to be patient, that her gran was in the emergency ward and they would be in touch as soon as she came out. So Lori reluctantly went back to the waiting room with her sisters, all of them too upset to talk to one another, but remained together in quiet companionship. Hours passed as they waited, eating junk food from the vending machine and gazing numbly at everyone who walked past.

Jean looked at her phone. "The girls should be in bed by now." She swiped the screen and gazed at images on some social media platform.

"Who's looking after them?" Lori yawned and stretched, her back, which ached from sitting on uncomfortable waiting-room chairs. Her body was tired, but her mind was alert looking at the door each time it opened. And each time her heart sank with disappointment as no news came.

"Karen has them. I feel so bad, but she was there with us at Gran's. She said she'd take them into school tomorrow on her way to work."

"She's such a good friend. I didn't realise you knew each other so well?" Lori welcomed the distraction of getting her mind off the hospital.

"Yeah the girls love her, we've been to see her at the shop

a few times now, as well as the Highland games the other day. Which reminds me, how did things go with Callum? He left the shinty match rather promptly, saying he was coming to see you. But before I could say anything, he was gone, just like that!" Jean clicked her fingers for effect.

"We... just talked." Lori lied, avoiding eye contact with Jean. "Then Michael came in with Gran."

"Oh?" Jean put her phone away and folded her arms waiting for further embellishment, but Lori made it clear with a single glance that she was giving away nothing further at this stage. After dozing for some time, Tammy had opened her eyes and quietly listened in to the conversation, hoping she hadn't missed anything. Jean shifted in her seat as their youngest sister woke, avoiding Lori's eyes. "I... may need to tell you something, Lo. I chatted to Callum before you guys left to go island-hopping."

Lori looked up to quiz Jean, but was interrupted by a man in a white coat.

"Are you Mary's granddaughters?" They nodded and followed the man down a long corridor. He gestured to them to go into Gran's room, where she lay, eyes closed and bandages smothering one side of her head. She looked so weak, with her makeup removed and wires fastened to her frail body. The girls went over to her, and she murmured something briefly, her eyes remaining closed. The doctor closed the door behind him "She had a blockage which deprived her brain of oxygen. As far as we can tell, it was simply due to her age. Given the history Jean has given me, there doesn't seem to be anything anyone could have done to avoid this. Even healthy people like your gran can have a stroke."

Tammy gasped and buried her head into Lori's shoulder. Lori patted Tammy's hair. "Will she be OK?"

With hands in pockets, the doctor glanced over to Gran, then back to Lori, making her heart stop, waiting for an answer. "It's difficult to know at this stage." A nurse came into the room and busied herself around Gran, checking her pillow and the screen that stood beside the bed. The doctor nodded to the nurse. "What she needs is rest. The paramedics got her in record-timing, and we were alerted she was coming so we could prepare for the operation immediately. She needs monitoring, time to see how far she can recover, and you three to make sure you're ready to keep her spirits up when she comes round properly. The nurses will let you have some time with her, and then we can give you a little bit more information and advice once we see what progress she's making." He gave a grim smile, then left the room with the nurse at his side.

The sisters remained by Gran and Lori held onto her hand gently. She had made up her mind, she would stay. Gran wouldn't be left alone. She sat on one of the chairs next to the bed, and continued to hold onto the frail pink hand lying limp on the bedspread.

Callum was consumed by the game before him. The opposition were winning, and he couldn't let that happen. The Lochalsh boys would make going to the pub a nightmare with their taunts and constant gloating. The referee threw the ball up high and the players were instantly in the air, in hot pursuit. Callum ran along the edge of the field, waiting for his team-mate to pass, and ready to take it up to the line. He was going to win this game, he told himself as the crowd cheered. Then the ball came at him with such speed that he was almost blown off his feet. It was Alan's pass, he had a force behind him that no-one else could match. Callum didn't waste a second, as the opposition would be on his tail, so he darted left and right, trying to rid himself of the players that were now closing in on all sides. He was fast, this was what he was good at, what he had always been good at, and all that mattered right now was just him, the ball and the goal. He ploughed on, and time slowed right down, making the seconds feel like minutes. He was so close to the goal; this was it, now was the time. He smashed the ball from a side-angle into the goal, but to his shock, he didn't score. The goalie blocked it, and the opposition had the ball now, which was quickly moving back to the other side of the field. Callum focused back in on the game, crushing the disappointment down into his stomach, his hands tense around the caman, waiting for his next opportunity. But that opportunity never came, and not long after the miss the referee blew the whistle: the game was over.

Back in the changing rooms, after hearing the gloats from the other team, Callum knew he needed to get out, to clear his head. His hands had been tense and rigid for days, and he needed some sort of release which neither the game, nor the promise of alcohol after it, would fulfil.

"You're losing your touch, Cal-mac," jested Ryan, one of his team's players. "We might need to get a younger model if you keep this up, old man." He laughed, then muttered something in gaelic that Callum didn't hear. They had never got on, though Callum didn't really understand why. They had much in common, but for some reason Ryan made Callum want to punch his lights out at any given moment. In principle, Callum agreed: he was the oldest team member, but only by a few years. Something Ryan always made sure to mention, insisting on calling him "Cal-mac", a nickname he'd come up with which referred to the name of the local old ferry boat, and infuriated Callum all the more. He tried to not let it bother him, and usually it didn't. But today, he was not in the mood, and if Ryan kept up the gibes, he would be sorry.

"Oh aye, Ryan," Callum scratched his wet head of hair with his towel. "You've not scored us a goal in -" He paused. "Actually I cannae think the last time you got us *any* points. Anyone would think you can't play!" He scoffed. "Maybe it helps that your uncle is a sponsor!"

Ryan stood up, throwing his towel to the floor and moving towards Callum, who was ready for him. But before anything could happen, Alan got in between the two, his tall stature casually diffusing the situation instantly. "Now boys, shall we head to the pub? The guys are wanting to drown their sorrows." He looked at the two men sternly, until they nodded. "Good, right are ye fit? Let's go."

Callum had a few drinks with the boys, but left the pub when no one was looking. He was in no mood for socialising, particularly after losing the game. He walked down the street and was happy to find it empty. At this time of year the town was fairly quiet, but once winter came with snowfall, the place would be inundated with skiers and the like. Being a part of the tourist trade himself, he enjoyed the rare pockets of peace to be found on occasion exploring a different part of the Highlands. He had planned to have Lori with him. Time away together, rekindling whatever he thought had been left to rekindle. But now? As far as he was concerned, she was heading back to New York with her fiancé. He thought of the afternoon he had stumbled upon her running away from the Highland cattle, and snorted to himself. New York would suit her far better than Arlochy, that was for sure.

Dusk had settled over the town, and in the distance he

heard sheep calling to one another, and cows settling for the night. He strolled past a quaint little church and town hall, until he came to his hotel, lit-up and welcoming in the twilight. Perhaps an early night would do the trick, especially since they would be playing another game the next day. Maybe he was old after all; the thoughts of drinking the night before a match weren't the least bit appealing to him. He entered the building, marched past the burbling pub inside, and continued upstairs. All he wanted was a shower, his pillow and to stop thinking about Lori's smile.

Lori had woken to the smells of coffee, as Jean came into the room holding three paper cups. Lori wiped her bleary eyes and panicked when she saw Gran still in bed, bandaged and very still.

"It's alright - she's been asleep the whole time." Jean handed Lori and Tammy their cups. "Well I mean, whatever time I woke up earlier, she's been the same".

"Have any of the nurses or doctors been in?" Tammy asked pulling back her long hair into a ponytail.

"Every hour I think, just to do the standard checks." Jean pulled out her phone and shook her head. "Damn it, my battery has gone. I can't leave Karen with the kids for another night, it's not fair on her."

"No of course not. We'll figure something out." Lori squeezed Jean's shoulder. Having Jean there made Lori feel better - she was sensible, someone to lean on, but she had a family of her own that she couldn't neglect. A nurse with a round friendly face popped her head around the door:

"How are you girls this morning?" She was the same nurse as the night before, and must have just started her shift. Lori noted how refreshed she looked - in comparison to all three sisters.

"Fine, I guess. Gran seems just the same, we think." Tammy looked on the verge of tears again, and the nurse gave her a look of sympathy.

"Let me have a look at her notes and have a chat with the doctor, he'll come and check on her soon." She walked off on the squeaky clean floor back down the corridor.

The girls sat around Gran once again and talked quietly to one another until they saw a small sign of movement, and heard a soft groan. Lori held her hand again.

"Gran it's OK. It's Lori, I'm here with Tammy and Jean. You've had a stroke, you're in hospital. But you're being well-cared for, you're getting better, it's all going to be alright." Her gran made a gentle moan, making Lori hope she understood. All three girls held onto Gran in some way, to let her feel their love surrounding her.

"I'd better tell the nurse." Lori let go of her grandmother's hand and rose from her seat, just as she made another slight groan, and her eyes flickered open.

"She's waking up!" Tammy cried out at the same time the nurse and doctor marched in at Lori's signal. Gran started to come to, gradually looking at them all and making whimpering sounds.

The girls had been told to go to the waiting room once again by the nursing staff as they were going to keep Gran under closer observation. They sat in the hospital café eating cold bacon sandwiches and sipping weak coffee. Lori ate what was on her plate but couldn't taste anything, her mind foggy as she tried to focus on the little jobs that needed taken care of.

"Oh my god, Bracken!" she gasped abruptly. "I didn't think of Bracken!" She winced at the idea of the old dog, sitting waiting for them all in the house, needing fed and let out to use the toilet.

Jean and Tammy looked at each other in equal alarm.

"Who do we call?" Lori bit her lip thinking of all Gran's possible neighbours who might help.

"I could ask Karen to call over and let him out?" Jean suggested. "But I've already asked so much of her."

"Maybe if she could just check on him?" Lori sighed. "Or I could go home and collect him, to take him here?"

"To a hospital?" Tammy screwed up her face.

"Maybe I can go later, I could let him out, and then come back with the girls the next day?" Jean ventured. "Or I could ask around, what about Mrs Smith? She could pop in?"

Lori gasped at the thought. "Flora Smith? They aren't friends, Gran would hate that!"

"What?" Jean looked incredulously at her sister. "They *are* friends, Gran is friends with everyone!"

"No, Flora always beats Gran at the baking competitions. They don't get on." Tammy stated and Lori nodded in agreement.

"Well... she lives close by, and I know her number, she helps with school fundraisers." Jean looked at her battery-dead phone. "Tammy, you call her?"

Tammy got out her phone, but handed it straight to Jean. "Flora scares me, she was always so bossy and matronly."

Jean turned her face away and sipped her coffee, retorting angrily: "So what? You've to do *something* in this family Tammy!"

Tammy looked close to tears again. "I *do* do things for

this family!" Her bottom lip started to wobble, and Lori, who couldn't bear to see everyone descend into snapping and sniffles for a second day running, took the phone out of Tammy's hands.

"I'll do it! Now look after each other please!"

After spending so many hours waiting, and despite Lori's best efforts, all three sisters found themselves getting frustrated with one another, so much that they had to take it in turns to walk around the hospital grounds alone. But finally, to their relief the doctor had taken the girls aside.

"Your gran is talking, that's really good news at this stage." The consultant dug his hands into his white coat again, Lori noticed, perhaps it was a nervous tick.

"So, um... you think she's going to be OK? Like, back to normal some time?" Tammy bit her fingernails as the three girls crowded around the doctor.

"Let's just say she is doing surprisingly well. She's talking with the nurses and myself, and there appears to be nothing wrong with her speech, which can be affected with a stroke. We just need to assess her over the next few days, but she is stable. She is likely to be a little more physically frail from now on, and she might need a bit of help around the house, but," he nodded and smiled, "if back to normal means, hassling me like a mother-duck to let you all in again, then yes - OK."

"We can go to her?" Lori grabbed a tight hold of Tammy and Jean. The doctor nodded and the girls went in to find Gran sitting up in bed, with the nurse giving her a cup and straw to drink from. Her white hair was uncharacteristically messy, and she still looked pale, but her eyes were open, and she smiled as the girls entered and began fussing around her.

"Aren't I well cared for?" She gestured sleepily to the nurse. "Thank you Abby."

"Your gran is a trooper," the nurse reassured the concerned sisters. "She's on the mend." She winked, straightened the bedclothes, and left the room promptly.

"Well, how are my wee women?" Gran asked in a quiet voice, and laid her head back gingerly on the pillows. Lori watched as the afternoon sun streamed through the fogged-up window and shone over Gran's white hair, making it glow. Dust particles floated in the light, and gave the scene such a peaceful air it made Lori reflect on how close she was to losing the woman lying before her, the woman who had shaped her whole world - a world that Lori had willingly chosen to leave.

The girls each took their turn to gently kiss her on the head, and stood around her, holding hands.

"Oh come now, why the glum faces." She swallowed, her voice croaky. Lori picked up the cup of water with the straw and let her gran take another drink.

"Gran, we were so worried. How are you feeling?" Lori waited until the old woman was finished, who sighed deeply, and smiled up at her granddaughter.

"Och, I am fine and dandy." She chuckled, then coughed weakly. "Just a wee bit tired".

∾

"I think Gran will be OK." Lori hugged her sisters in the corridor, and insisted they go home to rest, and to check in on Bracken. Lori had decided to stay with Gran until she recovered, there was no need to have them all at the hospital getting no sleep and eating awful food. Lori waved farewell as their car rolled out of the car park, with Tammy dabbing at her red eyes, and Jean eager to see her girls. She went back to spend the evening with Gran for visiting hours, and booked a nearby BnB for a long hot shower and a night-cap.

25

The boys suffered a second epic loss; playing another team, but yielding the same results. Callum's heart had not been in the game, and he looked forward to leave his failures and return back to Morvaig. He was eager to spend time out on the sea, blissfully kayaking the remainder of the summer nights away before autumn set in. He stepped onto the bus with the other boys for the long trip back home, and gazed out the window as the endless chatter that surrounded him began to make him weary. Perhaps he should do something else with his life? He mused to himself and studied the dramatic landscape on the other side of the steamed-up windows. He wiped his sleeve back and forth to show a clear vision of hills and lochs rolling past; not a tree in sight. The barren landscape would have once featured many ancient forests before they were all cut down to make room for private estates. Shooting deer and grouse were important to wealthy landowners, and the Highlands were well-known as a playing ground for the few landlords who hung onto their assets ever-tightly. Keeping it for themselves, they shared their miles and miles of desolate land with only their own hand-picked crew of elite peers. *People like Hector*, anger churned automatically in Callum's throat. What he should do is plant trees - hundreds, thousands of trees. Bring back the native Caledonian forests, which would attract indigenous species like red squirrels, capercaillies and the wild cat that had once thrived here. *Would that be worthwhile?* He thought hard as he breathed softly on the glass, and wrote his initials with his finger. He needed to put his energy somewhere that would grow with him. Maybe he should travel to new lands, meet someone new, someone completely different? His heart felt heavy, like someone was pressing down on his chest with the flat of their palm. Someone completely different to Lori, that was *really* what he meant. He wanted to laugh at himself there on the bus: what an eejit, he couldn't shift her from his thoughts, even now. He was sure that whatever Lori was doing at this very moment, it was not thinking of him. The bus sped past jagged hills on either side, containing a certain spot known as the Devil's Staircase, after travellers from long ago would say nothing grew there, not even wild flowers. They continued on through Glencoe - the gloomy hills always a welcome sight for Callum. The day was dark and overcast, but even though the sun didn't shine, he loved how this place made him feel, encouraging him to crack himself open and discover the secrets that were lurking underneath. This land was steeped in history and magic, and whenever he saw these familiar hills, it made him seek that inescapable connection with himself and the vastness around him, come rain or shine.

Callum woke after one of his team mates shook him. It was late when they arrived back, the town quiet and the street lights on. He saluted to any stragglers coming off the bus after him, but received little in the form of a response; the guys must have been eager to get home, to dinner and to a warm bed. He, on the other hand, didn't have much waiting for him. Just an out-of-date-kipper in his fridge, and a can of lager. The nearby grocery was closed, so he got a fish supper from the local chip shop, passed the locked-up *Adventurous Tours*, and finally arrived back home. He spent the next hour clicking buttons on the TV remote, never settling on anything to watch, drank his beer, and then went to bed.

The next day he headed in to work to find Karen chatting earnestly to Jean over the back counter. Jean's face had lost it's usual warm glow, and he was struck at how different she seemed.

"What's happened?" Callum knew there was something not quite right.

"It's Gran." Jean gave a deep sigh, her shoulders rising and falling heavily.

Callum went to her, his hand gently on her elbow. "Is she OK?" He couldn't imagine something being wrong with Mary, she was always fitter and healthier than most folk, running about cooking, looking after everyone, and generally enjoying life.

"She had a stroke." Karen offered, and stood with her arms crossed defensively, a concerned look on her face.

Callum couldn't bear to take in the news, but he needed to know everything. A tear fell down Jean's cheek and Karen went to hug her. Callum stepped back, expecting the worst. He shook his head "No, Jean. No, no."

Karen let go of her friend and rubbed her back as Jean breathed out again.

"It's okay – I mean, she's awake, she's speaking. Her speech isn't affected, just her body, a bit."

"Thank Christ!"

"The doctors got to her in time. We don't know what is affected exactly just yet. Lori has said the side of her right arm and her right leg might be not be fully functioning. She's just so tired, but she's resting for now."

Callum fidgeted, needing to do something. He wanted to see Mary, but would that overstep the mark? This was a family thing after all. But he needed to be involved somehow. "Can I do something? Maybe take Gran's things to her?" He offered.

Jean looked over at Karen with a small smile. "You've both been so generous. Karen was so good to look after the girls, since my ex couldn't even take the time to help me out." She was on the verge of tears again, and Callum didn't know if he should look away or give her comfort.

"Anything you need Jean, I'd do anything for the family." Callum thought of Gran, lying there lonely in the hospital, but then suddenly stopped - *Jean had said Lori was with her. Of course she'd be there to help her grandmother. She was the best person to be there.* Jean was a calm and stable person, but Lori was cool under pressure, and would get the things done that needed doing. He had always loved that about her. But he winced, *that must mean Michael was there too.* There was certainly no room for him if her fiancé was there. And it would look odd, if the local handyman turned up with Gran's clothes, or so Gran had inadvertently led Michael to believe, that day of the Highland games.

"Callum, that would be very kind if you could take her things. Tammy has to work today at the bakery, apparently she can't get another shift, and I haven't seen the girls properly yet, I was too late last night. Karen stayed over." She bit her lip then hesitated, "Also... well, Lori might need some clothes, as she left her flight in such a rush. I think her suit-case will be in New York by now!"

"Well that's settled then. I can go in a few hours after I close up the shop?" Callum nodded at Karen. "Sounds to me you need a rest Karen, why don't you take the day off?"

Karen's alarmed face spoke volumes. "No, we have a group booking today, we can't close!" She pointed up on the whiteboard of the day's events, which was above some children's drawings that Callum hadn't seen before.

"Don't worry, I'll take care of it Karen. You need some time. Why not take tomorrow off too, I'll make sure I'm back here to open."

Karen smiled at Jean. "Maybe I *could* take the time off."

Callum didn't need to tell her twice, and within minutes she had packed up her things and left. He got himself a cup of tea, and looked over the paperwork before him. A job that he did himself usually, but now wished he had an accountant to deal with. He took a big gulp of tea and thought to himself, *better late than never*, ploughing into the stodgy figures with his usual stoicism.

Mary slept into the early evening, lulled by the sounds of people walking by her room as the light outside faded gradually to a deep grey night. Lori had left her to sleep; she was so glad her recently-returned granddaughter was there beside her, but she would tell her tomorrow to go home. Yes, she needed rest too, what an ordeal they all had. The doctors had said she was to stay for perhaps a couple more days, just to get her body to waken up a little, and that would do the job. Mary hadn't slept well the night before, so the lovely nurse Abby had given her medicine to help her through to morning. She didn't know if she was really sleeping or not, but she felt more rested, without a doubt. Dream-like thoughts came to her, memories and faces she knew well. She saw so clearly her husband Jim, with his laughing eyes, and the way he always looked like he was up to some sort of mischief. She had always loved that about him, but had never told him – that would never have done. Her hand had held his tightly, all through the night before he had passed. She had watched him fade before her, but now she felt his hand on hers again, strong and warm.

"It's alright Mary," came a deep voice. "Everything is going to be just fine."

She forgot where she was. Her eyelids were heavy, and she couldn't move. But the deep voice remained close, and that was comforting enough. "Jim?" She murmured.

"I'm here, Mary." The hand pressed hers with a reassuring squeeze. Gran felt as if she were floating and soon fell into a deep sleep with ease.

Callum gently folded his other hand over hers and watched her drift off into a peaceful slumber.

26

Lori had been talked into going back home, while Gran recovered. The doctors had said she was on the mend, and they could start with plans for rehabilitation, and find out exactly what she needed to exercise. Gran readily insisted Lori leave, and allow her time to catchup on sleep. Reluctantly, Lori did as she was told, and hired a car back to Arlochy to see Bracken, then would visit Gran again in the next couple of days. On the journey back her thoughts finally focused on New York. *Shit!* She had forgotten to contact the office. They had been expecting her yesterday to present her ideas. "Oh bugger!" Lori cried. She dreaded what would be waiting for her at the other end of the line. Her insides tightened, and she couldn't think of anything else until she reached home. It was late, but not in New York, so she called the office on the landline, and desperately and anxiously awaited Frankie's voice.

"Yup...?" Came some particularly frosty tones.

"Oh Frankie, I'm so so sorry!"

"Lori, what happened? We've been calling you and leaving you messages! We were all waiting to see your presentation. Now I'll have to reschedule everything! The board is not happy. *I'm not happy!*" Frankie spoke loudly, and Lori butted in as soon as she could.

"I'm so sorry! It was my gran. She had a stroke just when I was due to fly back, and I've been so preoccupied with her and the family I... I lost my phone, and it completely slipped my mind to call and cancel the presentation."

"You forgot?" Frankie said, in disbelief. "I'm sorry about your gran Lori, but you have responsibilities. You can't just have *forgotten*!"

Lori was taken aback by her boss's tone. "I know that, but that's the truth of it."

There was silence on the other end and Lori didn't know if she had hung up on her.

"Lori, these are very important times for the company. You had a duty to show up. I have to say I'm really surprised at how you've behaved. You always put work first, I was sure big things were going to happen for you here."

Lori was in shock at what her boss was saying, her mouth was dry. After all the time and extra effort she had put in, this is how she was being treated?

"Frankie, my gran's health is very important. And I'm sorry, but it's much more important than clothes. I was always in the office, I've given you late nights and weekends for years! And now because I have taken a few extra days off in the middle of an assignment that we can easily reschedule, to care for my family, one of whom is in hospital, having come close to dying! I'm shocked that you don't care for your employees well-being!"

"We all have social lives, but you need to put your career ahead of all that if you want to succeed in this type of world." Frankie was stern, and bellowed at her receptionist to leave the room.

"I *have* put my career first, and all it gave me was missed years from my family – it certainly hasn't yielded much personal support from you! It doesn't have to be that way Frankie. Things are meant to have a better balance."

The next words came over the phone like sharp drops of ice: "Listen Lori. I have no time for this. You can forget that promotion I was talking about. I see no future for you here anymore. You have let me down and embarrassed me in front of the Board! In fact - you're fired. Feel free to prioritise your life anyway you want to. I have chosen my path in life and stuck to it, I suggest you do the same."

Frankie rang off, and Lori leaned against the wall with the receiver in hand and slid down slowly to the floor. Bracken shuffled over to her and laid his head in her lap. She stroked his soft black-and-white fur absentmindedly. She had given years of her life to a company that had dismissed her without a moment's hesitation. *Just like Michael.* What was wrong with her? Through all the times she had supported Frankie, she had thought there was a bond between them, an understanding as women - helping one another in the workforce. Maybe she had been careless; since returning home, family matters had taken over her mind bit by bit, making New York fade into a distant memory. What should she do now? Maybe look for another fashion job, perhaps with a rival company? *Frankie would hate that.* If Lori wanted to make her suffer then that was surely something she could do. But that just wasn't her; she was naturally loyal-minded, and now to see her loyalty dismissed as quickly as a fleeting thought, made her angry. She got up off the floor and paced the kitchen. Bracken made whining noises because she had stopped her petting, but she ignored him, and went to the cupboard to look for something strong to drink. Her gran had lots of healthy snacks, organic this and gluten-free that, in which Lori had no interest. There was nothing to soothe the soul or drown her sorrows. *Damn it, Gran!* She thought of the fit, lively old woman, and relented; perhaps all her years eating well and exercising would pay off, and she'd recover from this stroke with more of her strong mind and body present than most people her age. Lori put the kettle on and decided to have a cup of tea and a slice of banana loaf instead. The night trickled by, and Lori found herself itching to do something more the following morning. She spent the majority of the day cleaning the house from top to bottom and made the beds, but her energy had not disappeared. She put away her gran's scarves, and a jumper in the cupboard, clearing the room to make it nice for her homecoming. Then she saw her mum's sewing machine at the back of the cupboard, the prized, if archaic piece of equipment she had used for Tammy's wedding dress. The old singer was black, with intricate patterns in gold across its surface; *a beautiful piece of kit,* Lori reflected. She crouched down to touch its curves and remembered her mother at the kitchen table sewing dresses for her girls. Just looking at the machine now, made her feel closer to her mother and her creative ways. She stood up, and before closing the wardrobe door she caught a glimpse of a particular long blue skirt which was oddly familiar. The light cotton material had a strip down the sides in a deep orange, with orange stitching along the bottom of the hem. Its vibrant colour popped out against the blue, and gave the garment a structure and elegance that stood it apart. She had made this for Gran so long ago, but as she looked at it now, found it could be worn today, and not look out of fashion. Lori closed the wardrobe and made herself another cup of tea, then sat at the kitchen table, with pen and notebook in front of her. The pen darted about the paper in frantic scratches, forming silhouettes and shapes flowing over one another. She scribbled evermore notes and ideas. Fabrics she'd use for a swing jacket, a tea-dress, a pleated skirt - more and more ideas poured out onto the pages. The black and white sketches continued, and Lori felt the release she needed, but she also knew there was more within her.

~

Jean answered the door to a breathless Lori, with her car still running outside.

"You're home! We were going to come in tomorrow to see you and Gran!" Jean said, gesturing for Lori to follow her inside.

"I can't Jean, I'm in the middle of something. Do you have coloured pencils? Crayons, pens - anything?"

Jean looked at her sister in confusion. "Crayons?" She mockingly touched her sister's forehead, but was shrugged off.

"I'm fine, I'm sketching, but I need to colour them in Jean! Do the girls have anything I can use, I'll give them back ASAP!" Lori's face was so earnest that her sister wasted no time, and went off in pursuit of the desired articles. Lori stood on the step nudging the doorframe with her foot, eager to get back home.

Karen's face peered from the hallway.

"I thought I heard your voice!" Karen stood smiling, looking a little exposed in a thin white t-shirt and pyjama bottoms. She looked very much at home, Lori noted, and a little flushed, but she checked herself and quickly decided to make the most of Karen's presence and do a little casual digging.

"Yes, just me – not staying though, just getting some things from Jean. How are you Karen? Oh, I meant to ask you - I've been trying to find Callum - he's not answering his phone, and he wasn't at his house earlier either. Is he OK?" Lori felt like a stalker, and cringed at her lack of decorum.

Karen blinked. "Oh, he should be at home. I've seen him around, he's just been out with clients quite a lot while I've had time off - perhaps that's why he's not been in touch?"

That, or he doesn't want anything to do with a non-commit-tal, two-timing floozy like me? Lori thought to herself, and was about to say more, when Jean came back holding up a plastic bag with a bemused smile on her face.

"Thanks sis! OK, I must be off, nice to see you Karen!" She waved and left promptly.

Lori woke to Bracken licking her chin as the morning light hit her face. She squinted and pushed the dog away. Rising from the sofa, she padded across the room, skidding slightly on the sketches scattered all over the floor. She made herself a cup of coffee, looking at the fruits of her labour the night before. She had worked well into the night, drafting up patterns from her designs, creating practice mockups and finally sewing the actual garment into being. Gran had kept everything of her mother's, and Lori couldn't believe all the odds and ends she had found; her mum's old sketches and notes on patterns, measurements of her girls, and ideas of what she'd make for them over the next few seasons. The box of fabric was a mixture of various cottons, silks and wools. Over the course of the evening, Lori made a cape from two dark wools - a stylish grey and black herringbone weave. She had stitched the two different fabrics together, giving a subtle patchwork effect, and lined it in a soft burgundy silk. She just needed to add a fastening at the front.

Lori lifted the cape and scrutinised it; smoothing the soft wool between her fingers. Without thinking she picked up the phone and called Betty. The woman seemed surprised to hear her, and asked about New York. Lori had to confess about her job.

"Oh well, I'm sure something good will come out of things. Yes, we're still getting orders, especially since we're coming into autumn, people want tweed for winter."

"Right – yeah, that's why I'm calling. I'm looking to buy some!"

Lori had rang off once her fabric order was placed and gulped down the last of the coffee. She put on makeup, and wore one of her grey dresses, then looking in the mirror realised how much she missed colour. All her clothes from New York were black, grey or white, to fit in with the company setting. She needed to make a change, and wanted to incorporate more shades and textures into her wardrobe. For now, she tied a piece of turquoise silk around her neck, which she found in the scrap pile, and without further delay, hopped in the car in pursuit of Callum. With no answer at his apartment, she wandered down to the shop, again Karen's smiling face welcomed her but informed her he was out with customers. Lori wrote a note for him, and left, defeated.

Feeling a bit sorry for herself, she walked along the waterfront on the way back to her car, and came across an empty shop front. It's large curved window was painted a deep green, which was peeling with years of untended exposure to the salt air. Lori had recalled it had once been a book shop, but after the owners had left the area, the shop had switched hands many times with no real business success. She peeked inside to see a plain white space and a wooden floor. It looked very serviceable, if a bit mucky, with boxes and rubbish lying around on the floor. A small sign on the door had a name and number, with "To Let" in larger biro letter. Lori wrote down the number, and feeling more optimistic about the day ahead, headed home to use Gran's trusty landline.

As Callum waited on his clients, he leaned against the van and gazed out over the calm shallow loch. He had decided to let them kayak unguided, giving them the space to enjoy a romantic trip together. He expected the couple to be back any minute now, to collect bicycles for their cycle back to Morvaig. His phone buzzed, and he saw a curt message from Karen - Lori had been in the shop asking for him again. He didn't want to bring Karen into things, but he had no interest in being part of Lori's games, whatever they were these days. He knew at the same time, that she was only really there to help Gran, and it was good that the old lady had support from her granddaughters. After he had visited Mary at the hospital, it had left him a bit out of sorts. She had been so frail, and muttering such strange things, that he didn't know what to think or how to react afterwards. He had never felt so powerless, unable to offer anything more than calming words.

Voices grew louder and louder, snapping Callum out of his daydream, and the couple came into view paddling back to him. Callum unloaded the bikes, took their kayaks and stacked them in the trolley behind the van. As he left them to set off on the last leg of their journey, he saw them kiss in his rear-view mirror, making him long for something more; something he had thought he almost had found again. He went back gloomily to the shop, where he found Karen sitting at the computer.

"So, she's been here again asking for you!" Karen gave him a look like his old teacher Mrs Lang used to, whenever he had tried out a new excuse for not doing his homework. "I think you should just speak to her, for my sake at least!" She waved her hands in frustration. "I don't want to be asked about your comings and goings every time I see her!"

"Don't worry about it Karen, I'll take care of it." He started unpacking the van into the back cabin behind the shop. Perhaps it wasn't such a bad idea to go away for a while, he could leave for a few weeks – explore another country. He had always wanted to see Brazil. Lost in his thoughts, unloading paddles and life jackets, he heard a cough behind him. Karen was standing at the cabin door, cross armed with a non-indulgent look directed at him once again.

"You have a visitor." She leaned against the door frame.

His heart thumped, he couldn't face Lori again.

Karen sighed and rolled her eyes. "It's just Alan! For crying out loud, Callum, you gotta man up!"

He bristled but followed her out to the shop front, where Alan stood looking at the kids' drawings on the wall.

He spun around, but not in his usual cheery manner. "Hey Cal. I didn't know if you had heard about Gran." His face was downcast as he exhaled "It's bad news."

Callum stood frozen on the spot. A wave hit him, like he was being pushed in all directions. It couldn't be that...?

"What happened?" Callum placed his hand on the desk to steady himself. He had to go to them, he had to comfort

Lori. She had been looking for him, grieving, and all the while he had been ignoring her like a petulant child.

Alan nodded slowly. "She had a stroke, she was taken to hospital on Tuesday night."

"And -?" Callum waited for the dreaded news.

Alan's eyes widened. "You heard?"

"Yes I - I did!" Callum couldn't contain the urgency in his voice any longer. "Has she -?" The lump in his throat was there, just under the surface.

"What?" Alan briefly shook his head. "Oh no, don't worry Cal, she's okay, still in hospital, they were able to operate in time to save any severe damage. It turns out she's coming back tomorrow." His face was still one of confusion. "I just wasn't sure if you knew, sorry, I've been out on the boat since our last shinty match."

Callum took his hand away from the table and ran it through his hair. Within seconds he had thought the worst news, and now the sense of relief was overwhelming. Brazil could wait another week or so, he told himself with a sigh.

27

Lori's heart was fluttering like an excited bird desperate to get out and fly. She had spent two long evenings sewing, and somehow had come up with the bones of a project that would allow her to move forwards out of the shadow of Costner's, and onto her own path. She had received a call that morning from Frankie, who had apologised very politely for her outburst the day before, and asked her back to work – when she was ready. But the clarity Lori felt now was like nothing she had ever experienced before. Her old life in the city was fun, but had never *really* made her happy – not in the skin-tingling, hopeful way that the last two weeks in Arlochy had done. After a much deeper conversation with Frankie; the older woman drinking wine on one side while Lori drank tea, she laid out her reasons and her plan of action. Lori couldn't wait to get started, her mind racing with the initial arrangements, but had to put things on hold for the time being. More important duties needed to take priority. At the insistence of her sisters, she took them both in the car to collect

Gran, who sat waiting on her freshly-made bed with her overnight bag at her feet. Lori laughed and shook her head:

"Gran, you wouldn't be ready to leave, would you?"

Her gran still looked tired, but the familiar rosy hue was back in her cheeks. She stood up slowly. "Yes please, take me home. I'm desperate to get a proper cuppa tea!"

Tammy and Jean supported her on either side, and helped her out to the car. Lori thanked the now-familiar nurse, and soon after hopped in the car homewards to Arlochy. Gran sat in the front seat, gazed out the window quietly and dozed from time to time, while the sisters chatted.

"Alan said he went in to see Callum today." Tammy said breezily from the backseat. "He thinks Callum seems strange, looks a bit distracted."

Jean raised an eyebrow. "Isn't that just Callum? Mr Brooding - always looking like he's thinking of deep, serious things!" She sniggered, but was cut short by Lori's stern look in the rear-view mirror.

"I've been trying to see him. He's not forgiven me for Michael turning up out of the blue. He must think I'm some sort of a cheater."

"We can go rough him up then!" Tammy nudged Jean. "Eh sis, we'll get him to talk to Lori!"

"No! I don't want either of you interfering." Lori snapped. "I will speak to him eventually, just leave him be, OK? There's been enough damage done already." She glanced at Jean, who sheepishly looked away.

After some hours of steady travel, they finally began to approach Arlochy. The sweet smell of trees and the sea hit them almost tenderly, and Lori slowly parked up outside the house. The sisters supported their gran and led her inside to her bedroom.

"Oh - it looks lovely in here, you cleaned!" Gran chuckled and positioned herself on the bed. Her eyes squinted at what was hanging up in the wardrobe. "That's new?" She pointed at the item, and Lori pulled it out into view with a wide grin on her face.

"You don't miss anything!"

"I raised you three girls didn't I? Kept me on my toes!" she joked, and touched the tweed fabric that was presented to her.

"Do you like it? I made it for you, thought it might be nice for winter." Lori pulled the grey tweed cape off the hanger and swung it around Gran's shoulders.

"It's beautiful, Lori. You made this for me?" Her eyes reddened as she nuzzled into its soft velvet collar.

"You'll be the most glamorous woman in the area!" Jean said admiringly, sitting next to Gran.

"She already is!" Declared Tammy, and sat on the other side of Gran. Lori went back into the wardrobe, pulling out two scarves and handed them to her sisters; one in deep green and one in pale blue.

"I got a wee bit carried away with sewing, thought you guys might like these too."

"You *have* been busy!" Jean remarked and wrapped the green scarf with fleece lining around her neck.

"Just like your mother," Gran mused, beaming at her granddaughter.

"OK Gran, enough of the fashion show" Lori clapped her hands together. "What do you want to do? Shall we leave you to rest?"

"I'd love to see the kids." She said with a sparkle in her eye, and Lori knew in that moment she was making the right decision to stay.

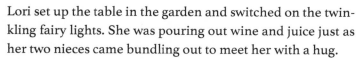

Lori set up the table in the garden and switched on the twinkling fairy lights. She was pouring out wine and juice just as her two nieces came bundling out to meet her with a hug.

"Aw my wee darlings! I told you I would see you again soon!"

"We missed you so much!" Anne said, bobbing up and down on the spot.

"Have you come back to take us to Disneyland?" Maggie cried out, smudging her hair back from her face.

Lori laughed and rolled her eyes. "Not quite yet, but I'm back – and that means more disastrous biking, ice creams, and hot-chocolate duvet days!" She ruffled Maggie's hair. "Now away you two, go get Gran – she's been looking forward to seeing you."

The two girls ran off in the direction of Gran's bedroom, pushing past their mother who came out carrying paper bags, with Karen at her side.

"I got a bit of everything – but mostly fish and chips!" Jean unpacked the newspaper packages gleefully before laying them down on the table. The smell of fried batter and sticky salt and vinegar made Lori's mouth water, and hastily she shouted for everyone to come out for dinner.

Karen sat next to Jean, and Lori caught a look pass between them. Ever since they had started seeing more of Karen, Jean had seemed so much more relaxed. Karen was proving to be a good friend, and Lori was thankful to have her there at this time as a part of the family.

Gran appeared at the entrance to the verandah, with walking stick in hand, about to descend just as Alan and Tammy arrived in a flurry.

"Only us!" Tammy shouted, and Alan marched up to

help Gran down the steps. She gratefully took his arm as he steadied her.

Lori and Gran sat at either end of the table, with the chattering group in between them. Lori took in the scene - everyone together, enjoying their meal, a usual family dinner, but this time, *she* was here with them. A proper part of it too.

"May I make an announcement?" Tammy piped up, smiling at Alan, as though thinking exactly the same thought as Lori. "It's time hun".

He nodded, and beamed proudly at her.

"I am...or I should say that *we are...* having a baby!" Tammy cried out joyfully and Alan kissed her on the cheek.

"And it's a boy!" he followed.

"No no! That part was secret, Alan!" Tammy nudged him in the ribs.

"Woops!" He put an arm around her. "It's fine, they won't tell anyone." He buried his face into her neck, as she rolled her eyes.

"We get a cousin!" Anne wriggled on her seat and Maggie made whooping noises.

Gran turned to Tammy and cupped her face in her hands. "Oh darling, I'm so happy for you both, that is the best news." She sniffed away a tear, and Tammy leaned in to give her a hug. "You've made me so proud." Gran gently leaned over the table and clasped hands with Alan. "Alan, you make my granddaughter very happy, and I will always be thankful for that. Congratulations, having a child is one of the most beautiful blessings in life".

～

Lori was at the sink washing glasses after the last cold chip had been claimed. Gran came in and leaned against the worktop carefully. "What can I do?" She scanned the room to find a job.

"Nothing Gran, everything's taken care of!" Lori heard her nieces in the background playing with Bracken. She tilted her head back to see the girls in the lounge, dressing the poor dog in a blanket and one of Lori's hats. But Bracken sat still, clearly happy to have the attention.

Jean and Tammy came in with more dishes, as Gran flicked on the kettle. Lori let the dishes soak in the sink and turned to them all.

"Now that I have you three in front of me, I have my own announcement to make."

Silence greeted her, the only sound was the kettle gently boiling its water.

"You're pregnant too?" Jean snorted, then looked apprehensive.

"Not funny Jean. No, I'm not pregnant. But I have some news. It's taken me a while to get to this place, but for the first time in a long time, I feel.." She paused, trying to find the words, but shrugged. "I'm happy. I'm glad I came home when I did, and I now see what I've missed all these years away." She took off her rubber gloves realising she had the full attention of her captivated audience. "I've decided to stay here in Arlochy."

All three women gasped around her.

"But... but what about your big-dollar job in New York?" Tammy sat down on the kitchen stool, gaping.

"Yeah, there was New York, once - but now the only things I really care about are here. Home."

Jean and Tammy cheered together.

"You owe me that twenty pounds back, Tam!" Jean fist-pumped the air in triumph.

Tammy groaned, and reached into her jeans' pocket, pulling out her purse and handing the note to her sister, who fanned the money over her face with glee.

"OK fine stop gloating!" Tammy said, and looked back at Lori with caution.

"You made a bet?" Lori's mouth opened at the very thought of her sisters profiting from *her* life.

"Aye, I bet you'd stay after this trip!" Jean pursed her lips together and gyrated on her chair in a way only a bratty sister could.

Lori shook her head and turned to find Gran looking down at her feet.

"Gran are you OK?" Lori moved over and rubbed her arm.

"Yes sweetheart." She breathed out and rested her hand on the counter. "Why are you staying, Lori?"

Lori was taken aback by the question. Did her gran not want her here? She had assumed she could stay on in the family house, help her gran get back to normal, and start her new life. But looking into Gran's weary eyes, Lori was astounded to see that maybe that chain of events wasn't a given after all.

"Because... well, because of what I said, Gran. It feels right to be here now."

Gran touched her forehead. "I'm sorry, I feel very tired. Can we talk about this tomorrow?" She shuffled off in the direction of her room.

Lori glanced at her sisters for an explanation, but was confronted with shrugs and confused expressions.

She knocked on Gran's door and a small voice from the other side called: "Come in."

Gran was perched on her bed, and with a tissue in hand she wiped her eyes.

"Gran, do you need a hand with undressing?" Lori had been told by the nurses that it would take a while for her grandmother to get back to her usual self.

The old lady sighed heavily, and the tears fell from her eyes more freely.

"I'm sorry Lori!" Gran's shoulders shook and the emotion erupted from her, like nothing Lori had ever seen before. Gran was usually the strongest one in their family, but Lori put an arm around her shoulder, it was now *her* turn to be strong, and give comfort.

"Don't be daft, why are you sorry?" Lori stroked her gran's white hair and rubbed her shoulder gently.

"That... you feel you need to stay and look after me." Gran sniffed, and Lori produced another tissue from a pouch that she always kept on her person.

"No, I don't Gran." She scratched her head then turned to face her. "OK, maybe I feel you need help, and I'm here to do it."

Gran shook her head. "I can't be the reason you're leaving your life in New York. You have your fiancé, and your wonderful job." She dabbed her eyes. "It's not right!"

"Oh Gran." Lori could have easily started crying herself, but knew she must remain calm and collected to convince her gran that everything was for the best. "I don't have any of those things any more, actually. I am wanting to start my own business here. And Michael, well - I realised we weren't right for each other pretty much as soon as he tried to convince me I should stay on the plane, and leave you to your fate! I'm so unbelievably glad I found that out before it was too late!"

Gran gently tapped Lori's hand. "Oh sweetheart, I'm so sorry. You've been going through a lot recently haven't you?"

They sat in silence for a few moments, Lori rubbing her gran's shoulders as she composed herself.

"You want to start your own business?" Gran sniffed abruptly, only just processing Lori's declaration.

Lori nodded and smiled. "Aye, I've made a business plan."

"Of course you have." Gran laughed and tucked the tissue up her cardigan sleeve. "I just want to make sure you're not coming home simply to look after me." She spoke in a more alert tone now.

"No Gran, I imagine you'll be on your feet in no time. You can't sit still, there will be yoga and coffee mornings galore to come, but just for now, I will help you get to that point again." Lori smiled. "I have ideas Gran, so many ideas floating around my head. I even thought about maybe doing something with the other rooms in the house. Maybe a B&B? I've also seen an empty shop in Morvaig - I want to sell handmade clothing. My own little boutique."

Gran chuckled. "If your garments are anything like that cape you made me," she pointed to the tweed garment hanging in the wardrobe, "I'm sure you'll have people queuing out the door! As for this B&B idea, you'll need to show me what you're thinking. I'm not sure about our home being opened up to strangers – not just yet." Gran bit the inside of her mouth.

"Gran don't worry, there's plenty of time to go over things so everyone's comfortable. And I'd never disrupt your life in any way and make things difficult for you – family comes first! For now, just you focus on getting better."

There were murmurs in the garden, the after-dinner party

was still going strong, so Lori made coffee for the guests, and laid out some tablet her gran always kept stored in the fridge. *Amen for tablet*, Lori thought. It was one of Gran's specialities, a sweet treat that would make your head spin from the smallest of morsels. Lori made a mental note to learn some baking skills from Gran, and to make time to share them with her nieces too. She stepped over a sprawled-out Bracken, and walked out into the garden of twinkling lights and laughter.

28

Lori opened the empty shop and walked around in the echoey cold. In the corner of the room, was an old fireplace, its tiles of swirling patterns reminded her somewhat of Rennie Mackintosh, a pretty feature, purely decorative however. There was a small back room, which had a sink and little else, judging by the size, she was sure she could fit in a little fridge there too, and maybe a cooker. At the far side of the smaller room was a compact bathroom, and back door that led out onto a tiny patch of grass. A wooden fence sheltered the space, but the view ahead was not obstructed, they were right on the harbour, looking out onto the ferry port. Lori couldn't help but jump for joy and cheer loudly over the sound of seagulls and boat horns. She had spoken to the owner, and thanks to her gran's sterling local reputation, he had welcomed her offer to lease the shop. She had big plans for this space. Her imagination conjured up window displays for winter - fairy lights draped over tree branches, and mannequins show-casing red woollen jackets. Lori would be inside, sewing and welcoming people with cups of mulled wine as they browsed the clothing rails. There would be a lot to do, but she relished the challenge to make something fully her own and almost skipped outside the door as she locked up. Nothing would bring her down today, even as droplets of rain fell on her head, she looked up to the dark clouds and welcomed the shower. Unable to suppress her happiness, Lori smiled to herself and headed in the direction of Callum's shop. She dashed in through the door just as the downpour and flashes of lightning ensued. Karen was there, packing boxes on the desk.

"Lori! How are you?" Karen came over and hugged her. Lori felt at ease instantly; her warm manner was so infectious that just a few moments with her would make anyone feel calm and focused.

"What's going on?" Lori looked from Karen to the boxes. "Are you having a big clear-out?"

"Yes." Karen bobbed her head side to side. "Well - sort of." She pursed her lips together and clasped her hands. "You don't know then?"

"Know what?" Lori's heart skipped a beat.

"I thought Callum had told you? Our lease is coming to an end." Karen went over to the desk, removing boxes from the chair to make more room.

"No, I didn't know." Lori sat down on a spare chair, confused. She had imagined Callum and her would reconnect, especially since he was to be on the same street as her new venture. But everything was changing for him, just as Lori was starting to get her life in order. "But your job, Karen? What are you going to do?"

Karen nodded. "I knew it was coming, and I've made plans. I'm thinking of going back to college."

"It's so sad, you guys had a great partnership." Lori looked down. "What is Callum going to do?"

"He's got ideas too, I know he's ready to travel. Some-where... totally different." The phone rang loudly, and Karen picked it up immediately. "Oh, hey you" Karen smiled and mouthed to Lori that it was Jean on the other end of the line.

Lori needed to see Callum, talk to him. She got up abruptly, just as Karen placed the receiver down, calling after her.

"Lori, are you OK?"

"I'm sorry, I need to go." She opened the door, but turned back; a part of her curiosity needed answered. "Karen... you - and my sister?"

Karen stood up rigidly, her smile fading. "Yes?"

"I may be overstepping the mark here, but: you make her happy. And I wish you both the best." Lori tapped the door slightly and left Karen standing open-mouthed, packing tape hanging loosely by her side.

Callum put the letter in its envelope and addressed it to Lori. He had been up half the night trying to find the words he needed, and after much time scoring out and rewriting, he was finally as happy as he ever would be with the result. He leaned back in his chair, stretching his legs out under the small foldaway table in his living-room. He looked around the small space; his apartment had served him well, but it was time for a change. He needed a different environment to help him decide what his next project would be. Some-where his mind could focus, and forget about the opinions of others. As he sealed the envelope, he summoned up the final push of willpower to deliver it before Lori got home, knowing that if he saw her, he'd never be able to explain how he felt properly. He found himself tongue-tied whenever she was in his presence. This way, she could make her own decision, and he could finally get on with his life, no matter the answer. He suppressed the nagging feeling that he was giving in to the coward's way of doing things, but he couldn't look at her and say what would make things right – this was the best way, he was sure of that.

He went to Arlochy, through heavy rain fall and behind a stream of cars, their headlights gliding along the watery road. Callum drove slowly to the Robertson's front door, and was confronted, almost the second he pulled in, with the flashback of them intertwined at the end of the hallway the day of the Highland games. He saw only Mary's small car parked at the front, so he knocked on the door, hoping to see her, if only for a moment. He peered through the windows but saw no-one, so without further thought he pushed the small envelope under the door and left. He hopped back in his van and drove down the lane towards the main street. The rain still lashed, making his windows steam up; blurring his vision. He wiped the window, feeling a pang of regret for leaving only a letter. He hesitated as he started to accelerate along the road, his mind foggy like the view before him. Distracted, he didn't see the figure standing in the middle of the road until it was too late.

Lori was soaked through, standing outside Callum's door; there was no answer. Was she ever going to get hold of him? She just wanted a chance to explain. *He was beginning to act unfairly.* With her good mood now wavering, Lori ran back to her car and headed for home.

Back in the warmth of their family home, she found

Gran sitting on the sofa with a cup of tea and a slice of cake halfway to her mouth.

"I see you're recovering nicely?" Lori chuckled, momentarily forgetting her troubles, and placing her bag on the kitchen table.

"I needed some energy!" she said defensively.

"I'm sure you did!" Lori shook her head and turned around to see Bracken shuffling towards her with something in his jaws. Lori teased the letter out of his mouth and gently placed the wet envelope on the table, focusing her attention back on Gran. "You've been taking things easy, I hope?"

Her gran sighed with an exasperated air. "Lori, dear - I have been relaxing just like the doctor told me to. I was only out in the garden briefly, then when the rain fell I came in."

Lori eyed Gran suspiciously. "You weren't doing any gardening, were you?"

"No of course not!" Gran tutted. "I pulled out a few weeds, that's all!"

"Gran!" Lori protested.

"It was nothing! Things are getting easier. I can't be sitting the whole time - I need to be exercising my leg and arms – Abby told me to!" She gestured to the two sturdy walking sticks that lay beside her.

"What if you had fallen? Gran, please be careful!" Lori tried her best not to nag, but found it difficult - Gran was determined to be back to normal sooner than was advisable.

"I am, Lori. Remember I still have my wits about me, I'm not an invalid."

"I didn't say you were!" Lori felt the frustration rise up inside her. "Gran please, we need to help each other out. I don't want to be worried every time I'm not here with you."

"And I don't want to be mollycoddled, I'm used to doing

things my own way". She nodded as if the conversation was over.

Lori sighed and sat down on the sofa. "OK, I will do my best to let you get on with things. I'm here for you, I just want you to be careful. That's all."

Gran patted Bracken as he nuzzled his nose between them both. "I just want my independence back, I'm sorry." She took her hand from Bracken and placed it on Lori's gently. "I'll help you, if you help me?"

Lori let out a giggle and shook the extended hand. "Deal" Then, remembering the wet envelope on the kitchen table, she ambled over to the counter-top and tore open the seal, trying to avoid the traces of Bracken's saliva. "Did someone drop by to see me?" Lori looked around the room, searching for any evidence of a visitor.

"No, no one came here." Gran placed her empty cup on the plate of leftover crumbs. "Although..." She hesitated. "Now I come to think of it, I thought I heard a car earlier. But wasn't sure, I may have dozed off."

Lori smiled, and glanced down at the note in her hands:

> *Dear Lori,*
> *I don't know when you'll read this but I want you*
> *to know: all the years apart, and the seas that*
> *were between us, they never stopped me*
> *loving you. It's you I see everywhere – in the*
> *mossy moors and rolling waters.*
> *It's strange to realise that even as we grew apart*
> *and lived our own lives, I felt we were meant*
> *to come together again one day. We both may*
> *have changed, in our wants and our needs,*
> *but I'm glad for it. I only ever wanted you to*

be happy, and if I could make you happy -
please be mine.
I am planning to go away for a while, so your
decision is an easy one - if you don't share my
feelings, please put me out of my misery and
let me let you go. Otherwise, in my heart, you
will always be my lass; my love.
Callum

Lori clutched the letter, her heart beating wildly. "When did you hear the car, Gran?" She picked up her car keys.

"I don't know, only just before you walked in really I think." Gran's eyes widened "How? Is everything OK?"

Lori put the keys down, maybe he was in the village? Driving in this rain would be difficult, so she took a chance, and hoped he was still near. She didn't want to miss him, not this time, not ever again. She dashed out, running under the rumbling sky, splashing through puddles as she turned onto the main street, hoping he might have parked the van somewhere, waiting for her. Her heart raced just thinking about him, at the thought of seeing his face. She wanted him. It felt so simple and came so easily to her, that the certainty frightened her a little. Why had she waited so long? She wiped her wet hair back and ran past a long line of cars, only noticing that there was an obstruction up ahead as she neared towards it. She ran past the bright lights that flooded the watery road, slowing to a walk when she saw Callum's van up ahead. She felt the scene unfold in slow motion. People got out of their cars to see what the commotion was. The van at the front was parked at an odd angle, blocking the road. A strong wind whipped Lori's hair over her face, as she approached the van slowly, and saw through the window a figure slumped over the steering wheel. She gasped, her blood running cold as the sounds of car horns boomed from impatient drivers in the lineup behind her. In a daze, she shrunk back, afraid of how she would find him. But there had been no crash, no blood; *what was wrong?* Then, quickly as she tried to register the scene before her, the figure suddenly looked up and slowly steered the van towards the side of the road. Callum got out and slammed the door behind him. He pinched the bridge of his nose, leaning against the van. Cars slowly passed by and he shook his head. With confusion on his face, eyes darting around him, he suddenly looked up and locked eyes with Lori. Her heart raced again and she stepped up onto the pavement, edging towards him. Feeling like a drowned rat, she was sure her hair was a sopping disaster, and probably her mascara was dripping in black threads down her cheeks by now, but she didn't care. This was her, in all honesty. And the relief at seeing Callum unhurt engulfed her completely. The rain continued to fall as Callum came towards her wearing an unsure expression, with his hands shoved in his jeans pockets. Still panting after her run, Lori clutched the letter tightly in her hand, its words now surely washed away.

"What happened? Are you...OK?" she asked, in between big breaths.

"It's OK. I'm OK.." He looked back at the passing traffic. "Someone appeared on the road, I thought for a moment... but it's fine...they weren't hurt. I just had a scare." He scratched his neck, unable to look her in the eyes.

"Callum... I've been trying to see you!"

He looked around and shrugged. "I needed time, Lori."

"Yes." She bit her lip.

"Lori -" His face was at an angle, looking down and still hesitating to meet her eyes.

"I think I've been hiding from myself for years," she blurted out, not wanting to waste the moment between them. "I didn't realise it, but I was so preoccupied of how I thought I should live my life, trying to avoid the mistakes I thought my parents made; trying to avoid being trapped by the memories, and what I thought I didn't want. I was so fixated on those things that I didn't listen to what my heart wanted." She gulped, unsure of what her next words would be, but continued. "I'm sorry I left you all those years ago, it'll be something I'll always regret. We could have shared so much more, back then. But I hope that... I hope that we can start again...?" Lori wanted to reach out to him, to feel his arms around her, but something stopped her, and she stood still waiting.

"You're not with Michael?"

"No. When you came to mine the day of the games, I honestly thought Michael and I were no longer together. I was surprised to see him, and I suppose I accepted his being there because I felt guilty for what was about to happen between us - then he pulled out a ring. Again – not really listening to how I felt, just trying to manage the situation like some paranoid life-coach." Lori explained, without stopping to take a breath. "I'm sorry it took me such a long time to see everything clearly. I thought I was making the right decision to be with him, whatever that meant, but my heart felt empty. Everything felt wrong."

Callum moved a step towards her, and his hand reached out to take hers. Holding her hand he moved closer, leaving them only inches apart. His hand moved up her arm to her chin, and he held her face in his hands as he came even closer. Every bit of Lori tingled with anticipation, knowing this was the moment she had been waiting for, for the last ten years of her life.

"You got my letter then?" he said quietly, glancing down at the sodden paper in her hands, and moving her wet hair out of her eyes.

"Yes, and... I feel the same! I want to be with you, wherever it takes us. I want to be with you. I just... want you."

Callum's serious face suddenly exploded into a beam of light, smiling back at her.

"Aren't you going to kiss me, before I get swept away by this rain?" Lori demanded with a grin.

Callum pulled her closer. "I will kiss you when I'm good and ready Lori Robertson." He touched her face again, enjoying the moments that passed, taunting Lori deliciously until he finally murmured, "My bonnie lass," and kissed her slowly and deliberately on the lips. Lori closed her eyes as the new-but-familiar heat hit her, falling into it with open arms, wanting to stay in this place of dreamy contentment forever. "My love" he murmured in-between kisses, and they embraced tightly, locking lips and bodies together.

EPILOGUE

"It seems a bit rushed to be traveling doesn't it? I mean, you literally just opened the shop!" Tammy remarked, as she riffled through the newly-made garments on the rails, her huge pregnant belly jutting out before her.

A few months ago Lori would have agreed with her sister, but now she delighted in her new found spontaneity. "Well it's not forever, Tam!" Lori picked up a few dresses and headed to the small changing room next to the back desk. Tammy sighed, and slowly eased herself down onto the antique French sofa, which Lori had repurposed with vintage silk, in hues of duck egg and patterns of red roses. The shop was Lori's pride and joy, and seeing women try on garments and falling in love with them, made her feel more uplifted and happier than she had ever been in her life. Even as the seasons changed and the start of a New Year was approaching, she felt light and free. To her amazement, her shop had already brought in business during the quiet months, and within the next twelve months she hoped to turn her first profit. She had built something that was hers, and she could make any decisions she wanted to about how it was run, and what creativity she indulged in each quarter. In the corner of the room, her mother's old Singer sewing machine was nestled in beside shelves displaying different coloured tweeds, looking every bit an organic part of the shop. Above the Singer, old framed photographs of her mother and her gran clung to the wall, her two biggest inspirations.

Tammy stretched her legs out in front of her. "Once this wee guy comes, I will be able to see my feet again. I can't wait!"

"I didn't know you were fond of your feet. The size they are, I'm surprised you don't see them peeping out under your belly!"

"Hey!" Tammy spun her head around just as Lori closed the curtain of the changing room. Being the tallest of the three sisters, Tammy also had the biggest feet, much to her annoyance, especially after the endless teasing in high-school. But on the positive side of things, she had never needed to worry about her sisters stealing her shoes. "You're such a cheeky besom!" Tammy bellowed, dispelling any energy she might have had left.

The door-bell jangled as Callum walked in. Since becoming the boyfriend of an up-and-coming designer, he had gradually been introduced to the world of fashion by Lori. Today he wore a smart navy coat, made by the designer herself, buttoned up with a striped scarf wrapped around his neck, above slim grey chinos. He rubbed his hands together and stomped his snow-covered boots on the mat, but when he saw Tammy sprawled on the sofa, he took up a new role with a playful bow and a flourish of his scarf: "I'm here to escort you ladies to dinner!"

Tammy pushed herself up slightly, but gave up almost immediately. "I need help to even get off this thing!" she shrieked, and Callum hauled her up with ease from the sofa. "Alan isn't with you? I see; he thought he'd leave his poor unfortunate wife to make her way to Gran's herself?"

"Tam... you're hardly a defenceless creature! Anyway, I said I'd take you both, I've plenty of room in the new van, and he'll see us at Gran's. I hear she's put on a huge spread, inviting more than a few folk! We're getting quite the send-off!" Callum offered Tammy his arm to lean on.

"Gran shouldn't be doing too much," Tammy tutted.

"You think Mary can be told what to do!" Callum shook his head incredulously. "At least you and Alan will be there to mind her while we're away."

"I'm not sure who'll be minding who, especially when this baby comes. I'll be needing all the help I can get!"

"Well thanks for being understanding, about us going at this time. But you are acting a little bit selfishly really, Tam – you should've had the baby last week!" Callum hunched his shoulders and winked.

"Hey, you are just as cheeky as that one!" She pointed to the changing room behind her.

"I learned from the best." He chuckled. "But we'll be back before you know it, two months will end up being no time at all."

"Oh aye, two months exploring and lounging around on tropical islands. Hard life, that!"

"Well yeah, you're right. It's going to be terribly, gut-wrenchingly hard, but we'll send you guys a postcard!"

"Ha!" Tammy squeezed his arm playfully, and quietly marvelled to herself at the muscle under his coat. Callum was indeed made of iron.

"Right, com'on Lori!" Tammy urged. "We can't be waiting here all day for you!"

"Yes - your gran will kill us if we're late to this soiree!"

"Oh '*this soirée*' is it? - how very posh!" called Lori from the changing room.

Callum rolled his eyes at Tammy. "I can't help it if I'm distinguished and worldly compared to some people".

Lori's indignant exclamations from behind the curtain could be heard all too clearly.

"When are you coming out, Lori MacNori?" Callum winked at Tammy.

"Are you seriously calling me that, I hated that nickname!" Lori pulled the curtain open and emerged wearing a mustard yellow woollen dress, a dark grey silk scarf, and black knee-high boots. She had been exploring with different colours for some months now, and had cast aside her old monochrome preferences, replacing them with a palate of endless vibrancy.

Tammy shook her head and made her way to the door. Callum breathed out looking at Lori as if for the first time:

"OK my love, I won't call you that name again."

"Really? What, just like that? You'd honestly stop calling me that if I asked you?"

"Yes I would, whatever you want from me, I'll give it to you completely." His face turned serious.

Lori chuckled and grabbed him by the collar. "Perhaps a kiss would do...for now?"

He put his arms around her, and she could feel the cold on him from outside as he pressed against her. "Whatever I can do to make you happy, my lass... my love".

THANK YOU

If you enjoyed reading this, please leave a review on Amazon, it really helps new readers discover my books.

ALSO BY CLAIRE GILLIES

On The Edge

CLAIRE GILLIES

Sometimes running
away only brings us
closer to home

on the
edge

AFTERWORD

This book really came from the heart. I wanted to write an authentic depiction of how I see the Highlands and the characters that you can find there. I wanted to portray realistic life in rural Scotland and hopefully you get a wee flavour of it from the bustling village of Arlochy.

Arlochy is inspired by a few spots on the west coast - these places do get very busy with tourists and in the summer months a lot goes on!

The Robertson family came to me naturally. I wanted to capture the complexities of family life, and the dynamics and heart that can be found within them.

I hope to check in on the Robertson family again soon, and hope you will come back for more of their trials and tribulations.

ACKNOWLEDGMENTS

Grace - You have been an incredible help and the best editor I could wish for!

Eamonn - My support and guiding light. It means so much that you are in my corner and inspiring me to write everyday.

Torrin - Thanks for taking long naps so I can write!

ABOUT THE AUTHOR

Claire Gillies was born and raised in the Highlands of Scotland, Claire's homeland continues to be a stream of inspiration.

Claire splits her time between Scotland and Australia with her lovely Irish husband and their son.

She is a cat lover (without the cat) and takes her other interests very seriously - a connoisseur of coffee, cake and gin!

This is Claire's second book, and the first instalment in the Arlochy Series.

 facebook.com/ClaireGilliesAuthor

 twitter.com/ClaireGillies13

 instagram.com/clairegillies_